# THE REVENANT

1823: Hugh Glass is among the Rocky Mountain Fur Company's finest men, an experienced frontiersman and expert tracker. When a scouting mission puts him face to face with a grizzly bear, he is viciously mauled and not expected to survive. The company's captain dispatches two of his men to stay behind and tend to Glass before he dies, and to give him the respect of a proper burial. But instead the men abandon him, taking his only means of protecting himself, including his precious gun and hatchet. With grit and determination, Glass begins to crawl inch by inch across more than three thousand miles of uncharted American frontier, negotiating predators both human and inhuman, the threat of starvation, and the agony of his horrific wounds . . . driven to survive by one desire: revenge.

# SPECIAL MESSAGE TO READERS

## THE ULVERSCROFT FOUNDATION
**(registered UK charity number 264873)**
was established in 1972 to provide funds for research, diagnosis and treatment of eye diseases. Examples of major projects funded by the Ulverscroft Foundation are:-

- The Children's Eye Unit at Moorfields Eye Hospital, London
- The Ulverscroft Children's Eye Unit at Great Ormond Street Hospital for Sick Children
- Funding research into eye diseases and treatment at the Department of Ophthalmology, University of Leicester
- The Ulverscroft Vision Research Group, Institute of Child Health
- Twin operating theatres at the Western Ophthalmic Hospital, London
- The Chair of Ophthalmology at the Royal Australian College of Ophthalmologists

You can help further the work of the Foundation by making a donation or leaving a legacy. Every contribution is gratefully received. If you would like to help support the Foundation or require further information, please contact:

**THE ULVERSCROFT FOUNDATION**
**The Green, Bradgate Road, Anstey**
**Leicester LE7 7FU, England**
**Tel: (0116) 236 4325**

**website: www.foundation.ulverscroft.com**

# THE REVENANT

## MICHAEL PUNKE

LARGE
PRINT

First published in Great Britain 2015
by
The Borough Press
an imprint of HarperCollins*Publishers*

First Isis Edition
published 2016
by arrangement with
HarperCollins*Publishers*

This novel is entirely a work of fiction. The names,
characters and incidents portrayed in it, while at times
based on historical events and figures, are the work of
the author's imagination.

Map © 2002 by Jeffrey L. Ward

A catalogue record for this book is available
from the British Library.

ISBN 978–1–78541–236–3 (hb)
ISBN 978–1–78541–242–4 (pb)

*For my parents, Marilyn and Butch Punke*

Avenge not yourselves, but rather give place unto wrath: for it is written, Vengeance is mine; I will repay, saith the Lord.

— Rom. 12:19

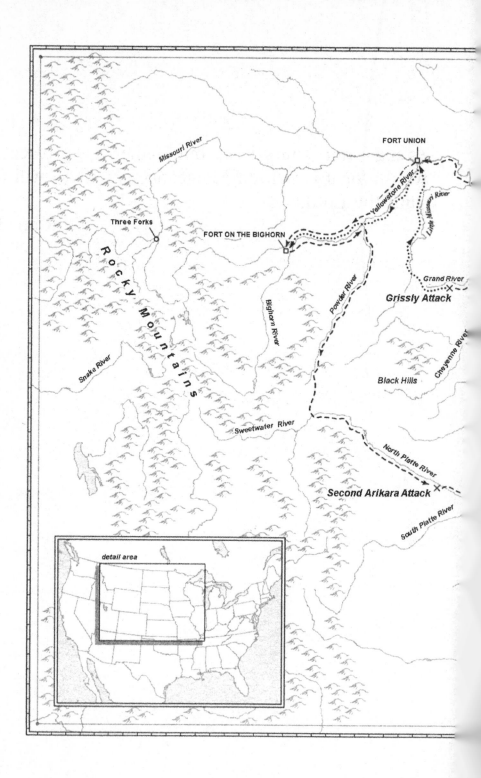

FORT UNION

Missouri River

Three Forks

FORT ON THE BIGHORN

*Rocky Mountains*

Yellowstone River

Little Missouri River

Grand River
X
**Grissly Attack**

Snake River

Bighorn River

Powder River

Black Hills

Cheyenne River

Sweetwater River

North Platte River

**Second Arikara Attack**
X

South Platte River

detail area

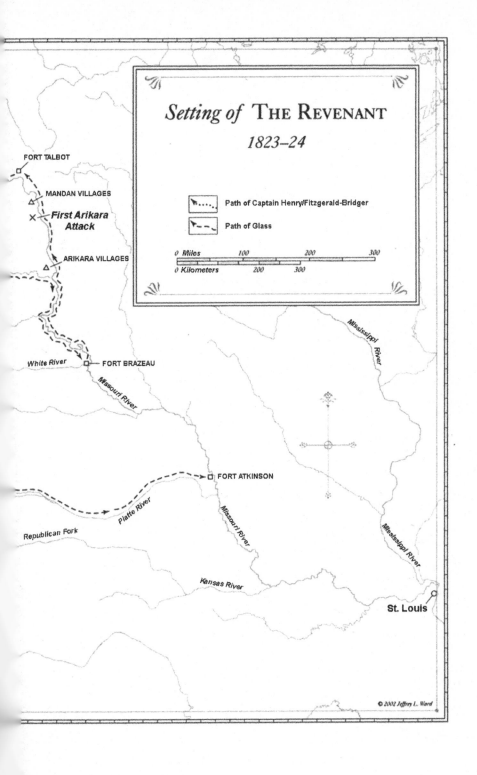

Setting of THE REVENANT
1823–24

Path of Captain Henry/Fitzgerald-Bridger

Path of Glass

0 Miles 100 200 300
0 Kilometers 200 300

FORT TALBOT

MANDAN VILLAGES

First Arikara Attack

ARIKARA VILLAGES

White River FORT BRAZEAU

Missouri River

Mississippi River

FORT ATKINSON

Missouri River

Platte River

Republican Fork

Mississippi River

Kansas River

St. Louis

© 2002 Jeffrey L. Ward

# September 1, 1823

They were abandoning him. The wounded man knew it when he looked at the boy, who looked down, then away, unwilling to hold his gaze.

For days, the boy had argued with the man in the wolf-skin hat. *Has it really been days?* The wounded man had battled his fever and pain, never certain whether conversations he heard were real, or merely by-products of the delirious wanderings in his mind.

He looked up at the soaring rock formation above the clearing. A lone, twisted pine had managed somehow to grow from the sheer face of the stone. He had stared at it many times, yet it had never appeared to him as it did at that moment, when its perpendicular lines seemed clearly to form a cross. He accepted for the first time that he would die there in that clearing by the spring.

The wounded man felt an odd detachment from the scene in which he played the central role. He wondered briefly what he would do in their position. If they stayed and the war party came up the creek, all of them would die. *Would I die for them ... if they were certain to die anyway?*

"You sure they're coming up the creek?" The boy's voice cracked as he said it. He could effect a tenor most of the time, but his tone still broke at moments he could not control.

The man in the wolf skin stooped hurriedly by the small meat rack near the fire, stuffing strips of partially dried venison into his parfleche. "You want to stay and find out?"

The wounded man tried to speak. He felt again the piercing pain in his throat. Sound came forth, but he could not shape it into the one word he sought to articulate.

The man in the wolf skin ignored the sound as he continued to gather his few belongings, but the boy turned. "He's trying to say something."

The boy dropped on one knee next to the wounded man. Unable to speak, the man raised his working arm and pointed.

"He wants his rifle," said the boy. "He wants us to set him up with his rifle."

The man in the wolf skin covered the ground between them in quick, measured steps. He kicked the boy hard, square in the back. "Move, goddamn you!"

He strode quickly from the boy to the wounded man, who lay next to the meager pile of his possessions: a possibles bag, a knife in a beaded scabbard, a hatchet, a rifle, and a powder horn. As the wounded man watched helplessly, the man in the wolf skin stooped to pick up the possibles bag. He dug inside for the flint and steel, dropping them into the pocket on the front of his leather tunic. He grabbed the powder horn and slung it over his shoulder. The hatchet he tucked under his broad leather belt.

"What're you doing?" asked the boy.

The man stooped again, picked up the knife, and tossed it to the boy.

"Take that." The boy caught it, staring in horror at the scabbard in his hand. Only the rifle remained. The man in the wolf skin picked it up, checking quickly to ensure it was charged. "Sorry, old Glass. You ain't got much more use for any of this."

The boy appeared stunned. "We can't leave him without his kit." The man in the wolf skin looked up briefly, then disappeared into the woods.

The wounded man stared up at the boy, who stood there for a long moment with the knife — his knife. Finally, the boy raised his eyes. At first it appeared that he might say something. Instead, he spun around and fled into the pines.

The wounded man stared at the gap in the trees where they had disappeared. His rage was complete, consuming him as fire envelops the needles of a pine. He wanted nothing in the world except to place his hands around their necks and choke the life from them.

Instinctively he started to yell out, forgetting again that his throat produced no words, only pain. He raised himself on his left elbow. He could bend his right arm slightly, but it would support no weight. The movement sent agonizing bolts through his neck and back. He felt the strain of his skin against the crude sutures. He looked down at his leg, where the bloody remnants of an old shirt were tightly wrapped. He could not flex his thigh to make the leg work.

Marshaling his strength, he rolled heavily to his stomach. He felt the snap of a suture breaking and the warm wetness of new blood on his back. The pain diluted to nothing against the tide of his rage.

Hugh Glass began to crawl.

# PART ONE

PART ONE

# CHAPTER
# ONE

## *August 21, 1823*

"My keelboat from St. Louis is due here any day, Monsieur Ashley." The portly Frenchman explained it again in his patient but insistent tone. "I'll gladly sell the Rocky Mountain Fur Company the entire contents of the boat — but I can't sell you what I don't have."

William H. Ashley slammed his tin cup on the crude slats of the table. The carefully groomed gray of his beard did not conceal the tight clench of his jaw. For its part, the clenched jaw seemed unlikely to contain another outburst, as Ashley found himself confronting again the one thing he despised above all else — waiting.

The Frenchman, with the unlikely name of Kiowa Brazeau, watched Ashley with growing trepidation. Ashley's presence at Kiowa's remote trading post presented a rare opportunity, and Kiowa knew that the successful management of this relationship could lay a permanent foundation for his venture. Ashley was a prominent man in St. Louis business and politics, a man with both the vision to bring commerce to the West and the money to make it happen. "Other people's money," as Ashley had called it. Skittish money. Nervous money. Money that would flee easily from one speculative venture to the next.

Kiowa squinted behind his thick spectacles, and though his vision was not sharp, he had a keen eye for reading people. "If you will indulge me, Monsieur Ashley, perhaps I can offer one consolation while we await my boat."

Ashley offered no affirmative acknowledgment, but neither did he renew his tirade.

"I need to requisition more provisions from St. Louis," said Kiowa. "I'll send a courier downstream tomorrow by canoe. He can carry a dispatch from you to your syndicate. You can reassure them before rumors about Colonel Leavenworth's debacle take root."

Ashley sighed deeply and took a long sip of the sour ale, resigned, through lack of alternative, to endure this latest delay. Like it or not, the Frenchman's advice was sound. He needed to reassure his investors before news of the battle ran unchecked through the streets of St. Louis.

Kiowa sensed his opening and moved quickly to keep Ashley on a productive course. The Frenchman produced a quill, ink, and parchment, arranging them in front of Ashley and refilling the tin cup with ale. "I'll leave you to your work, monsieur," he said, happy for the opportunity to retreat.

By the dim light of a tallow candle, Ashley wrote deep into the night:

Fort Brazeau,
On the Missouri

August 21, 1823

James D. Pickens, Esquire
Pickens and Sons
St. Louis

Dear Mr. Pickens,

It is my unfortunate responsibility to inform you of the events of the past two weeks. By their nature these events must alter — though not deter — our venture on the Upper Missouri.

As you probably know by now, the men of the Rocky Mountain Fur Company were attacked by the Arikara after trading in good faith for sixty horses. The Arikara attacked without provocation, killing 16 of our men, wounding a dozen, & stealing back the horses they had feigned to sell to us the day before.

In face of this attack, I was forced to retreat downstream, while at the same time requesting the aid of Colonel Leavenworth & the US Army in responding to this clear affront to the sovereign right of US citizens to traverse the Missouri unimpeded. I also requested the support of our own men, who joined me (led by Capt. Andrew Henry) at great peril, from their position at Fort Union.

By August 9th, we confronted the Arikara with a combined force of 700 men, including 200 of Leavenworth's regulars (with two howitzers) and forty men of the RMF Co. We also found allies (albeit temporary) in 400 Sioux warriors, whose enmity for the

Arikara stems from historical grudge, the origin of which I do not know.

Suffice it to say that our assembled forces were more than ample to carry the field, punish the Arikara for their treachery, & reopen the Missouri for our venture. That such results did not occur we owe to the unsteady timber of Colonel Leavenworth.

The details of the inglorious encounter can await my return to St. Louis, but suffice it to say that the Colonel's repeated reluctance to engage in an inferior foe allowed the entire Arikara tribe to slip our grasp, the result being the effective closure of the Missouri between Fort Brazeau & the Mandan villages. Somewhere between here and there are 900 Arikara warriors, newly entrenched, no doubt, & with new motive to foil all attempts up the Missouri.

Colonel Leavenworth has returned to garrison at Fort Atkinson, where he no doubt will pass the winter in front of a warm hearth, carefully mulling his options. I do not intend to wait for him. Our venture, as you know, can ill-afford the loss of eight months.

Ashley stopped to read his text, unhappy with its dour tone. The letter reflected his anger, but did not convey his predominant emotion — a bedrock optimism, an unwavering faith in his own ability to succeed. God had placed him in a garden of infinite bounty, a Land of Goshen in which any man could prosper if only he had the courage and the fortitude to try. Ashley's weaknesses, which he confessed forthrightly, were simply barriers to be overcome by some creative combination of his strengths. Ashley expected setbacks, but he would not tolerate failure.

We must turn this misfortune to our benefit, press on while our competitors take pause. With the Missouri effectively closed, I have decided to send two groups West by alternate route. Captain Henry I have already dispatched up the Grand River. He will ascend the Grand as far as possible and make his way back to Fort Union. Jedidiah Smith will lead a second troop up the Platte, his target the waters of the Great Basin.

You no doubt share my intense frustration at our delay. We must now move boldly to recapture lost time. I have instructed Henry and Smith that they shall *not* return to St. Louis with their harvest in the Spring. Rather, *we* shall go to *them* — rendezvous in the field to exchange their furs for fresh supplies. We can save four months this way, & repay at least some portion of our debt to the clock. Meanwhile, I propose a new fur troop be raised in St. Louis & dispatched in the Spring, led by me personally.

The remnants of the candle sputtered and spit foul black smoke. Ashley looked up, suddenly aware of the hour, of his deep fatigue. He dipped the quill and returned to his correspondence, writing firmly and quickly now as he drew his report to its conclusion:

I urge you to communicate to our syndicate — in strongest possible terms — my complete confidence in the inevitable success of our endeavor. A great bounty

**11**

has been laid by Providence before us, & we must not fail to summon the courage to claim our rightful share.
Your Very Humble Servant,
William H. Ashley

Two days later, August 16, 1823, Kiowa Brazeau's keelboat arrived from St. Louis. William Ashley provisioned his men and sent them west on the same day. The first rendezvous was set for the summer of 1824, the location to be communicated through couriers.

Without understanding fully the significance of his decisions, William H. Ashley had invented the system that would define the era.

# CHAPTER
# TWO

## *August 23, 1823*

Eleven men hunkered in the camp with no fire. The camp took advantage of a slight embankment on the Grand River, but the plain afforded little contour to conceal their position. A fire would have signaled their presence for miles, and stealth was the trappers' best ally against another attack. Most of the men used the last hour of daylight to clean rifles, repair moccasins, or eat. The boy had been asleep from the moment they stopped, a crumpled tangle of long limbs and ill-shod clothing.

The men fell into clusters of three or four, huddled against the bank or pressed against a rock or clump of sage, as if these minor protusions might offer protection.

The usual banter of camp had been dampened by the calamity on the Missouri, and then extinguished altogether by the second attack only three nights before. When they spoke at all they spoke in hushed and pensive tones, respectful of the comrades who lay dead in their trail, heedful of the dangers still before them.

"Do you think he suffered, Hugh? I can't get it out of my head that he was suffering away, all that time."

Hugh Glass looked up at the man, William Anderson, who had posed the question. Glass thought for a while before he answered, "I don't think your brother suffered."

"He was the oldest. When we left Kentucky, our folks told *him* to look after *me*. Didn't say a word to me. Wouldn't have occurred to them."

"You did your best for your brother, Will. It's a hard truth, but he was dead when that ball hit him three days ago."

A new voice spoke from the shadows near the bank. "Wish we'd have buried him then, instead of dragging him for two days." The speaker perched on his haunches, and in the growing darkness his face showed little feature except a dark beard and a white scar. The scar started near the corner of his mouth and curved down and around like a fishhook. Its prominence was magnified by the fact that no hair grew on the tissue, cutting a permanent sneer through his beard. His right hand worked the stout blade of a skinning knife over a whetstone as he spoke, mixing his words with a slow, rasping scrape.

"Keep your mouth shut, Fitzgerald, or I swear on my brother's grave I'll rip out your bloody tongue."

"Your brother's grave? Not much of a grave now, was it?"

The men within earshot paid sudden attention, surprised at this conduct, even from Fitzgerald.

Fitzgerald felt the attention, and it encouraged him. "More just a pile of rocks. You think he's still in there, moldering away?" Fitzgerald paused for a moment, so that the only sound was the scraping of the blade on the stone. "I doubt it — speaking for myself." Again he

14

waited, calibrating the effect of his words as he spoke them. "Course, could be the rocks kept the varmints off. But I think the coyotes are dragging little bits of him across . . ."

Anderson lunged at Fitzgerald with both hands extended.

Fitzgerald brought his leg up sharply as he rose to meet the attack, his shin catching Anderson full-force in the groin. The kick folded Anderson in two, as if some hidden cord drew his neck to his knees. Fitzgerald drove his knee into the helpless man's face and Anderson flipped backward.

Fitzgerald moved spryly for someone his size, pouncing to pin his knee against the chest of the gasping, bleeding man. He put the skinning knife to Anderson's throat. "You want to go join your brother?" Fitzgerald pressed the knife so that the blade drew a thin line of blood.

"Fitzgerald," Glass said in an even but authoritative tone. "That's enough."

Fitzgerald looked up. He contemplated an answer to Glass's challenge, while noting with satisfaction the ring of men that now surrounded him, witnesses to Anderson's pathetic position. Better to claim victory, he decided. He'd see to Glass another day. Fitzgerald removed the blade from Anderson's throat and rammed the knife into the beaded sheath on his belt. "Don't start things you can't finish, Anderson. Next time I'll finish it for you."

Captain Andrew Henry pushed his way through the circle of spectators. He grabbed Fitzgerald from behind and ripped him backward, pushing him hard into the embankment. "One more fight and you're out, Fitzgerald." Henry pointed beyond the perimeter of the camp to the distant horizon. "If you've got an extra store of piss you can go try making it on your own."

The captain looked around him at the rest of the men. "We'll cover forty miles tomorrow. You're wasting time if you're not asleep already. Now, who's taking first watch?" No one stepped forward. Henry's eyes came to rest on the boy, oblivious to the commotion. Henry took a handful of determined steps to the crumpled form. "Get up, Bridger."

The boy sprang up, wide-eyed as he grasped, bewildered, for his gun. The rusted trading musket had been an advance on his salary, along with a yellowed powder horn and a handful of flints.

"I want you a hundred yards downstream. Find a high spot along the bank. Pig, the same thing upstream. Fitzgerald, Anderson — you'll take the second watch."

Fitzgerald had stood watch the night before. For a moment it appeared he would protest the distribution of labor. He thought better of it, sulking instead to the edge of the camp. The boy, still disoriented, half stumbled across the rocks that spilled along the river's edge, disappearing into the cobalt blackness that encroached on the brigade.

The man they called "Pig" was born Phineous Gilmore on a dirt-poor farm in Kentucky. No mystery surrounded his nickname: he was enormous and he was filthy. Pig smelled so bad it confused people. When they encountered his reek, they looked around him for the

16

source, so implausible did it seem that the odor could emanate from a human. Even the trappers, who placed no particular premium on cleanliness, did their best to keep Pig downwind. After hoisting himself slowly to his feet, Pig slung his rifle over his shoulder and ambled upstream.

Less than an hour passed before the daylight receded completely. Glass watched as Captain Henry returned from a nervous check of the sentries. He picked his way by moonlight among the sleeping men, and Glass realized that he and Henry were the only men awake. The captain chose the ground next to Glass, leaning against his rifle as he eased his large frame to the ground. Repose took the weight off his tired feet, but failed to relieve the pressure he felt most heavily.

"I want you and Black Harris to scout tomorrow," said Captain Henry. Glass looked up, disappointed that he could not respond to the beckoning call of sleep.

"Find something to shoot in late afternoon. We'll risk a fire." Henry lowered his voice, as if making a confession. "We're way behind, Hugh." Henry gave every indication that he intended to talk for a while. Glass reached for his rifle. If he couldn't sleep, he might as well tend his weapon. He had doused it in a river crossing that afternoon and wanted to apply fresh grease to the trigger works.

"Cold'll set in hard by early December," continued the captain. "We'll need two weeks to lay in a supply of meat. If we're not on the Yellowstone before October we'll have no fall hunt."

If Captain Henry was racked by internal doubt, his commanding physical presence betrayed no infirmity. The band of leather fringe on his deerskin tunic cut a swath across his broad shoulders and chest, remnants of his former profession as a lead miner in the Saint Genevieve district of Missouri. He was narrow at the waist, where a thick leather belt held a brace of pistols and a large knife. His breeches were doeskin to the knee, and from there down red wool. The captain's pants had been specially tailored in St. Louis and were a badge of his wilderness experience. Leather provided excellent protection, but wading made it heavy and cold. Wool, by contrast, dried quickly and retained heat even when wet.

If the brigade he led was motley, Henry at least drew satisfaction from the fact they called him "captain." In truth, of course, Henry knew the title was an artifice. His band of trappers had nothing to do with the military, and scant respect for any institution. Still, Henry was the only man among them to have trod and trapped the Three Forks. If title meant little, experience was the coin of the realm.

The captain paused, waiting for acknowledgment from Glass. Glass looked up from his rifle. It was a brief look, because he had unscrewed the elegantly scrolled guard that covered the rifle's twin triggers. He cupped the two screws carefully in his hand, afraid of dropping them in the dark.

The glance sufficed, enough to encourage Henry to continue. "Did I ever tell you about Drouillard?"

"No, Captain."

"You know who he was?"

"George Drouillard — Corps of Discovery?"

Henry nodded his head. "Lewis and Clark man, one of their best — a scout and a hunter. In 1809 he signed up with a group I led — he led, really — to the Three Forks. We had a hundred men, but Drouillard and Colter was the only ones who'd ever been there.

"We found beaver thick as mosquitoes. Barely had to trap 'em — could go out with a club. But we ran into trouble with the Blackfeet from the start. Five men killed before two weeks was up. We had to fort up, couldn't send out trapping parties.

"Drouillard holed up there with the rest of us for about a week before he said he was tired of sitting still. He went out the next day and came back a week later with twenty plews."

Glass paid the captain his full attention. Every citizen of St. Louis knew some version of Drouillard's story, but Glass had never heard a first-person account.

"He did that twice, went out and came back with a pack of plews. Last thing he said before he left the third time was, 'Third time's charmed.' He rode off and we heard two gunshots about half an hour later — one from his rifle and one from his pistol. Second shot must have been him shooting his horse, trying to make a barrier. That's where we found him, behind his horse. There must have been twenty arrows between him and the horse. Blackfeet left the arrows in, wanted to send us a message. They hacked him up, too — cut off his head."

The captain paused again, scraping at the dirt in front of him with a pointed stick. "I keep thinking about him."

Glass searched for words of reassurance. Before he could say anything the captain asked, "How long do you figure this river's gonna keep running west?"

Glass stared intently, now, searching for the captain's eyes. "We'll start making better time, Captain. We can follow the Grand for the time being. We know the Yellowstone's north and west." In truth, Glass had developed significant doubts about the captain. Misfortune seemed to hang on him like day-before smoke.

"You're right." The captain said it and then he said it again, as if to convince himself. "Of course you're right."

Though his knowledge was born of calamity, Captain Henry knew as much about the geography of the Rockies as almost any man alive. Glass, though an experienced plainsman, had never set foot on the Upper Missouri. Yet Henry found something steady and reassuring in Glass's voice. Someone had told him that Glass had been a mariner in his youth. There was even a rumor that he'd been a prisoner of the pirate Jean Lafitte. Perhaps it was those years on the empty expanse of the high seas that left him comfortable on the featureless plain between St. Louis and the Rocky Mountains.

"We'll be lucky if the Blackfeet haven't wiped out the whole lot at Fort Union. The men I left there aren't exactly the cream of the crop." The captain continued

20

now with his usual catalog of concerns. On and on into the night. Glass knew that it was enough just to listen. He looked up or grunted from time to time, but focused in the main on his rifle.

Glass's rifle was the one extravagance of his life, and when he rubbed grease into the spring mechanism of the hair trigger, he did so with the tender affection that other men might reserve for a wife or child. It was an Anstadt, a so-called Kentucky flintlock, made, like most of the great arms of the day, by German craftsmen in Pennsylvania. The octagonal barrel was inscribed at the base with the name of its maker, "Jacob Anstadt," and the place of its manufacture, "Kutztown, Penn." The barrel was short, only thirty-six inches. The classic Kentucky rifles were longer, some with barrels stretching fifty inches. Glass liked a shorter gun because shorter meant lighter, and lighter meant easier to carry. For those rare moments when he might be mounted, a shorter gun was easier to maneuver from the back of a horse. Besides, the expertly crafted rifling of the Anstadt made it deadly accurate, even without the longer barrel. A hair trigger enhanced its accuracy, allowing discharge with the lightest touch. With a full charge of 200 grains of black powder, the Anstadt could throw a .53 caliber ball nearly 200 yards.

His experiences on the western plains had taught Glass that the performance of his rifle could mean the difference between life and death. Of course, most men in the troop had reliable weapons. It was the Anstadt's elegant beauty that set his gun apart.

21

It was a beauty that other men noticed, asking, as they often did, if they might hold the rifle. The iron-hard walnut of the stock took an elegant curve at the wrist, but was thick enough to absorb the recoil of a heavy powder charge. The butt featured a patchbox on one side and a carved cheek piece on the other. The stock turned gracefully at the butt, so that it fit against the shoulder like an appendage of the shooter's own body. The stock was stained the deepest of browns, the last tone before black. From even a short distance, the grain of the wood was imperceptible, but on close examination, irregular lines seemed to swirl, animated beneath the hand-rubbed coats of varnish.

In a final indulgence, the metal fittings of the rifle were silver instead of the usual brass, adorning the gun at the butt-plate, the patchbox, the trigger guard, the triggers themselves, and the cupped fittings on the ends of the ramstaff. Many trappers pounded brass studs into their rifle stocks for decoration. Glass could not imagine such a gaudy disfigurement of his Anstadt.

Satisfied that his rifle's works were clear, Glass returned the trigger guard to its routed groove and replaced the two screws that held it. He poured fresh powder in the pan beneath the flint, ensuring that the gun was primed to fire.

He noticed suddenly that the camp had fallen still, and wondered vaguely when the captain had stopped talking. Glass looked toward the center of the camp. The captain lay sleeping, his body twitching fitfully. On the other side of Glass, closest to the camp's perimeter,

Anderson lay against a chunk of driftwood. No sound rose above the reassuring flow of the river.

The sharp crack of a flintlock pierced the quiet. It came from downstream — from Jim Bridger, the boy. The sleeping men lurched in unison, fearful and confused as they scrambled for weapons and cover. A dark form hurtled toward the camp from downstream. Next to Glass, Anderson cocked and raised his rifle in a single motion. Glass raised the Anstadt. The hurtling form took shape, only forty yards from the camp. Anderson sighted down the barrel, hesitating an instant before pulling the trigger. At the same instant, Glass swung the Anstadt beneath Anderson's arms. The force knocked Anderson's barrel skyward as his powder ignited.

The hurtling form stopped cold at the explosion of the shot, the distance now close enough to perceive the wide eyes and heaving chest. It was Bridger. "I . . . I . . . I . . ." A panicked stammer paralyzed him.

"What happened, Bridger?" demanded the captain, peering beyond the boy into the darkness downstream. The trappers had fallen into a defensive semicircle with the embankment behind them. Most had assumed a firing position, perched on one knee, rifles at full cock.

"I'm sorry, Captain. I didn't mean to fire. I heard a sound, a crash in the brush. I stood up and I guess the hammer slipped. It just went off."

"More likely you fell asleep." Fitzgerald uncocked his rifle and rose from his knee. "Every buck for five miles is headed our way now."

Bridger started to speak, but searched in vain for the words to express the depth of his shame and regret. He stood there, open-mouthed, staring in horror at the men arrayed before him.

Glass stepped forward, pulling Bridger's smoothbore from his hands.

He cocked the musket and pulled the trigger, catching the hammer with his thumb before the flint struck the frisson. He repeated the action. "This is a poor excuse for a weapon, Captain. Give him a decent rifle and we'll have fewer problems on watch." A few of the men nodded their heads.

The captain looked first at Glass, then at Bridger, and he said, "Anderson, Fitzgerald — it's your watch." The two men took their positions, one upstream and one down.

The sentries were redundant. No one slept in the few hours remaining before dawn.

# CHAPTER
# THREE

## *August 24, 1823*

Hugh Glass stared down at the cloven tracks, the deep indentions clear as newsprint in the soft mud. Two distinct sets began at the river's edge, where the deer must have drunk, and then trailed into the heavy cover of the willows. The persistent work of a beaver had carved a trail, now trod by a variety of game. Dung lay piled next to the tracks, and Glass stooped to touch the pea-sized pellets — still warm.

Glass looked west, where the sun still perched high above the plateau that formed the distant horizon. He guessed there were three hours before sunset. Still early, but it would take the captain and the rest of the men an hour to catch up. Besides, it was an ideal campsite. The river folded gently against a long bar and gravel bank. Beyond the willows, a stand of cottonwoods offered cover for their campfires and a supply of firewood. The willows were ideal for smoke racks. Glass noticed plum trees scattered among the willows, a lucky break. They could grind pemmican from the combined fruit and meat. He looked downriver. *Where's Black Harris?*

In the hierarchy of challenges the trappers faced each day, obtaining food was the most immediate. Like other challenges, it involved a complicated balancing of benefits and risks. They carried virtually no food with them, especially since abandoning the flatboats on the Missouri and proceeding on foot up the Grand. A few men still had tea or sugar, but most were down to a bag of salt for preserving meat. Game was plentiful on this stretch of the Grand, and they could have dined on fresh meat each night. But harvesting game meant shooting, and the sound of a rifle carried for miles, revealing their position to any foe within earshot.

Since leaving the Missouri, the men had held closely to a pattern. Each day, two scouted ahead of the others. For the time being their path was fixed — they simply followed the Grand. The scouts' primary responsibilities were to avoid Indians, select a campsite, and find food. They shot fresh game every few days.

After shooting a deer or buffalo calf, the scouts prepared the camp for the evening. They bled the game, gathered wood, and set two or three small fires in narrow, rectangular pits. Smaller fires produced less smoke than a single conflagration, while also offering more surface for smoking meat and more sources of heat. If enemies did spot them at night, more fires gave the illusion of more men.

Once flames were burning, the scouts butchered their game, pulling choice cuts for immediate consumption and cutting thin strips with the rest. They constructed crude racks with green willow branches, rubbed the meat strips with a little salt and hung them just above the flames. It wasn't the type of jerky they would make in a permanent camp, which would keep for months. But the meat would keep for several days, enough to last until the next fresh game.

Glass stepped from the willows into a clearing, scanning for the deer he knew must be just ahead.

He saw the cubs before he saw the sow. There was a pair, and they tumbled toward him, bawling like playful dogs. The cubs had been dropped in the spring, and at five months weighed a hundred pounds each. They nipped at each other as they bore down on Glass, and for the briefest of instants the scene had a near comic quality. Transfixed by the whirling motion of the cubs, Glass had not raised his glance to the far end of the clearing, fifty yards away. Nor had he yet to calculate the certain implication of their presence.

Suddenly he knew. A hollowness seized his stomach half an instant before the first rumbling growl crossed the clearing. The cubs skidded to an immediate stop, not ten feet in front of Glass. Ignoring the cubs now, Glass peered toward the brush line across the clearing.

He heard her size before he saw it. Not just the crack of the thick underbrush that the sow moved aside like short grass, but the growl itself, a sound deep like thunder or a falling tree, a bass that could emanate only through connection with some great mass.

The growl crescendoed as she stepped into the clearing, black eyes staring at Glass, head low to the ground as she processed the foreign scent, a scent now mingling with that of her cubs. She faced him head-on, her body coiled and taut like the heavy spring on a buckboard. Glass marveled at the animal's utter muscularity, the thick stumps of her forelegs folding into massive shoulders, and above all the silvery hump that identified her as a grizzly.

Glass struggled to control his reaction as he processed his options. His reflex, of course, screamed at him to flee. Back through the willows. Into the river. Perhaps he could dive low and escape downstream. But the bear was already too close for that, barely a hundred feet in front of him. His eyes searched desperately for a cottonwood to climb; perhaps he could scramble out of reach, then shoot from above. No, the trees were behind the bear. Nor did the willows provide sufficient cover. His options dwindled to one: Stand and shoot. One chance to stop the grizzly with a .53 caliber ball from the Anstadt.

The grizzly charged, roaring with the focused hate of protective maternal rage. Reflex again nearly compelled Glass to turn and run. Yet the futility of flight was instantly apparent as the grizzly closed the ground between them with remarkable speed. Glass pulled the hammer to full-cock and raised the Anstadt, staring through the pronghorn sight in stunned horror that the animal could be, at the same time, enormous and lithe. He fought another instinct — to shoot immediately. Glass had seen grizzlies absorb half a dozen rifle balls without dying. He had one shot.

Glass struggled to sight on the bouncing target of the sow's head, unable to align a shot. At ten paces, the grizzly lifted herself to a standing position. She towered three feet over Glass as she pivoted for the raking swipe of her lethal claws. Point-blank, he aimed at the great bear's heart and pulled the trigger.

The flint sparked the Anstadt's pan, setting off the rifle and filling the air with the smoke and smell of exploding black powder. The grizzly roared as the ball entered her chest, but her attack did not slow. Glass dropped his rifle, useless now, and reached for the knife in the scabbard on his belt. The bear brought down her paw, and Glass felt the sickening sensation of the animal's six-inch claws dredging deep into the flesh of his upper arm, shoulder, and throat. The blow threw him to his back. The knife dropped, and he pushed furiously against the earth with his feet, futilely seeking the cover of the willows.

The grizzly dropped to all fours and was on him. Glass rolled into a ball, desperate to protect his face and chest. She bit into the back of his neck and lifted him off the ground, shaking him so hard that Glass wondered if his spine might snap. He felt the crunch of her teeth striking the bone of his shoulder blade. Claws raked repeatedly through the flesh of his back and scalp. He screamed in agony. She dropped him, then sank her teeth deep into his thigh and shook him again, lifting him and throwing him to the ground with such force that he lay stunned — conscious, but unable to resist any further.

He lay on his back staring up. The grizzly stood before him on her hind legs. Terror and pain receded, replaced by a horrified fascination at the towering animal. She let out a final roar, which registered in Glass's mind like an echo across a great distance. He was aware of enormous weight on top of him. The dank smell of her coat overwhelmed his other senses. *What*

29

*was it?* His mind searched, then locked on the image of a yellow dog, licking a boy's face on the plank porch of a cabin.

The sunlit sky above him faded to black.

Black Harris heard the shot, just ahead around a bend in the river, and hoped that Glass had shot a deer. He moved forward quickly but quietly, aware that a rifle shot could mean many things. Harris began to trot when he heard the roar of the bear. Then he heard Glass scream.

At the willows, Harris found the tracks of both the deer and Glass. He peered into the path cut by a beaver, listening intently. No sound rose above the hushed trickle of the river. Harris pointed the rifle from his hip, his thumb on the hammer and his forefinger near the trigger. He glanced briefly at the pistol on his belt, assuring himself it was primed. He stepped into the willows, carefully placing each moccasin as he peered ahead. The bawling of the cubs broke the silence.

At the edge of the clearing Black Harris stopped to absorb the scene before him. An enormous grizzly lay sprawled on her belly, eyes open but dead. One cub stood on hind legs, pressing against the sow with its nose, futilely seeking to evoke some sign of life. The other cub rooted at something, tugging with its teeth. Harris realized suddenly it was a man's arm. *Glass*. He raised his rifle and shot the nearer of the two cubs. It fell limp. The sibling scampered for the cottonwoods

**30**

and disappeared. Harris reloaded before walking forward.

Captain Henry and the men of the brigade heard the two shots and hurried upstream. The first shot didn't worry the captain, but the second one did. The first shot was expected — Glass or Harris bringing down game as they had planned the night before. Two shots closely spaced also would be normal. Two men hunting together might come upon more than one target, or the first shooter might miss. But several minutes separated the two shots. The captain hoped that the hunters were working apart. Perhaps the first shooter had flushed game to the second. Or perhaps they had been lucky enough to come across buffalo. Buffalo would sometimes stand, unfazed by the clap of a rifle, allowing a hunter to reload and casually pick a second target. "Keep tight, men. And check your arms."

For the third time in a hundred paces, Bridger checked the new rifle that Will Anderson had given to him. "My brother don't need this no more," was all he had said.

In the clearing, Black Harris looked down at the body of the bear. Only Glass's arm protruded from underneath. Harris glanced around before setting his rifle on the ground, tugging at the bear's foreleg in an attempt to move the carcass. Heaving, he pulled the animal far enough to see Glass's head, a bloody tangle of hair and flesh. *Jesus Christ!* He worked urgently, fighting against the fear of what he would find.

Harris moved to the opposite side of the bear, climbing across the animal to grab its foreleg, then tugging, his knees pressed against the grizzly's body for leverage. After several attempts, he managed to roll the front half of the bear so that the giant animal lay twisted at the midsection. Then he pulled several times at the rear leg. He gave a final heave, and the bear tumbled heavily onto her back. Glass's body was free. On the sow's chest, Black Harris noticed the matted blood where Glass's shot had found its mark.

Black Harris knelt next to Glass, unsure of what to do. It was not through lack of experience with the wounded. He had removed arrows and bullets from three men, and twice had been shot himself.

But he had never seen human carnage like this, fresh in the wake of attack. Glass was shredded from head to foot. His scalp lay dangling to one side, and it took Harris an instant to recognize the components that made up his face. Worst was his throat. The grizzly's claws had cut three deep and distinct tracks, beginning at the shoulder and passing straight across his neck. Another inch and the claws would have severed Glass's jugular. As it was, they had laid open his throat, slicing through muscle and exposing his gullet. The claws had also cut the trachea, and Harris watched, horrified, as a large bubble formed in the blood that seeped from the wound. It was the first clear sign that Glass was alive.

Harris rolled Glass gently on his side to inspect his back. Nothing remained of his cotton shirt. Blood oozed from deep puncture wounds at his neck and shoulder. His right arm flopped unnaturally. From the middle of his back to his waist, the bear's raking claws left deep, parallel cuts. It reminded Harris of tree trunks he had seen where bears mark their territory, only these marks were etched in flesh instead of wood. On the back of Glass's thigh, blood seeped through his buckskin breeches.

Harris had no idea where to begin, and was almost relieved that the throat wound appeared so obviously mortal. He pulled Glass a few yards to a grassy, shaded spot and eased him to his back. Ignoring the bubbling throat, Harris focused on the head. Glass at least deserved the dignity of wearing his scalp. Harris poured water from his canteen, attempting to wash away as much of the dirt as possible. The skin was so loose that it was almost like replacing a fallen hat on a bald man. Harris pulled the scalp across Glass's skull, pressing the loose skin against his forehead and tucking it behind his ear. They could stitch it later if Glass lasted that long.

Harris heard a sound in the brush and drew his pistol. Captain Henry stepped into the clearing. The men filed grimly behind, eyes moving from Glass to the sow, from Harris to the dead cub.

The captain surveyed the clearing, oddly numb as his mind filtered the scene through the context of his own past. He shook his head and for a moment his eyes, normally sharp, seemed not to focus. "Is he dead?"

"Not yet. But he's tore to pieces. His windpipe's cut."

"Did he kill the sow?"

Harris nodded. "I found her dead on top of him. There's a ball in her heart."

"Not soon enough, eh." It was Fitzgerald.

The captain knelt next to Glass. With grimy fingers he poked at the throat wound, where bubbles continued to form with each breath. The breathing had grown more labored, and a tepid wheeze now rose and fell with Glass's chest.

"Somebody get me a clean strip of cloth and some water — and whiskey in case he wakes up."

Bridger stepped forward, rummaging through a small satchel from his back. He pulled a wool shirt from the bag, and handed it to Henry. "Here, Captain."

The captain paused, hesitant to take the boy's shirt. Then he grabbed it, tearing strips from the coarse cloth. He poured the contents of his canteen on Glass's throat. Blood washed away, quickly replaced by the wound's heavy seep. Glass began to sputter and cough. His eyes fluttered, then opened wide, panicky.

Glass's first sensation was that he was drowning. He coughed again as his body attempted to clear the blood from his throat and lungs. He focused briefly on Henry as the captain rolled him to his side. From his side, Glass was able to swallow two breaths before nausea overwhelmed him. He vomited, igniting excruciating pain in his throat. Instinctively, Glass reached to touch his neck. His right arm wouldn't function, but his left hand found the gaping wound. He was overcome with horror and panic at what his fingers discovered. His eyes became wild, searching for reassurance in the faces surrounding him. Instead he saw the opposite — awful affirmation of his fears.

Glass tried to speak, but his throat could muster no sound beyond an eerie wail. He struggled to rise on his elbows. Henry pinned him to the ground, pouring whiskey on his throat. A searing burn replaced all other pain. Glass convulsed a final time before again losing consciousness.

"We need to bind his wounds while he's down. Cut more strips, Bridger."

The boy began ripping long lengths from the shirt. The other men watched solemnly, standing like casket bearers at a funeral.

The captain looked up. "Rest of you get moving. Harris, scout a wide circle around us. Make sure those shots didn't draw attention our way. Someone get the fires going — make sure the wood's dry — we don't need a damn smoke signal. And get that sow butchered."

The men moved off and the captain turned again to Glass. He took a strip of cloth from Bridger and threaded it behind Glass's neck, tying it as tightly as he dared. He repeated the action with two more strips. Blood soaked the cloth instantly. He wound another strip around Glass's head in a crude effort to hold his scalp in place. The head wounds also bled heavily, and the captain used water and the shirt to mop the blood pooling around Glass's eyes. He sent Bridger to refill the canteen from the river.

When Bridger returned, they again rolled Glass onto his side. Bridger held him, keeping his face from the ground, while Captain Henry inspected his back. Henry poured water on the puncture wounds from the bear's fangs. Though deep, they bled very little. The five parallel wounds from the bear's claws were a different story. Two in particular cut deep into Glass's back, exposing the muscle and bleeding heavily. Dirt mixed freely with the blood, and the captain again dumped water from the canteen. Without the dirt, the wounds seemed to bleed even more, so the captain left them alone. He cut two long strips from the shirt, worked them around Glass's body and tied them tightly. It didn't work. The strips did little to stop his back from bleeding.

The captain paused to think. "These deep wounds need to be stitched or he'll bleed to death."

"What about his throat?"

"I ought to sew that up too, but it's such a damn mess I don't know where to start." Henry dug into his possibles bag and pulled out coarse black thread and a heavy needle.

The captain's thick fingers were surprisingly nimble as he threaded the needle and tied an end knot. Bridger held the edges of the deepest wound together and watched, wide-eyed, as Henry pressed the needle into Glass's skin. He worked the needle from side to side, four stitches pulling the skin together in the center of the cut. He tied off the ends of the thick thread. Of the five claw wounds on Glass's back, two were deep enough to need stitches. For each wound, the captain made no effort to sew the entire length. Instead, he simply bound the middle together, but the bleeding slowed.

"Now let's look at his neck."

They rolled Glass onto his back. Despite the crude bandages, the throat continued to bubble and wheeze.

Beneath the open skin Henry could see the bright white cartilage of the gullet and windpipe. He knew from the bubbles that the windpipe was cut or nicked, but he had no idea how to repair it. He held his hand over Glass's mouth, feeling for breath.

"What are you gonna do, Captain?"

The captain tied a new end knot in the thread on the needle. "He's still getting some air through his mouth. Best we can do is close up the skin, hope for the rest he can heal himself." At inchwide intervals, Henry sewed stitches to close Glass's throat. Bridger cleared a piece of ground in the shade of the willows and arranged Glass's bedroll. They laid him there as gently as they could.

The captain took his rifle and walked away from the clearing, back through the willows toward the river.

When he reached the water he set his rifle on the bank and removed his leather tunic. His hands were coated in sticky blood, and he reached into the stream to wash them. When some spots would not come clean, he scooped sand from the bank and scrubbed it against the stains. Finally he gave up, cupping his hands and pressing the icy stream water to his bearded face. Familiar doubt crept back. *It's happening again.*

It was no surprise when the green succumbed to the wilderness, but it came as a shock when the veterans fell victim. Like Drouillard, Glass had spent years on the frontier. He was a keel, steadying others through his quiet presence. And Henry knew that by morning he would be dead.

The captain thought back to his conversation with Glass the night before. *Was it only last night?* In 1809, Drouillard's death had been the beginning of the end. Henry's party abandoned the stockade in the Valley of the Three Forks and fled south. The move put them out of range of the Blackfeet, but did not protect them from the harshness of the Rockies themselves. The party endured savage cold, near starvation, and then robbery at the hands of the Crow. When they finally limped from the mountains in 1811, the viability of the fur trade remained an unsettled question.

More than a decade later, Henry again found himself leading trappers in pursuit of the Rockies' elusive wealth. In his mind Henry flipped through the pages of his own recent past: A week out of St. Louis, he lost a keelboat with $10,000 in trading goods. The Blackfeet killed two of his men near the Great Falls of the Missouri. He had rushed to Ashley's aid at the Arikara villages, participated in the debacle with Colonel Leavenworth, and then watched the Arikara close the Missouri. In a week of overland travel up the Grand, three of his men had been killed by Mandans, normally peaceful Indians who attacked by mistake in the night. Now Glass, his best man, lay mortally wounded after stumbling upon a bear. *What sin has plagued me with this curse?*

Back in the clearing, Bridger arranged a blanket over Glass and turned to look at the bear. Four men worked at butchering the animal. The choicest cuts — the liver, heart, tongue, loin, and ribs — were set aside for immediate consumption. The rest they cut into thin strips and rubbed with salt.

Bridger walked up to the great bear's paw and removed his knife from its scabbard. As Fitzgerald looked up from his butchering, Bridger began to cut the largest of the claws from the paw. He was shocked at its size — nearly six inches long and twice as thick as his thumb. It was razor sharp at the point and still bloody from the attack on Glass.

"Who says you get a claw, boy?"

"It ain't for me, Fitzgerald." Bridger took the claw and walked to Glass.

Glass's possibles bag lay next to him. Bridger opened it and dropped in the claw.

The men gorged for hours that night, their bodies craving the rich nutrients of the greasy meat. They knew it would be days before they ate fresh meat again, and they took advantage of the feast. Captain Henry posted two sentries. Despite the relative seclusion of the clearing, he worried about the fires.

Most of the men sat within reach of the flames, tending skewers of willow branches laden with meat. The captain and Bridger took turns checking on Glass. Twice his eyes were open, unfocused and glazed. They reflected the firelight, but seemed not to spark from within. Once he managed to swallow water in a painful convulsion.

They fed the fire in the long pits often enough to keep heat and smoke on the racks of drying meat. In the hour before dawn, Captain Henry checked on Glass and found him unconscious. His breathing had become labored, and he rasped as if each breath required the sum total of his strength.

Henry returned to the fire and found Black Harris there, gnawing on a rib. "Coulda been anyone, Captain — stepping on Old Ephraim like that. There's no accounting for bad luck."

Henry just shook his head. He knew about luck. For a while they sat in silence, as the first hint of another day was born in a barely perceptible glow on the eastern horizon. The captain gathered his rifle and powder horn. "I'll be back before the sun's up. When the men wake up, pick two to dig a grave."

An hour later the captain returned. The shallow beginnings of a grave had been dug, but apparently abandoned. He looked at Harris. "What's the hitch?"

"Well, Captain — for starters he ain't dead. Didn't seem right to keep digging with him laying there."

They waited all morning for Hugh Glass to die. He never gained consciousness. His skin was pallid from the loss of blood and his breathing remained labored. Still, his chest rose and fell, each breath stubbornly followed by another.

Captain Henry paced between the stream and the clearing, and by midmorning sent Black Harris to scout upstream. The sun stood directly overhead when Harris returned. He had seen no Indians, but a game trail on the opposite bank was covered with the tracks of men and horses. Two miles upstream Harris had found a deserted campsite. The captain could wait no more.

He ordered two men to cut saplings. With Glass's bedroll, they would fashion a litter.

"Why don't we make a travois, Captain? Use the mule to pull it?"

"Too rough to pull a travois by the river."

"Then let's move off the river."

"Just build the damn litter," said the captain. The river was the sole marker across unknown terrain. Henry had no intention of veering so much as an inch from its banks.

# CHAPTER
# FOUR

## *August 28, 1823*

One by one the men reached the obstacle and stopped. The Grand River flowed directly into the steep face of a sandstone cliff, which forced it to turn. The waters swirled and pooled deeply against the wall before spreading widely toward the opposite shore. Bridger and Pig arrived last, bearing Glass between them. They eased the litter to the ground. Pig plopped heavily to his rump, panting, his shirt stained dark with sweat.

Each man looked up as he arrived, quickly appreciating the two choices for moving forward. One was to climb along the steep face of the cliff. It was possible, but only by using hands as well as feet. This was the path taken by Black Harris when he had passed two hours before them. They could see his tracks and the broken branch on the sagebrush that he had grabbed to pull himself up. It was obvious that neither the litter bearers nor the mule could make the climb.

The other option was to cross the river. The opposite bank was level and inviting, but the problem was getting there. The pool created by the embankment appeared at least five feet deep, and the current ran swift. Seam water toward the middle of the river marked the place where the stream shallowed. From there it was an easy wade to the other side. A surefooted man might keep his feet in the deep water, holding his rifle and powder above his head; the less agile might fall, but could certainly swim the few yards to the shallower water.

Getting the mule in the river was no problem. So famous was the animal's love of water that the men called her "Duck." At the end of the day she would stand for hours in water up to her sagging belly. In fact, it was this odd predilection that kept the Mandans from stealing her along with the rest of their stock. While the other animals were grazing or sleeping along the shore, Duck was standing in shallow water on a sandbar. When the bandits tried to take her, she was firmly stuck in the mud. It ultimately took half the brigade to pull her out.

So the problem wasn't the mule. The problem, of course, was Glass.

It would be impossible to hold the litter above the water while crossing.

Captain Henry mulled his choices, cursing Harris for not leaving a sign to cross earlier. They had passed an easy ford a mile downstream. He hated to divide the men, even for a few hours, but it seemed silly to march them all back. "Fitzgerald, Anderson — it's your turn on the litter. Bernot — you and me will go back with 'em to the crossing we passed. Rest of you cross here and wait."

Fitzgerald glared at the captain, muttering under his breath. "You got something to say, Fitzgerald?"

"I signed on to be a trapper, Captain — not a goddamned mule."

"You'll take your turn like everybody else."

"And I'll tell you what everybody else is afraid to say to your face. We're all wondering if you intend to drag this corpse all the way to the Yellowstone."

"I intend to do the same with him that I'd do for you or any other man in this brigade."

"What you'll be doing for all of us is digging graves. How long do you figure we can parade through this valley before we stumble on some hunting party? Glass ain't the only man in this brigade."

"You ain't the only man either," said Anderson. "Fitzgerald don't speak for me, Captain — and I bet he don't speak for many others."

Anderson walked to the litter, placing his rifle next to Glass. "You gonna make me drag him?"

For three days they had carried Glass. The banks of the Grand alternated between sandbar and jumbled rock. Occasional stands of cottonwood gave way at the high water line to the graceful branches of willows, some reaching ten feet in height. Cut banks forced them to climb, giant scoops where erosion sliced away the earth as neatly as a cleaver. They maneuvered around the tangled debris left piled behind the spring flood — mounded stones, tangled branches, and even entire trees, their sun-bleached trunks as smooth as glass from the beating of water and stone. When the terrain became too rugged, they crossed the river to continue

44

upstream, wet buckskins compounding the weight of their load.

The river was a highway on the plains, and Henry's men were not the only travelers on its banks. Tracks and abandoned campsites were numerous. Black Harris had twice seen small hunting parties. The distance had been too great to determine if they were Sioux or Arikara, though both tribes presented danger. The Arikara were certain enemies since the battle on the Missouri. The Sioux had been allies in that fight, but their current disposition was unknown. With only ten able men, the small party of trappers offered little deterrent to attack. At the same time, their weapons, traps, and even the mule were attractive targets. Ambush was a constant danger, with only the scouting skills of Black Harris and Captain Henry to steer them clear.

*Territory to cross quickly*, thought the captain. Instead, they plodded forward at the leaden pace of a funeral procession.

Glass slipped in and out of consciousness, though one state differed little from the other. He could occasionally take water, but the throat wounds made it impossible to swallow solid food. Twice the litter spilled, dumping Glass on the ground. The second spill broke two of the stitches in his throat. They stopped long enough for the captain to resuture the neck, red now with infection. No one bothered to inspect the other wounds. There was little they could do for them, anyway. Nor could Glass protest. His wounded throat

**45**

rendered him mute, his only sound the pathetic wheeze of his breathing.

At the end of the third day they arrived at the confluence of a small creek with the Grand. A quarter mile up the creek, Black Harris found a spring, surrounded by a thick stand of pines. It was an ideal campsite. Henry dispatched Anderson and Harris to find game.

The spring itself was more seep than font, but its icy water filtered over mossy stones and collected in a clear pool. Captain Henry stooped to drink while he thought about the decision he had made.

In three days of carrying Glass, the captain estimated they had covered only forty miles. They should have covered twice that distance or more. While Henry believed they might be beyond Arikara territory, Black Harris found more signs each day of the Sioux.

Beyond his concerns about where they were, Henry fretted about where they needed to be. More than anything, he worried that they would arrive too late on the Yellowstone. Without a couple of weeks to lay in a supply of meat, the whole brigade would be at jeopardy. Late fall weather was as capricious as a deck of cards. They might find Indian summer, or the howling winds of an early blizzard.

Aside from their physical safety, Henry felt enormous pressure for commercial success. With luck, a few weeks of fall hunting, and some trading with the Indians, they might net enough fur to justify sending one or two men downriver.

46

The captain loved to imagine the effect of a fur-laden pirogue arriving in St. Louis on some bright February day. Stories of their successful establishment on the Yellowstone would headline the *Missouri Republican*. The press would bring new investors. Ashley could parley fresh capital into a new fur brigade by early spring. By late summer, Henry envisioned himself commanding a network of trappers up and down the Yellowstone. With enough men and trading goods, maybe he could even buy peace with the Blackfeet, and once again trap in the beaver-rich valleys of the Three Forks. By next winter it would take flatboats to carry the plews they would harvest.

But it all depended upon time. Being there first and in force. Henry felt the press of competition from every point on the compass.

From the north, the British North West Company had established forts as far south as the Mandan villages. The British also dominated the western coast, from which they now pushed inland along the Columbia and its tributaries. Rumors circulated that British trappers had penetrated as far as the Snake and the Green.

From the south, several groups spread northward from Taos and Santa Fe: the Columbia Fur Company, the French Fur Company, StoneBostwick and Company.

Most visible of all was the competition from the east, from St. Louis itself. In 1819, the U.S. Army began its "Yellowstone Expedition" with the express goal of enlarging the fur trade. Though extremely limited, the army's presence emboldened entrepreneurs already eager to pursue the fur trade. Manuel Lisa's Missouri Fur Company opened trade on the Platte. John Jacob Astor revived the remnants of his American Fur Company, driven from the Columbia by the British in the War of 1812, by establishing a new headquarters in St. Louis. All competed for limited sources of capital and men.

Henry glanced at Glass, lying on the litter in the shade of the pines.

He had never returned to the task of properly stitching Glass's scalp. It still lay haphazardly atop his head, purple-black around the edges where dried blood now held it in place, a grotesque crown on a shattered body. The captain felt anew the polarizing mix of sympathy and anger, resentment and guilt.

He could not blame Glass for the grizzly attack. The bear was simply a hazard in their path, one of many. When the troop left St. Louis, Henry knew that men would die. Glass's wounded body merely underscored the precipice that each of them walked every day. Henry considered Glass his best man, the best mix of seasoning, skills, and disposition. The others, with the possible exception of Black Harris, he viewed as subordinates. They were younger, dumber, weaker, less experienced. But Captain Henry saw Glass as a peer. If it could happen to Glass, it could happen to anyone; it could happen to him. The captain turned from the dying man.

He knew that leadership required him to make tough decisions for the good of the brigade. He knew that the frontier respected — required — independence and self-sufficiency above all else. There were no entitlements west of St. Louis. Yet the fierce individuals who comprised his frontier community were bound together by the tight weave of collective responsibility. Though no law was written, there was a crude rule of law, adherence to a covenant that transcended their selfish interests. It was biblical in its depth, and its importance grew with each step into wilderness. When the need arose, a man extended a helping hand to his friends, to his partners, to strangers. In so doing, each knew that his own survival might one day depend upon the reaching grasp of another.

The utility of his code seemed diminished as the captain struggled to apply it to Glass. *Haven't I done my best for him?* Tending his wounds, portaging him, waiting respectfully so that he might at least have a civilized burial. Through Henry's decisions, they had subordinated their collective needs to the needs of one man. It was the right thing to do, but it could not be sustained. Not here.

The captain had thought of abandoning Glass outright. In fact, so great was Glass's suffering that Henry wondered briefly whether they should put a bullet in his head, bring his misery to an end. He quickly dismissed any notion of killing Glass, but he wondered if he could somehow communicate with the wounded man, make him understand that he could no longer risk the entire brigade. They could find him shelter, leave him with a fire, weapons, and provisions. If his condition improved, he could join them on the Missouri. Knowing Glass, he suspected this was what the man would ask for if he could speak for himself. Surely he wouldn't jeopardize the lives of the other men.

Yet Captain Henry couldn't bring himself to leave the wounded man behind. There had been no coherent conversation with Glass since the bear attack, so ascertaining his wishes was impossible. Absent such clear guidance, he would make no assumptions. He was the leader, and Glass was his responsibility.

*But so are the other men.* So was Ashley's investment. So was his family back in St. Louis, a family that had waited more than a decade for the commercial success that seemed always as distant as the mountains themselves.

That night the men of the brigade gathered around the three small fire pits. They had fresh meat to smoke, a buffalo calf, and the shelter of the pines gave them added confidence in building fires. The late August evening cooled quickly after sunset: not cold, but a reminder that a change of season lurked just over the horizon.

The captain stood to address the men, a formality that foreshadowed the seriousness of what he would say. "We need to make better time. I need two volunteers to stay with Glass. Stay with him here until he dies, give him a proper burial, then catch up. The Rocky Mountain Fur Company will pay $70 for the risk of staying back."

A pine knot burst from one of the fires, catapulting sparks into the clear night sky. Otherwise the camp fell silent as the men pondered the situation and the offer.

It was eerie to contemplate Glass's death, however certain. A Frenchman named Jean Bernot crossed himself. Most of the others simply stared at the fire.

No one said anything for a long time. They all thought about the money. Seventy dollars was more than a third of their wage for the entire year. Viewed through the cold prism of economics, Glass would surely die soon. Seventy dollars to sit in a clearing for a few days, then a week of tough marching to catch up with the brigade. Of course they all knew there was a real risk in staying back. Ten men were little deterrent from attack. Two men were none. If a war party happened upon them . . . Seventy dollars bought you nothing if you were dead.

"I'll stay with him, Captain." The other men turned, surprised that the volunteer was Fitzgerald.

Captain Henry was unsure how to react, so suspicious was he of Fitzgerald's motive.

Fitzgerald read the hesitation. "I ain't doing it for love, Captain. I'm doing it for money, pure and simple. Pick somebody else if you want somebody to mother him."

Captain Henry looked around the loose circle of men. "Who else'll stay?" Black Harris threw a small stick on the fire. "I will, Captain." Glass had been a friend to Harris, and the idea of leaving him with Fitzgerald didn't sit right.

None of the men liked Fitzgerald. Glass deserved better.

The captain shook his head. "You can't stay, Harris."

"What do you mean I can't stay?"

"You can't stay. I know you were his friend, so I'm sorry. But I need you to scout."

Another long silence followed. Most of the men stared blankly into the fire. One by one they arrived at the same uncomfortable conclusion: It wasn't worth it. The money wasn't worth it. Ultimately, Glass wasn't worth it. Not that they didn't respect him, like him even. Some, like Anderson, felt an additional debt, a sense of obligation for gratuitous acts of past kindness. It would be different, thought Anderson, if the captain were asking them to defend Glass's life — but that was not the task at hand. The task at hand was waiting for Glass to die, then burying him. It wasn't worth it.

Henry began to wonder if he would have to entrust the job to Fitzgerald alone, when suddenly Jim Bridger rose clumsily to his feet. "I'll stay."

Fitzgerald snorted sarcastically. "Jesus, Captain, you can't leave me to do this with some pork-eating boy! If it's Bridger that stays you better pay me double for tending to two."

The words jabbed at Bridger like punches. He felt his blood rise in embarrassment and anger. "I promise you, Captain — I'll pull my weight."

This was not the outcome the captain had expected. A part of him felt that leaving Glass with Bridger and Fitzgerald differed little from abandonment. Bridger was barely more than a boy. In his year with the Rocky Mountain Fur Company, he had proved himself to be honest and capable, but he was no counterweight to Fitzgerald. Fitzgerald was a mercenary. But then, thought the captain, wasn't that the essence of the course he had chosen? Wasn't he simply buying proxies, purchasing a substitute for their collective responsibility? For his own responsibility? What else could he do? There was no better choice.

"All right, then," said the captain. "Rest of us leave at dawn."

# CHAPTER
# FIVE

## *August 30, 1823*

It was the evening of the second day since the departure of Captain Henry and the brigade. Fitzgerald had dispatched the boy to gather wood, leaving himself and Glass alone in the camp. Glass lay near one of the small fires. Fitzgerald ignored him.

A rock formation crowned the steep slope above the clearing. Massive boulders stood in a rocky stack, as if titanic hands had piled them one on top of the other and then pressed.

From a crack between two of the great stones grew a lone, twisted pine.

The tree was a sibling to the lodgepole pines that the local tribes used to frame their teepees, but the seed of its origin had been lifted high above the fertile soil of the forest below. A sparrow had pried it from a pine cone decades before, carrying it to a lofty height above the clearing. The sparrow lost the seed to a crevice between the rocks. There was soil in the crevice, and a timely rain for germination. The rocks drew heat in the daytime, compensating in part for the exposure of the outcropping. There was no straight path to sunlight, so the pine grew sideways before it grew upward, worming its way from the crevice before turning toward the sky. A few gnarled branches extended from the warped trunk, each capped with a scruffy tuft of needles. The lodgepoles below grew straight as arrows, some towering sixty feet above the floor of the forest. But none grew higher than the twisted pine on top of the rock.

Since the captain and the brigade left, Fitzgerald's strategy was simple: lay in a supply of jerked meat so they were ready to move fast when Glass died; in the meantime, stay away from their camp as much as possible.

Though they were off the main river, Fitzgerald had little confidence in their position on the creek. The little stream led straight to the clearing. The charred remains of campfires made it clear that others had availed themselves of the sheltered spring. In fact, Fitzgerald feared that the clearing was a well-known campsite. Even if it were not, the tracks of the brigade and the mule led clearly from the river. A hunting or war party couldn't help but find them if they came up the near bank of the Grand.

Fitzgerald looked bitterly at Glass. Out of morbid curiosity, he had examined Glass's wounds on the day the rest of the troop left. The sutures in the wounded man's throat had held since the litter spilled, but the entire area was red with infection. The puncture wounds on his leg and arm seemed to be healing, but the deep slashes on his back were inflamed. Luckily for him, Glass spent most of his time unconscious. *When will the bastard die?*

★　★　★

It was a twisted path that brought John Fitzgerald to the frontier, a path that began with his flight from New Orleans in 1815, the day after he stabbed a prostitute to death in a drunken rage.

Fitzgerald grew up in New Orleans, the son of a Scottish sailor and a Cajun merchant's daughter. His father put in port once a year during the ten years of marriage before his ship went down in the Caribbean. On each call to New Orleans he left his fertile wife with the seed of a new addition to the family. Three months after learning of her husband's death, Fitzgerald's mother married the elderly owner of a sundry shop, an action she viewed as essential to support her family. Her pragmatic decision served most of her children well. Eight survived to adulthood. The two eldest sons took over the sundry shop when the old man died. Most of the other boys found honest work and the girls married respectably. John got lost somewhere in the middle.

From an early age, Fitzgerald demonstrated both a reflex toward and a skill for engaging in violence. He was quick to resolve disputes with a punch or a kick, and was thrown out of school at the age of ten for stabbing a classmate in the leg with a pencil. Fitzgerald had no interest in the hard labor of following his father to sea, but he mixed eagerly in the seedy chaos of a port town. His fighting skills were tested and honed on the docks where he spent his teenage days. At seventeen, a boatman slashed his face in a barroom brawl. The incident left him with a fishhook scar and a new respect for cutlery. He became fascinated with knives, acquiring a collection of daggers and scalpers in a wide range of sizes and shapes.

At the age of twenty, Fitzgerald fell in love with a young whore at a dockside saloon, a French girl named Dominique Perreau. Despite the financial underpinnings of their relationship, the full implications of Dominique's métier apparently did not register with Fitzgerald. When he walked in on Dominique plying her trade with the fat captain of a keelboat, the young man fell into a rage. He stabbed them both before fleeing into the streets. He stole eighty-four dollars from his brothers' store and hired passage on a boat headed north up the Mississippi.

For five years he made his living in and around the taverns of Memphis. He tended bar in exchange for room, board, and a small salary at an establishment known, with pretensions that exceeded its grasp, as the Golden Lion. His official capacity as barkeep gave him something he had not possessed in New Orleans — a license to engage in violence. He removed disorderly patrons with a relish that startled even the rough-cut clientele of the saloon. Twice he nearly beat men to death.

Fitzgerald possessed some of the mathematical skills that made his brothers successful storekeepers, and he applied his native intelligence toward gambling. For a while he was content to squander his paltry stipend from the bar. Over time he was drawn to higher stakes. These new games required more money to play, and Fitzgerald found no shortage of lenders.

Not long after borrowing two hundred dollars from the owner of a rival tavern, Fitzgerald hit it big. He won a thousand dollars on a single hand of queens over tens, and spent the next week in a celebratory debauch. The payoff infused him with a false confidence in his gambling skills and a ravenous hunger for more. He quit his work at the Golden Lion and sought to make his living at cards. His luck veered sharply south, and a month later he owed two thousand dollars to a loan shark named Geoffrey Robinson. He dodged Robinson for several weeks before two henchmen caught him and broke his arm. They gave him a week to pay the balance due.

In desperation, Fitzgerald found a second lender, a German named Hans Bangemann, to pay off the first. With the two thousand dollars in his hands, however, Fitzgerald had an epiphany: He would flee Memphis and start someplace new. The next morning he took passage on another boat north. He landed in St. Louis late in the month of February 1822.

After a month in the new city, Fitzgerald learned that two men had been asking at pubs about the whereabouts of a "gambler with a scar on his face." In the small world of Memphis moneylenders, it had not taken long for Geoffrey Robinson and Hans Bangemann to discover the full measure of Fitzgerald's treachery. For one hundred dollars each, they hired a pair of henchmen to find Fitzgerald, kill him, and recover as much of their loans as possible. They harbored little hope of getting their money back, but they did want Fitzgerald dead. They had reputations to uphold, and word was spread of their plan through the network of Memphis taverns.

Fitzgerald was trapped. St. Louis was the northernmost outpost of civilization on the Mississippi. He was afraid to go south, where trouble awaited him in New Orleans and Memphis. That day Fitzgerald overheard a group of pub patrons talking excitedly about a newspaper ad in the *Missouri Republican*. He picked up the paper to read for himself:

To enterprising young men. The subscriber wishes to engage one hundred young men to ascend the Missouri river to its source, there to be employed for one, two, or three years. For particulars enquire of Captain Henry, near the lead mines in the country of Washington, who will ascend with, and command, the party.

Fitzgerald made a rash decision. With the paltry remnants of the money he had stolen from Hans Bangemann, he bought a weathered leather tunic, moccasins, and a rifle. The next day he presented himself to Captain Henry and requested a spot with the fur brigade. Henry was suspicious of Fitzgerald from the beginning, but pickings were slim. The captain needed a hundred men and Fitzgerald looked fit. If he'd been in a few knife fights, so much the better. A month later Fitzgerald was on a keelboat headed north up the Missouri River.

Although he fully intended to desert the Rocky Mountain Fur Company when the opportunity presented itself, Fitzgerald took to life on the frontier. He found that his skill with knives extended to other weapons. Fitzgerald had none of the tracking skills of the real woodsmen in the brigade, but he was an excellent shot. With a sniper's patience, he had killed two Arikara during the recent siege on the Missouri. Many of Henry's men had been terrified in their fights with various Indians. Fitzgerald found them exhilarating, even titillating.

Fitzgerald glanced at Glass, his eyes falling on the Anstadt lying next to the wounded man. He looked around to make sure that Bridger wasn't returning, then picked up the rifle. He pulled it to his shoulder and sighted down the barrel. He loved how the gun fit snug against his body, how the wide pronghorn sites found targets quickly, how the lightness of the weapon let him hold a steady bead. He swung from target to target, up and down, until the sights came to rest on Glass.

Once again Fitzgerald thought about how the Anstadt soon would be his. They hadn't talked about it with the captain, but who deserved the rifle more than the man who stayed behind? Certainly his claim was better than Bridger's. All the trappers admired Glass's gun. Seventy dollars was paltry pay for the risk they were taking — Fitzgerald was there for the Anstadt. Such a weapon should not be wasted on a boy. Besides, Bridger was happy enough to get William Anderson's rifle. Throw him some other crumb — Glass's knife, perhaps.

Fitzgerald mulled the plan he had formed since he volunteered to stay with Glass, a plan that seemed more compelling with each passing hour. *What difference does a day make to Glass?* On the other hand, Fitzgerald knew exactly the difference a day meant to his own prospects for survival.

Fitzgerald set the Anstadt down. A bloody shirt lay next to Glass's head. *Push it against his face for a few minutes — we could be on our way in the morning.* He looked again at the rifle, its dark brown striking against the orange hue of fallen pine needles. He reached for the shirt.

"Did he wake up?" Bridger stood behind him, his arms full of firewood. Fitzgerald startled, fumbling for an instant. "Christ, boy! Sneak up on me again like that and I swear to God I'll cut you down!"

Bridger dropped the wood and walked over to Glass. "I was thinking maybe we ought to try giving him some broth."

"Why, that's mighty kind of you, Bridger. Pour a little broth down that throat and maybe he'll last a week instead of dying tomorrow! Will that make you sleep better? What do you think, that if you give him a little soup he's going to get up and walk away from here?"

Bridger was quiet for a minute, then said, "You act like you want him to die."

"Of course I want him to die! Look at him. *He* wants to die!" Fitzgerald paused for effect. "You ever go to school, Bridger?" Fitzgerald knew the answer to his question.

The boy shook his head.

"Well, let me give you a little lesson in arithmetic. Captain Henry and the rest are probably making around thirty miles a day now that they're not dragging Glass. Let's figure we'll be faster — say we make forty. Do you know what's forty minus thirty, Bridger?" The boy stared blankly.

"I'll tell you what it is. It's ten." Fitzgerald held up the fingers of both hands in a mocking gesture. "This many, boy. Whatever their head start is — we only make up ten miles a day once we take after them. They're already a hundred miles ahead of us. That's ten days on our own, Bridger. And that assumes he dies today and we find them straight away. Ten days for a Sioux hunting party to stumble on us. Don't you get it? Every day we sit here is another three days we're on our own. You'll look worse than Glass when the Sioux are finished with you, boy. You ever see a man who got scalped?"

Bridger said nothing, though he had seen a man scalped. He was there near the Great Falls when Captain Henry brought the two dead trappers back to camp, butchered by Blackfeet. Bridger vividly remembered the bodies. The captain had tied them belly down to a single pack mule. When he cut them loose, they fell stiffly to the ground. The trappers had gathered round them, mesmerized as they contemplated the mutilated corpses of the men they had seen that morning at the campfire. And it wasn't just their scalps that were missing. Their noses and ears had been hacked away, and their eyes gouged out. Bridger remembered how, without noses, the heads looked more like skulls than faces. The men were naked, and their privates were gone, too. There was a stark tan line at their necks and wrists. Above the line their skin was as tough and brown as saddle leather, but the rest of their bodies was as white as lace. It looked funny, almost. It was the type of thing that one of the men would have joked about, if it hadn't been so horrible. Of course nobody laughed. Bridger always thought about it when he washed himself — how underneath, they all had this lacy white skin, weak as a baby.

Bridger struggled, desperately wanting to challenge Fitzgerald, but wholly incapable of articulating a rebuttal. Not for lack of words, this time, but rather for lack of reasons. It was easy to condemn Fitzgerald's motivation — he said himself it was money. But what, he wondered, was his own motivation? It wasn't money. The numbers all jumbled together, and his regular salary was already more wealth than he had ever seen. Bridger liked to believe that his motive was loyalty, fidelity to a fellow member of the brigade. He certainly respected Glass. Glass had been kind, watching out for him in small ways, schooling him, defending him against embarrassments. Bridger acknowledged a debt to Glass, but how far did it extend?

The boy remembered the surprise and admiration in the eyes of the men when he had volunteered to stay with Glass. What a contrast to the anger and contempt of that terrible night on sentry duty. He remembered how the captain had patted him on the shoulder when the brigade departed, and how the simple gesture had filled him with a sense of affiliation, as if for the first time he deserved his place among the men. Wasn't that why he was there in the clearing — to salve his wounded pride? Not to take care of another man, but to take care of himself? Wasn't he just like Fitzgerald, profiting from another man's misfortune? Say what you would about Fitzgerald, at least he was honest about why he stayed.

# CHAPTER
# SIX

## *August 31, 1823*

Alone in the camp on the morning of the third day, Bridger spent several hours repairing his moccasins, both of which had developed holes in the course of their travels. As a consequence, his feet were scraped and bruised, and the boy appreciated the opportunity for the repair work. He cut leather from a rawhide left when the brigade departed, used an awl to punch holes around the edge, and replaced the soles with the new hide on the bottom. The stitching was irregular but tight.

As he examined his handiwork his eyes fell on Glass. Flies buzzed around his wounds and Bridger noticed that Glass's lips were cracked and parched. The boy questioned again whether he stood on any higher moral plane than Fitzgerald. Bridger filled his large tin cup with cold water from the spring and put it to Glass's mouth. The wetness triggered an unconscious reaction, and Glass began to drink.

Bridger was disappointed when Glass finished. It was good to feel useful. The boy stared at Glass. Fitzgerald was right, of course. There was no question that Glass would die. *But shouldn't I do my best for him? At least provide comfort in his final hours?*

Bridger's mother could tease a healing property from anything that grew. He wished many times that he had paid more attention when she had returned from the woods, her basket filled with flowers, leaves, and bark. He did know a few basics, and on the edge of the clearing he found what he was looking for, a pine tree with its sticky gum oozing like molasses. He used his rusty skinning knife to scrape off the gum, working until his blade was smeared with a good quantity. He walked back to Glass and knelt next to him. The boy focused first on the leg and arm wounds, the deep punctures from the grizzly's fangs. While the surrounding areas remained black-and-blue, the skin itself appeared to be repairing. Bridger used his finger to apply the gum, filling the wounds and smearing the surrounding skin.

Next he rolled Glass to his side in order to examine his back. The crude sutures had snapped when the litter spilled, and there were signs of more recent bleeding. Still, it wasn't blood that gave Glass's back its crimson sheen. It was infection. The five parallel cuts extended almost the entire length of his back. There was yellow pus in the center of the cuts, and the edges practically glowed fiery red. The odor reminded Bridger of sour milk. Unsure what to do, he simply smeared the entire area with pine gum, returning twice to the trees to gather more.

Bridger turned last to the neck wounds. The captain's sutures remained in place, though to the boy they seemed merely to conceal the carnage beneath the skin. The wheezing rumble continued from Glass's unconscious breathing, like the loose rattle of broken parts in a machine. Bridger walked again into the pines, this time looking for a tree with loose bark. He found one and used his knife to pry loose the outer skin. The tender inner bark he gathered in his hat.

Bridger filled his cup again with water at the spring and set it in the coals of the fire. When it boiled, he added the pine bark, mashing the mixture with the pommel of his knife. He worked until the consistency was thick and smooth as mud. He waited for the poultice to cool slightly, then applied it to Glass's throat, packing the mixture against the slashes and spreading it outward toward his shoulder. Next Bridger walked to his small pack, pulling out the remnants of his spare shirt. He used the cloth to cover the poultice, lifting Glass's head to tie a knot firmly behind the man's neck.

Bridger let the wounded man's head return gently to the ground, surprised to find himself staring into Glass's open eyes. They burned with an intensity and lucidity that juxtaposed oddly against his broken body. Bridger stared back, searching to discern the message that Glass clearly intended to convey. *What is he saying?*

Glass stared at the boy for a minute before allowing his eyes to fall closed. In his fleeting moments of consciousness, Glass felt a heightened sensitivity, as if suddenly made aware of the secret workings of his body. The boy's efforts provided topical relief. The slight stinging of the pine gum had a medicinal quality, and the heat from the poultice created a steeping

**67**

comfort at his throat. At the same time, Glass sensed that his body was marshaling itself for another, decisive battle. Not at the surface, but deep within.

By the time Fitzgerald returned to camp, the shadows of late afternoon had stretched into the fading glow of early evening. He carried a doe over his shoulder. He had field-dressed the animal, slitting her neck and removing the entrails. He let the deer fall next to one of the fires. She landed in an unnatural pile, so different from her grace in life.

Fitzgerald stared at the fresh dressings on Glass's wounds. His face tensed. "You're wasting your time with him." He paused. "I wouldn't give a tinker's damn, except you're wasting my time too."

Bridger ignored the comment, though he felt the blood rise in his face. "How old are you, boy?"

"Twenty."

"You lying piece of horseshit. You can't even talk without squeaking. I bet you never seen a tit that wasn't your ma's."

The boy looked away, hating Fitzgerald for his bloodhound ability to sense weakness.

Fitzgerald absorbed Bridger's discomfort like the nourishment of raw meat. He laughed. "What! You never been with a woman? I'm right, aren't I, boy? What's the matter, Bridger — you didn't have two bucks for a whore before we left St. Louis?"

Fitzgerald eased his large frame to the ground, sitting down to better enjoy himself. "Maybe you don't like girls? You a bugger, boy? Maybe I need to sleep on my back, keep you from rutting at me in the night." Still Bridger said nothing.

"Or maybe you got no pecker at all."

Without thinking, Bridger jumped to his feet, grabbed his rifle, cocked it, and pointed the long barrel at Fitzgerald's head. "You son of a bitch, Fitzgerald! Say another word and I'll blow your damn head off!"

Fitzgerald sat stunned, staring at the dark muzzle of the rifle barrel. For a long moment he sat like that, just staring at the muzzle. Then his dark eyes moved slowly up to Bridger's, a smile creeping to join the scar on his face. "Well, good for you, Bridger. Maybe you don't squat when you piss, after all."

He snorted at his joke, pulled out his knife, and set to butchering the deer.

In the quiet of the camp, Bridger became aware of the heavy sound of his own breathing, and could feel the rapid beat of his heart. He lowered the gun and set the butt on the ground, then lowered himself. He felt suddenly tired, and pulled his blanket around his shoulders.

After several minutes, Fitzgerald said, "Hey, boy."

Bridger looked over, but said nothing in acknowledgment.

Fitzgerald casually wiped the back of a bloody hand against his nose.

"That new gun of yours won't fire without a flint."

Bridger looked down at his rifle. The flint was missing from the lock.

The blood rose again in his face, though this time he hated himself as much as Fitzgerald. Fitzgerald laughed quietly and continued his skillful work with the long knife.

In truth, Jim Bridger was nineteen that year, with a slight build that made him look younger still. The year of his birth, 1804, coincided with the launch of the Lewis and Clark expedition, and it was the excitement generated by their return that led Jim's father to venture west from Virginia in 1812.

The Bridger family settled on a small farm at Six-Mile-Prairie near St. Louis. For a boy of eight, the voyage west was a grand adventure of bumpy roads, hunting for supper, and sleeping beneath a canopy of open sky. In the new farm, Jim found a forty-acre playground of meadows, woods, and creeks. Their first week on the new property, Jim discovered a small spring. He remembered vividly his excitement as he led his father to the hidden seep, and his pride when they built the springhouse. Among many trades, Jim's father dabbled in surveying. Jim often tagged along, further fixing a taste for exploration.

Bridger's childhood ended abruptly at the age of thirteen, when his mother, father, and older brother all died of fever in the space of a single month. The boy found himself suddenly responsible for both himself and a younger sister. An elderly aunt came to tend for his sister, but the financial burden for the family fell upon Jim. He took a job with the owner of a ferry.

The Mississippi of Bridger's boyhood teemed with traffic. From the south, manufactured supplies moved upriver to the booming St. Louis, while downstream flowed the raw resources of the frontier. Bridger heard stories about the great city of New Orleans and the foreign ports beyond. He met the wild boatmen who pushed their craft upstream through sheer strength of body and will. He talked to teamsters who portaged products from Lexington and Terre Haute. He saw the future of the river in the form of belching steamboats, churning against the current.

Yet it wasn't the Mississippi River that captured Jim Bridger's imagination — it was the Missouri. A mere six miles from his ferry the two great rivers joined as one, the wild waters of the frontier pouring into the bromide current of the everyday. It was the confluence of old and new, known and unknown, civilization and wilderness. Bridger lived for the rare moments when the fur traders and voyageurs tied their sleek Mackinaws at the ferry landing, sometimes even camping for the night. He marveled at their tales of savage Indians, teeming game, forever plains, and soaring mountains.

The frontier for Bridger became an aching presence that he could feel, but could not define, a magnetic force pulling him inexorably toward something that he had heard about, but never seen. A preacher on a swaybacked mule rode Bridger's ferry one day. He asked Bridger if he knew God's mission for him in life. Without pause Bridger answered, "Go to the Rockies." The preacher was elated, urging the boy to consider missionary work with the savages. Bridger had no interest in bringing Jesus to the Indians, but the conversation stuck with him. The boy came to believe that going west was more than just a fancy for someplace new. He came to see it as a part of his soul, a missing piece that could only be made whole on some far-off mountain or plain.

Against this backdrop of an imagined future, Bridger poled the sluggish ferry. To and fro, back and forth, motion without progression, never venturing so much as a mile beyond the fixed points of the two landings. It was the polar opposite of the life he imagined for himself, a life of wandering and exploration through country unknown, a life in which he never once retraced his steps.

After a year on the ferry, Bridger made a desperate and ill-thought effort to make some progress westward, apprenticing himself to a blacksmith in St. Louis. The blacksmith treated him well, and even provided a modest stipend to send to his sister and aunt. But the terms of apprenticeship were clear — five years of servitude.

If the new job did not put him in the wilderness, at least St. Louis talked of little else. For half a decade Bridger soaked in frontier lore. When the plainsmen came to shoe their horses or repair their traps, Bridger overcame his reserve to ask about their travels. Where had they been? What had they seen? The boy heard tales of a naked John Colter, outracing a hundred Blackfeet intent on taking his scalp. Like everyone in St. Louis, he came to know details of successful traders like Manuel Lisa and the Chouteau brothers. Most exciting to Bridger were occasional glimpses of his heroes in the flesh. Once a month, Captain Andrew Henry visited the blacksmith to shoe his horse. Bridger made sure to volunteer for the work, if only for the chance that he might exchange a few words with the captain. His brief encounters with Henry were like a reaffirmation of faith, a tangible manifestation of something that otherwise might exist only as fable and tale.

The term of Bridger's apprenticeship ran to his eighteenth birthday, on March 17, 1822. To coincide with the Ides of March, a local actors' brigade played a rendition of Shakespeare's *Julius Caesar*. Bridger paid two bits for a seat. The long play made little sense. The men looked silly in full-length gowns, and for a long time Bridger was unsure whether the actors were speaking English. He enjoyed the spectacle, though, and after a while began to develop a feel for the rhythm of the stilted language. A handsome actor with a bellowing voice spoke a line that would stick with Bridger for the rest of his life:

There is a tide in the affairs of men,
Which, taken at the flood, leads on to fortune . . .

Three days later, the blacksmith told Bridger about a notice in the *Missouri Republican*. "To Enterprising Young Men . . ." Bridger knew his tide had come in.

The next morning Bridger awoke to find Fitzgerald bent over Glass, his hand pressed against the forehead of the wounded man.

"What're you doing, Fitzgerald?"

"How long's he had this fever?"

Bridger moved quickly to Glass and felt his skin. It was steamy with heat and perspiration. "I checked him last night and he seemed all right."

"Well, he's not all right now. It's the death sweats. The son of a bitch is finally going under."

Bridger stood there, unsure whether to feel upset or relieved. Glass began to shiver and shake. There seemed little chance that Fitzgerald was wrong.

"Listen, boy — we got to be ready to move. I'm going to scout up the Grand. You take the berries and get that meat pounded into pemmican."

"What about Glass?"

"What about him, boy? You become a doctor while we've been camping here? There's nothing we can do now."

"We can do what we're supposed to be doing — wait with him and bury him when he dies. That was our deal with the captain."

"Scrape out a grave if it'll make you feel better! Hell, build him a goddamn altar! But if I come back here and that meat's not ready, I'll whip on you till you're worse off than him!" Fitzgerald grabbed his rifle and disappeared down the creek.

The day was typical of early September, sunny and crisp in the morning, hot by afternoon. The terrain flattened where the creek met the river, its trickling waters spreading wide across a sandbar before joining the rushing current of the Grand. Fitzgerald's eyes were drawn downward to the scattered tracks of the fur brigade, still apparent after four days. He glanced upriver, where an eagle perched like a sentry on the

74

bare branch of a dead tree. Something startled the bird. It opened its wings, and with two powerful flaps lifted itself from its perch. Carving a neat pivot on the tip of its wing, the bird turned and flew upriver.

The screaming whinny of a horse cut the morning air. Fitzgerald spun around. The morning sun sat directly on the river, its piercing rays merging with water to form a dancing sea of light. Squinting against the glare, Fitzgerald could discern the silhouettes of mounted Indians. He dropped to the ground. *Did they see me?* He lay on the ground for an instant, his breath arriving in staccato spurts. He snaked toward the only cover available, a scrubby stand of willows. Listening intently, he heard again the whinny of the horse — but not the churning pound of charging horses. He checked to ensure his rifle and pistol were charged, removed his wolf-skin hat, and lifted his head to peer through the willows.

There were five Indians at a distance of about two hundred yards on the opposite bank of the Grand. Four of the riders formed a loose semicircle around the fifth, who quirted a balking pinto. Two of the Indians laughed, and all of them seemed transfixed by the struggle with the horse.

One of the Indians wore a full headdress of eagle feathers. Fitzgerald was close enough to see clearly a bear-claw necklace around his chest and the otter pelts that wrapped his braids. Three of the Indians carried guns; the other two bows. There was no war paint on the men or the horses, and Fitzgerald guessed they were hunting. He wasn't sure of the tribe, although his working assumption was that any Indians in the area would view the trappers with hostility. Fitzgerald calculated that they were just beyond rifle range. That would change quickly if they charged. If they came, he would have one shot with the rifle and one with the pistol. He might be able to reload his rifle once if the river slowed them down. *Three shots at five targets.* He didn't like the odds.

Belly to the ground, Fitzgerald wormed his way toward the cover of the higher willows near the creek. He crawled through the middle of the brigade's old tracks, cursing the markings that so clearly betrayed their position. He turned again when he reached the thicker willows, relieved that the Indians remained preoccupied with the stubborn pinto. Still, they would arrive at the confluence of the creek with the river in a matter of instants. They would notice the creek, and then they would notice the tracks. *The goddamn tracks!* Pointing like an arrow up the creek.

Fitzgerald worked his way from the willows to the pines. He pivoted to take one final look at the hunting party. The skittish pinto had settled, and all five Indians now continued up the river. *We have to leave now.* Fitzgerald ran up the creek the short distance to the camp.

Bridger was pounding venison against a stone when Fitzgerald burst into the clearing. "There's five bucks coming up the Grand!" Fitzgerald began wildly stuffing his few possessions into his pack. He looked up suddenly, his eyes focused in intensity and fear, then anger. "Move, boy! They'll be on our tracks any minute!"

Bridger stuffed meat into his parfleche. Next he threw his pack and possibles bag over his shoulders, then turned to grab his rifle, leaning against a tree next to Glass's Anstadt. *Glass.* The full implications of flight struck the boy like a sudden, sobering slap. He looked down at the wounded man.

For the first time that morning, Glass's eyes were open. As Bridger stared down, the eyes initially had the glassy, uncomprehending gaze of one awakening from deep sleep. The longer Glass stared, the more his eyes seemed to focus. Once focused, it was clear that the eyes stared back with complete lucidity, clear that Glass, like Bridger, had calculated the full meaning of the Indians on the river.

Every pore in Bridger's body seemed to pound with the intensity of the moment, yet to Bridger it seemed that Glass's eyes conveyed a serene calmness. *Understanding? Forgiveness? Or is that just what I want to believe?* As the boy stared at Glass, guilt seized him like clenched fangs. *What does Glass think? What will the captain think?*

"You sure they're coming up the creek?" Bridger's voice cracked as he said it. He hated the lack of control, the demonstrable weakness in a moment demanding strength.

"Do you want to stay and find out?" Fitzgerald moved to the fire, grabbing the remaining meat from the drying racks.

Bridger looked again at Glass. The wounded man worked his parched lips, struggling to form words through a throat rendered mute. "He's trying to say something." The boy knelt, struggling to understand. Glass slowly raised his hand and pointed a shaking finger. *He wants the Anstadt.* "He wants his rifle. He wants us to set him up with his rifle."

The boy felt the blunt pain of a forceful kick against his back and found himself lying facedown on the ground. He struggled to his hands and knees, looking up at Fitzgerald. The rage on Fitzgerald's face seemed to merge with the distorted features of the wolf-skin hat. "Move, goddamn you!"

Bridger scrambled to his feet, wide-eyed and startled. He watched as Fitzgerald walked to Glass, who lay on his back with his few possessions piled next to him: a possibles bag, a knife in a beaded scabbard, a hatchet, the Anstadt, and a powder horn.

Fitzgerald stooped to pick up Glass's possibles bag. He dug inside for the flint and steel, dropping them into the pocket on the front of his leather tunic. He grabbed the powder horn and slung it over his shoulder. The hatchet he tucked under his broad leather belt.

Bridger stared, uncomprehending. "What are you doing?"

Fitzgerald stooped again, picked up Glass's knife, and tossed it to Bridger. "Take that." Bridger caught it, staring in horror at the scabbard in his hand. Only the rifle remained. Fitzgerald picked it up, checking quickly

78

to ensure it was charged. "Sorry, old Glass. You ain't got much more use for any of this."

Bridger was stunned. "We can't leave him without his kit."

The man in the wolf skin looked up briefly, then disappeared into the woods.

Bridger looked down at the knife in his hand. He looked at Glass, whose eyes glared directly into him, animated suddenly like coals beneath a bellows. Bridger felt paralyzed. Conflicting emotions fought inside of him, struggling to dictate his action, until one emotion came suddenly and overwhelmingly to prevail: He was afraid.

The boy turned and ran into the woods.

# CHAPTER
# SEVEN

## *September 2, 1823 — Morning*

There was daylight. Glass could tell that much without moving, but otherwise he had no idea of the time. He lay where he collapsed the day before. His rage had carried him to the edge of the clearing, but his fever stopped him there.

The bear had carved away at Glass from the outside and now the fever carved away from within. It felt to Glass as if he had been hollowed out. He shivered uncontrollably, yearning for the seeping warmth of a fire. Looking around the campsite, he saw that no smoke rose from the charred remains of the fire pits. No fire, no warmth.

He wondered if he could at least scoot back to his tattered blanket, and made a tentative effort to move. When he summoned his strength, the reply that issued back from his body was like a faint echo across a wide chasm.

The movement irritated something deep in his chest. He felt a cough coming on and tensed his stomach muscles to suppress it. The muscles were sore from numerous earlier battles, and despite his effort, the cough burst forth. Glass grimaced at the pain, like the extraction of a deep-set fishhook. It felt like his innards were being ripped out through his throat.

When the pain of coughing receded, he focused again on the blanket.

*I have to get warm.* It took all his strength to lift his head. The blanket lay about twenty feet away. He rolled from his side to his stomach, maneuvering his left arm out in front of his body. Glass bent his left leg, then straightened it to push. Between his one good arm and his one good leg, he push-dragged himself across the clearing. The twenty feet felt like twenty miles, and three times he stopped to rest. Each breath drew like a rasp through his throat, and he felt again the dull throbbing in his cleaved back. He stretched to grab the blanket when it came within reach. He pulled it around his shoulders, embracing the weighty warmth of the Hudson Bay wool. Then he passed out.

Through the long morning, Glass's body fought against the infection of his wounds. He slipped between consciousness, unconsciousness, and a confusing state in between, aware of his surroundings like random pages of a book, scattered glimpses of a story with no continuity to bind them. When conscious, he wished desperately to sleep again, if only to gain respite from the pain. Yet each interlude of sleep came with a haunting precursor — the terrifying thought that he might never wake again. *Is this what it's like to die?*

Glass had no idea how long he had been lying there when the snake appeared. He watched with a mixture of terror and fascination as it slid almost casually from the woods into the clearing. There was an element of caution; the snake paused on the open ground of the clearing, its tongue slithering in and out to test the air. On the whole, though, this was a predator in its element, in confident pursuit of prey. The snake began to move again, the slow serpentine motion accelerating suddenly to propel it with surprising speed. It went straight for him.

Glass wanted to roll away, but there was something inevitable about the way the snake moved. Some part of Glass remembered an admonishment to hold still in the presence of a snake. He froze, as much from hypnosis as from choice. The snake moved to within a few feet of his face and stopped. Glass stared, trying to mimic the serpent's unblinking stare. He was no match. The snake's black eyes were as unforgiving as the plague. He watched, mesmerized, as the snake wrapped itself slowly into a perfect coil, its entire body made for the sole purpose of launching forward in attack. The tongue moved in and out, testing, probing. From the midst of the coil, the snake's tail began quivering back and forth, the rattle like a metronome marking the brief moments before death. The first strike came so quickly that Glass had no time to recoil. He stared down in horror as the rattler's head shot forward, jaws distended to reveal fangs dripping with poison. The fangs sunk into Glass's forearm. He screamed in pain as the venom coursed into his body. He shook his arm but the fangs held on, the snake's body flailing with Glass's arm through the air. Finally the snake dropped, its long body perpendicular to Glass's torso. Before Glass could roll away, the snake rewound itself and struck again.

Glass couldn't scream this time. The serpent had buried its fangs in his throat.

Glass opened his eyes. The sun stood directly above him, the only angle from which it could throw light onto the floor of the clearing. He rolled gingerly to his side to avoid the glare. Ten feet away, a six-foot rattlesnake lay fully extended. An hour before it had swallowed a cottontail kit. Now a large lump distorted the snake's proportions as the rabbit worked its way slowly down the serpent's digestive tract.

Panicked, Glass looked down at his arm. There were no fang marks.

Gingerly, he touched his neck, half expecting to find a serpent attached. Nothing. Relief flooded over him as he realized the snake — or at least the snake bites — were the imagined horror of a nightmare. He looked again at the snake, torpid, as its body worked to digest its prey.

He moved his hand from his throat to his face. He felt the thick coat of salty wetness from heavy sweat, yet his skin was cool. The fever had broken. *Water!* His body screamed at him to drink. He dragged himself to the spring. His shredded throat still permitted only the smallest of sips. Even these caused pain, although the icy water felt like tonic, replenishing and cleansing him from within.

Hugh Glass's remarkable life began unremarkably as the firstborn son of Victoria and William Glass, an English bricklayer in Philadelphia. Philadelphia was growing rapidly at the turn of the century, and builders found no shortage of work. William Glass never became wealthy, but he comfortably supported five children. With a bricklayer's eye, William viewed his responsibility to his children as the laying of a foundation. He considered his provision for their formal education as the crowning achievement of his life.

When Hugh demonstrated considerable academic aptitude, William urged him to consider a career in the law. Hugh, though, had no interest in the white wigs and musty books of lawyers. He did have a passion — geography.

The Rawsthorne & Sons Shipping Company kept an office on the same street as the Glass family. In the foyer of their building they displayed a large globe, one of the few in Philadelphia. On his way home from school each day, Hugh stopped in the office, spinning the globe on its axis, his fingers exploring the oceans and mountains of the world. Colorful maps adorned the office walls, sketching the major shipping routes of the day. The thin lines traversed broad oceans, connecting Philadelphia to the great ports of the world. Hugh liked to imagine the places and people at the ends of those thin lines: from Boston to Barcelona, from Constantinople to Cathay.

Willing to allow his son some rein, William encouraged Hugh to consider a career in cartography. But to Hugh, the mere drawing of maps seemed too passive. The source of Hugh's fascination lay not in the abstract representation of places, but rather in the places themselves, and above all the vast masses marked terra incognita. The cartographers of the day populated these unknown spaces with etchings of the most fanciful and terrifying monsters. Hugh wondered if such beasts could truly exist, or if they were mere fabrications of the mapmaker's pen. He asked his father, who told him, "No one knows." His father's intent was to frighten Hugh toward more practical pursuits. The tactic failed. At the age of thirteen, Hugh announced his intention to become the captain of a ship.

In 1802, Hugh turned sixteen, and William, afraid the boy might run off to sea, relented to the wishes of his son. William knew the Dutch captain of a Rawsthorne & Sons frigate, and asked that Hugh be taken aboard as a cabin boy. The captain, Jozias van Aartzen, had no children of his own. He took his responsibility for Hugh seriously, and for a decade worked to school him in the ways of the sea. By the time the captain died in 1812, Hugh had risen to the rank of first mate.

The War of 1812 interrupted Rawsthorne & Sons' traditional trade with Great Britain. The company quickly diversified into a dangerous but lucrative new business — blockade running. Hugh spent the war years dodging British warships as his speedy frigate transported rum and sugar between the Caribbean and embattled American ports. When the war ended in 1815, Rawsthorne & Sons maintained its Caribbean business, and Hugh became the captain of a small freighter.

Hugh Glass had just turned thirty-one the summer he met Elizabeth van Aartzen, the nineteen-year-old niece of the captain who had mentored him. Rawsthorne & Sons sponsored a Fourth of July celebration, complete with line dancing and Cuban rum. The style of dance did not lend itself to conversation, but it did result in dozens of brief, twirling, thrilling exchanges. Glass sensed something unique about Elizabeth, something confident and challenging. He found himself taken completely.

He called on her the next day, then whenever he docked in Philadelphia. She was traveled and educated, talking easily of far-off peoples and places. They could speak an abbreviated language, each able to complete the other's thoughts. They laughed easily at each other's stories. Time away from Philadelphia became torture, as Glass remembered her eyes in the sparkle of the morning sun, her pale skin in the light of the moon on a sail.

On a bright May day in 1818, Glass returned to Philadelphia with a tiny velvet bag in the breast pocket of his uniform. Inside was a gleaming pearl on a delicate, golden chain. He gave it to Elizabeth and asked her to marry. They planned a wedding for the summer.

Glass left a week later for Cuba. He found himself stuck in the port of Havana, awaiting the resolution of a local dispute over the tardy delivery of a hundred barrels of rum. After a month in Havana, another Rawsthorne & Sons ship arrived. It carried a letter from his mother with the news that his father had died. She implored him to return to Philadelphia immediately.

Hugh knew that the dispute over the rum might well take months to resolve. In that time he could travel to Philadelphia, settle his father's estate, and return to Cuba. If the legal proceedings in Havana proceeded more quickly, his first mate could pilot the ship back to Philadelphia. Glass booked passage on *Bonita Morena*, a Spanish merchant bound that week for Baltimore.

As it turned out, the Spanish merchant would never sail past the ramparts of Fort McHenry. And Glass would never again see Philadelphia. A day's sail from Havana there appeared on the horizon a ship with no flag. *Bonita Morena*'s captain attempted to flee, but his sluggish boat was no match for the speedy pirate cutter. The cutter came abreast of the merchant and fired five cannons loaded with grape. With five of his sailors dead on the decks, the captain took down his sails.

The captain expected his surrender to result in quarter. It did not.

Twenty pirates boarded *Bonita Morena*. The leader, a mulatto with a golden tooth and a golden chain, approached the captain who was standing formally on the quarterdeck.

The mulatto pulled a pistol from his belt and shot the captain point-blank in the head. The crew and passengers stood shocked, awaiting their fates. Hugh Glass stood among them, looking at the buccaneers and their ship. They spoke a jumbled mix of Creole, French, and English. Glass suspected, correctly, that they were Baratarians — foot soldiers in the growing syndicate of the pirate Jean Lafitte.

Jean Lafitte had plagued the Caribbean for years before the War of 1812. The Americans paid little attention, since his targets were primarily British. In 1814, Lafitte discovered a sanctioned avenue for his hatred of England. Major-General Sir Edward Pakenham and six thousand veterans of Waterloo laid siege to New Orleans. In command of the American army, General Andrew Jackson found himself outnumbered five to one. When Lafitte offered the services of his Baratarians, Jackson did not ask for references. Lafitte and his men fought valiantly in the Battle of New Orleans. In the heady wake of the American victory, Jackson recommended a full pardon of Lafitte's earlier crimes, which President Madison quickly granted.

Lafitte had no intention of abandoning his chosen profession, but he had learned the value of sovereign sponsorship. Mexico was at war with Spain. Lafitte established a settlement he called Campeche on the island of Galveston and offered his services to Mexico City. The Mexicans commissioned Lafitte and his small navy, authorizing the attack of any Spanish ship. Lafitte, in turn, won a license to plunder.

The brutal reality of this arrangement now played out before Hugh Glass's eyes. When two crew members stepped forward to aid the mortally wounded captain, they too were shot. The three women onboard, including an ancient widow, were carried to the cutter, where a leering crew welcomed them aboard. While one band of pirates went belowdecks to inspect the cargo, another group began a more systematic appraisal of the crew and passengers. Two elderly men and one obese banker were stripped of their possessions and pushed into the sea.

The mulatto spoke Spanish as well as French. He stood before the captured crew, explaining their options. Any man willing to renounce Spain could join the service of Jean Lafitte. Any man unwilling could join their captain. The dozen remaining sailors chose Lafitte. Half were taken to the cutter, half left to join a pirate crew on the *Bonita Morena*.

Though Glass spoke barely a word of Spanish, he understood the gist of the mulatto's ultimatum. When the mulatto approached him, pistol in hand, Glass pointed to himself and said one word in French: "*Marin*." Sailor.

The mulatto stared at him in silent appraisal. An amused smirk appeared at the corner of his mouth, and he said, "*Ah bon? Okay, monsieur le marin, hissez le foc.*" Hoist the jib.

Glass desperately rummaged the corners of his rudimentary French.

He had no idea of the meaning of *hissez le foc*. In context though, he understood quite clearly the high stakes connected with passing the mulatto's test. Assuming that the challenge involved his bona fides as a sailor, he strode confidently to the fore of the ship, reaching for the jib line that would set the ship into the wind.

"*Bien fait, monsieur le marin*," said the mulatto. It was August of 1819.

Hugh Glass had become a pirate.

Glass looked again at the gap in the woods where Fitzgerald and Bridger had fled. His jaw set as he thought about what they had done, and he felt again the visceral desire to strike out in pursuit. This time though, he also felt the weakness of his body. For the first time since the bear attack, his mind was clear. With clarity came an alarming assessment of his situation.

It was with considerable trepidation that Glass began an examination of his wounds. He used his left hand to trace the edges of his scalp. He'd caught a blurry glimpse of his face in the pooled waters of the spring, and he could see that the bear had nearly scalped him. Never a vain man, his appearance struck him as particularly irrelevant in his current state of affairs. If he survived, he supposed that his scars might even afford him a certain measure of respect among his peers.

What did concern him was his throat. Unable to see the throat wound except in the watery reflection of the spring, he could only probe gingerly with his fingers. Bridger's poultice had fallen off in his short crawl the day before. Glass touched the sutures and appreciated Captain Henry's rudimentary surgical skills. He had a vague memory of the captain working over him in the moments after the attack, although the details and chronology remained murky.

By craning his neck downward he could see the claw marks that extended from his shoulder to his throat. The bear had raked deeply through the muscles of his chest and upper arm. Bridger's pine tar had sealed the wounds. They looked relatively healthy, though a sharp muscular pain kept him from lifting his right arm. The pine tar made him think of Bridger. He remembered that the boy had tended his wounds. Still, it wasn't the image of Bridger nursing him that stuck in his mind. Instead, he saw Bridger looking back from the edge of the clearing, the stolen knife in his hand.

He looked at the snake and thought, *God, what I'd give for my knife*. The rattler had yet to move. He suppressed further thoughts about Fitzgerald and Bridger. *Not now*.

Glass looked down at his right leg. Bridger's tar smeared the puncture wounds in his upper thigh. Those wounds also looked relatively healthy. Cautiously, he straightened the leg. It was stiff as a corpse. He tested the leg by rolling slightly to shift his weight, then pushing down. Excruciating pain radiated outward from the wounds. Clearly, the leg would bear no weight.

Last of all, Glass used his left arm to explore the deep slashes on his back. His probing fingers counted the five parallel cuts. He touched the sticky mess of pine tar, suture, and scab. When he looked at his hand, there was fresh blood too. The cuts began on his butt and got deeper as they rose up his back. The deepest part of the wounds lay between his shoulder blades, where his hand could not reach.

Having completed his self-examination, Glass arrived at several dispassionate conclusions: He was defenseless. If Indians or animals discovered him, he could muster no resistance. He could not stay in the clearing. He wasn't sure how many days he had been in the camp, but he knew that the sheltered spring must be well known to any Indians in the area. Glass had no idea why he had not been discovered the day before, but he knew his luck could not last much longer.

Despite the risk of Indians, Glass had no intention of veering from the Grand. It was a known source for water, food, and orientation. There was, however, one critical question: Upstream or down? As much as Glass might want to embark in immediate pursuit of his betrayers, he knew that to do so would be folly. He was alone with no weapons in hostile country. He was weak from fever and hunger. He couldn't walk.

It pained him to consider retreat, even temporary retreat, but Glass knew there was no real option. The trading post of Fort Brazeau lay 350 miles downstream at the confluence of the White River and the Missouri. If he could make it there, he could reprovision himself, then begin his pursuit in earnest.

*Three hundred and fifty miles.* A healthy man in good weather could cover that ground in two weeks. *How far can I crawl in a day?* He had no idea, but he did not intend to sit in one place. His arm and leg did not appear inflamed, and Glass assumed they would mend with time. He would crawl until his body could support a crutch. If he only made three miles a day, so be it. Better to have those three miles behind him than ahead. Besides, moving would increase his odds of finding food.

The mulatto and his captured Spanish ship sailed west for Galveston Bay and Lafitte's pirate colony at

Campeche. They attacked another Spanish merchantman a hundred miles south of New Orleans, luring their prey into cannon range under the guise of the *Bonita Morena*'s Spanish flag. Once aboard this newest victim, the *Castellana*, the buccaneers again conducted their brutal triage. This time the urgency was greater, since the cannon barrage had ripped open the *Castellana* below the water-line. She was sinking.

The pirates' luck ran flush. The *Castellana* was bound from Seville to New Orleans with a cargo of small arms. If they could remove the guns from the ship before it sank, they would turn an enormous profit. Lafitte would be pleased.

The settlement of Texas had begun in earnest by 1819, and Jean Lafitte's pirate enclave on Galveston Island worked diligently to supply it. Towns sprouted from the Rio Grande to the Sabine, and all of them needed provisions. Lafitte's particular method of obtaining his wares cut out the middleman. In fact, it cut up the middleman. With this competitive advantage over more conventional traders, Campeche thrived, becoming a magnet for all manner of smugglers, slavers, picaroons, and anyone else seeking a tolerant environment for illicit trade. The ambiguous status of Texas helped to shelter the Campeche pirates from intervention by outside powers. Mexico benefited from the attacks on Spanish ships, and Spain was too weak to challenge them. For a while, the United States was willing to look the other way. After all, Lafitte left American ships alone, and he was a hero of the Battle of New Orleans to boot.

Though not physically shackled, Hugh Glass found himself thoroughly imprisoned by Jean Lafitte's criminal enterprise. Onboard ship, any form of mutiny would result in his death. His participation in various attacks on Spanish merchantmen left no doubt about the pirates' perspective on dissent. Glass managed to avoid spilling blood by his own hand; his other actions he justified by the doctrine of necessity.

Nor did Glass's time ashore in Campeche offer any reasonable opportunity for escape. Lafitte reigned supreme on the island. Across the bay on the Texas mainland, the dominant inhabitants were the Karankawa Indians, notorious for cannibalism. Beyond the territory of the Karankawa lay the Tonkawas, the Comanches, the Kiowas, and the Osage. None were hospitable to whites, though they were less inclined to eat them. The scattered pockets of civilization still included a large number of Spaniards, likely to hang as a pirate anyone who walked up from the coast. Mexican banditos and vigilante Texicans added final spice to the mainland mix.

Ultimately, there were limits on the civilized world's willingness to tolerate a thriving pirate state. Most significantly, the United States decided to improve its relations with Spain. This diplomatic endeavor was made more difficult by the constant harassment of Spanish ships, often in U.S. territorial waters. In November 1820, President Madison sent Lieutenant Larry Kearney, the *USS Enterprise*, and a fleet of American warships to Campeche. Lieutenant Kearney presented Lafitte with a succinct choice: Leave the island or be blown to pieces.

Jean Lafitte may have been a swashbuckler, but he was also a pragmatist. He loaded his ships with as much plunder as could be carried, set Campeche ablaze, and sailed away with his buccaneer fleet, never again to be glimpsed by history.

Hugh Glass stood in the chaotic streets of Campeche that November night and made an abrupt decision about the course of his future. He had no intention of joining the fleeing band of pirates. Glass had come to view the sea, which he once embraced as synonymous with freedom, as no more than the confining parameters of small ships. He resolved to turn a new direction.

The crimson glow of fire cast Campeche's last night in apocalyptic splendor. Men swarmed through the scattered buildings, grabbing for anything of value. Liquor, never in short supply on the island, flowed with particular abandon. Disputes over plunder found quick resolution through gunfire, filling the town with the staccato explosions of small arms. Wild rumors spread that the American fleet was about to shell the town. Men fought wildly to clamber aboard departing ships, whose crews used swords and pistols to fight off unwanted passengers.

As Glass wondered where to go, he ran headlong into a man named Alexander Greenstock. Like Glass, Greenstock was a prisoner, impressed into duty when his ship had been captured. Glass had served with him on a recent foray into the Gulf. "I know about a skiff on the South Shore," said Greenstock. "I'm taking it to the mainland." Among the contending poor options, the risks on the mainland seemed least bad. Glass and Greenstock picked their way through the town. Before them on a narrow road, three heavily armed men sat atop a horse-drawn cart, stacked precariously with barrels and crates. One man whipped the horse, while two others stood guard from the top of their loot. The cart hit a stone and a crate tumbled to the ground with a crash. The men ignored it, racing to catch their ship.

The top of the crate read "Kutztown, Pennsylvania." Inside were newly crafted rifles from the gunsmith shop of Joseph Anstadt. Glass and Greenstock each grabbed a gun, incredulous at their luck. They scavenged through the few buildings that hadn't been reduced to ashes, eventually finding ball, powder, and a few trinkets for trading.

It took them most of the night to row around the east end of the island and across Galveston Bay. The water caught the dancing light from the burning colony, making it appear as if the whole bay was ablaze. They could see clearly the hulking profiles of the American fleet and the fleeing ships of Lafitte. When they were a hundred yards from the mainland shore, a great explosion erupted from the island. Glass and Greenstock looked back to see mushrooming flames bellow forth from Maison Rouge, the residence and armory of Jean Lafitte. They rowed across the final few yards of the bay and jumped into the shallow surf. Glass waded ashore, leaving the sea behind him forever.

With no plan or destination, the two men picked their way slowly down the Texas coast. They set their course based more on that which they sought to avoid than on that which they sought to find. They worried constantly about the Karankawa. On the beach they felt exposed, but thick cane jungles and swampy bayous discouraged turning inland. They worried about Spanish troops and they worried about the American fleet.

After walking seven days, the tiny outpost of Nacogdoches appeared in the distance. News of the American raid on Campeche no doubt had spread. They guessed that the locals would view anyone approaching from Galveston as a runaway pirate, likely to be hanged on sight. Glass knew that Nacogdoches was the trailhead for the Spanish enclave of San Fernando de Bexar. They decided to avoid the village and cut inland. Away from the coast, they hoped, there would be less awareness of the events at Campeche.

Their hopes were misguided. They arrived at San Fernando de Bexar after six days and were promptly arrested by the Spanish. After a week in a stifling jail cell, the two men were brought before Major Juan Palacio del Valle Lersundi, the local magistrate.

Major Palacio gazed at them wearily. He was a disillusioned soldier, a would-be conquistador who instead found himself the administrator of a dusty backwater at the tail end of a war that he knew Spain would lose. As Major Palacio looked at the two men before him, he knew that the safest course would be to order them hanged. Wandering up from the coast with only their rifles and the clothes on their backs, he assumed they were pirates or spies, although both claimed to have been captured by Lafitte while traveling on Spanish ships.

But Major Palacio was not in a hanging mood. The week before, he had sentenced to death a young Spanish soldier for falling asleep while on sentry duty, the proscribed punishment for the infraction. The hanging had left him deeply depressed, and he had spent the better part of the past week in confession with the local *padre*. He stared at the two prisoners and listened to their story. Was it the truth? How could he know for sure, and not knowing, by what authority could he take their lives?

Major Palacio offered Glass and Greenstock a deal. They were free to leave San Fernando de Bexar on one condition — that they traveled north. If they traveled south, Palacio feared that other Spanish troops would pick them up. The last thing he needed was a reprimand for pardoning pirates.

The men knew little about Texas, but Glass found himself suddenly exhilarated, about to embark without compass into the interior of the continent.

And so they made their way north and east, assuming at some point they would collide with the great Mississippi. In more than a thousand miles of wandering, Glass and Greenstock managed to survive on the open plain of Texas. Game was plentiful, including thousands of wild cattle, so food was rarely a problem. The danger came from successive territories of hostile Indians. Having survived their traipse through the territory of the Karankawa, they succeeded in avoiding the Comanches, the Kiowas, the Tonkawas, and the Osage.

Their luck ran out on the banks of the Arkansas River. They had just shot a buffalo calf and were preparing to butcher it. Twenty mounted Loup Pawnees heard the shot and came thundering over the crest of a rolling butte. The treeless plain offered no cover, not even rocks. Without horses, they stood no chance. Foolishly, Greenstock raised his weapon and fired, shooting the horse from one of the charging braves. An instant later he lay dead, three arrows protruding from his chest. A single arrow struck Glass in the thigh.

Glass didn't even raise his rifle, staring in detached fascination as nineteen horses barreled toward him. He saw the flash of paint on the chest of the lead horse and black hair against the blue sky, but he barely felt the round stone of the coup stick that crashed against his skull.

Glass awoke in the Pawnee village. His head throbbed and he was tied at the neck to a post driven into the ground. They had bound his wrists and ankles, though he could move his hands. A crowd of children stood around him, chattering excitedly when he opened his eyes.

An ancient chief with stiffly spiked hair approached him, staring down at the strange man before him, one of the few white men he had ever seen. The chief, named Kicking Bull, said something that Glass could not understand, though the assembled Pawnee began whooping and howling in obvious delight. Glass lay on the edge of a great circle in the middle of the village. As his blurry vision began to focus, he noticed a carefully prepared pyre in the center of the circle and quickly surmised the source of the Pawnee glee. An old woman yelled at the children. They ran off as the Pawnee dispersed to prepare for the ceremonial conflagration.

Glass was left alone to assess his situation. Twin images of the camp floated before his eyes, merging only if he squinted or closed one eye. Looking down at his leg, he saw that the Pawnee had done him the favor of plucking out the arrow. It had not penetrated deeply, but the wound would certainly slow him down if he tried to flee. In short, he could barely see and he could barely walk, let alone run.

He patted the pocket in the front of his shirt, relieved that a small container of cinnabar paint had not fallen out. The cinnabar was one of the few trading goods he had grabbed in his escape from Campeche. Rolling to his side to conceal his actions, he pulled out the container, opened it, and spit into the powder, mixing it with his finger. Next he spread the paint on his face, careful to cover every inch of exposed skin from his forehead to the top of his shirt. He also smeared a large quantity of the thick paint into the palm of his hand. He recapped the small jar and buried it in the sandy soil beneath him. Finally finished, he rolled onto his stomach, resting his head on the crook of his arm so that his face remained hidden.

He stayed in that position until they came for him, listening to the excited preparations for his execution.

Night fell, though an enormous fire illuminated the circle in the center of the Pawnee camp.

Glass was never really sure whether he intended his act as some type of symbolic final gesture, or whether he actually hoped for the effect which in fact occurred. He had heard that most savages were superstitious. In any event, the effect was dramatic, and, as it turned out, saved his life.

Two Pawnee braves and Chief Kicking Bull came to carry him to the pyre. When they found him, facedown, they read it as a sign of fear. Kicking Bull cut the bindings to the post, while the two braves each reached for a shoulder to pull him upright. Ignoring the pain in his thigh, Glass sprang to his feet, facing the chief, the braves, and the assembled tribe.

The collected Pawnee tribe stood in front of him, open-mouthed in shock. Glass's entire face was blood red, as if his skin had been stripped away. The whites of his eyes caught the light of the fire and shone like a fall moon. Most of the Indians had never seen a white man, so his full beard added to the impression of a demonic animal. Glass slapped one of the braves with his open hand, leaving a vermillion hand print etched on his chest. The tribe let out a collective gasp.

For a long moment there was complete silence. Glass stared at the Pawnee and the stunned Pawnee stared back. Somewhat surprised at the success of his tactic, Glass wondered what he should do next. He panicked at the thought that one of the Indians might suddenly regain his composure. Glass decided to begin shouting, and unable to think of anything else to say, he launched into a screaming recitation of the Lord's Prayer: "Our Father, Who art in Heaven, hallowed be Thy Name . . ."

Chief Kicking Bull stared in complete confusion. He had seen a few whites before, but this man appeared to be some type of medicine man or devil. Now the man's strange chant appeared to be putting the entire tribe under some type of spell.

Glass ranted on: "For Thine is the Kingdom, and the Power, and the Glory, forever. Amen."

Finally the white man stopped yelling. He stood there, panting like a spent horse. Chief Kicking Bull looked around him. His people looked back and forth between the chief and the crazy devil man. Chief Kicking Bull could feel the tribe's blame. What had he brought upon them? It was time for a new course of action.

He walked slowly up to Glass, stopping directly in front of him. The chief reached around his neck, removing a necklace from which dangled a pair of hawk's feet. He placed the necklace around Glass's neck, staring questioningly into the devil man's eyes.

Glass looked into the circle before him. At its center, near the pyre, stood a row of four-low chairs made from woven willows. Clearly, these were the front-row seats to the spectacle that was to have been his ritual burning. He limped to one of the seats and sat down. Chief Kicking Bull said something, and two women scrambled to fetch food and water. Then he said something to the brave with the vermillion hand print

102

on his chest. The brave darted off, returning with the Anstadt, which he placed on the ground next to Glass.

Glass spent almost a year with the Loup Pawnee on the plains between the Arkansas and Platte Rivers. After overcoming his initial reticence, Kicking Bull adopted the white man like a son. What Glass had not learned about wilderness survival in his trek from Campeche, he learned from the Pawnee that year.

By 1821, scattered white men had begun to travel the plains between the Platte and the Arkansas. In the summer of that year, Glass was hunting with a party of ten Pawnee when they came across two white men with a wagon. Telling his Pawnee friends to stay behind, Glass rode slowly forward. The men were federal agents dispatched by William Clark, United States Superintendent of Indian Affairs. Clark invited the chiefs of all the surrounding tribes to St. Louis. To demonstrate the government's good faith, the wagon was loaded with gifts — blankets, sewing needles, knives, cast iron pots.

Three weeks later, Glass arrived in St. Louis in the company of Kicking Bull.

St. Louis lay at the frontier of the two forces tugging at Glass. From the east he felt anew the powerful pull of his ties to the civilized world — to Elizabeth and to his family, to his profession and to his past. From the west he felt the tantalizing lure of terra incognita, of freedom unmatched, of fresh beginnings. Glass posted three letters to Philadelphia: to Elizabeth, to his mother, and to Rawsthorne & Sons. He took a clerical job with the Mississippi Shipping Company and waited for replies.

It took more than six months. In early March 1822, a letter arrived from his brother. Their mother had died, he wrote, following their father after barely a month.

There was more. "It is also my sad duty to tell you that your dear Elizabeth has died. She contracted a fever last January, and, though she struggled, she did not recover." Glass collapsed into a chair. The blood drained from his face and he wondered if he would be sick. He read on: "I hope it will give you comfort to know that she was laid to rest near Mother. You should also know that her fidelity to you never wavered, even when we all believed that you had perished."

On March 20th, Glass arrived at the offices of the Mississippi Shipping Company to find a group of men huddled around an advertisement in the *Missouri Republican*. William Ashley was raising a fur brigade, bound for the upper Missouri.

A week later, a letter arrived from Rawsthorne & Sons, offering Glass a new commission as the captain of a cutter on the Philadelphia to Liverpool run. On the evening of April 14th, he read the offer one last time, then threw it on the fire, watching as the flames devoured this last tangible link to his former life.

The next morning, Hugh Glass embarked with Captain Henry and the men of the Rocky Mountain Fur Company. At thirty-six, Glass no longer considered himself a young man. And unlike young men, Glass did not consider himself as someone with nothing to lose. His decision to go west was not rash or forced, but as fully deliberate as any choice in his life. At the same time, he could not explain or articulate his reasons. It was something that he felt more than understood.

In a letter to his brother he wrote, "I am drawn to this endeavor as I have never before been drawn to anything in my life. I am sure that I am right to do this, though I cannot tell you precisely why."

# CHAPTER
# EIGHT

## *September 2, 1823 — Afternoon*

Glass took another long look at the rattlesnake, still lying torpid in the all-consuming state of digesting its prey. The snake hadn't moved an inch since Glass had been conscious. *Food*. His thirst quenched at the seeping spring, Glass became suddenly aware of a profound and gnawing hunger. He had no idea how long it had been since he had eaten, but his hands trembled from the lack of subsistence. When he lifted his head, the clearing spun a slow circle around him.

Glass crawled cautiously toward the snake, the imagery of his horrific dream still vivid. He moved to within six feet, stopping to pick up a walnut-size rock. With his left hand, he rolled the rock, which skipped toward the snake, bumping its body. The snake didn't move. Glass picked up a fist-size rock and crawled within reach. Too late, the snake made a sluggish move toward cover. Glass smashed the rock on its head, beating the serpent repeatedly until he was certain it was dead.

Having killed the rattlesnake, Glass's next challenge was to gut it out.

He looked around the camp. His possibles bag lay near the edge of the clearing. He crawled to it, emptying its remaining contents on the ground: a few rifle patches, a razor, two hawk's feet on a beaded necklace, and the six-inch claw of a grizzly bear. Glass picked up the claw, fixating on the thick coat of dried blood at its tip. He returned it to the bag, wondering how it got there. He picked up the patches, thinking that he might use them for tinder, bitter anew that they would not serve their intended purpose. The razor was the one true find. Its blade was too fragile to make of a weapon, but it could serve a number of useful purposes. Most immediately, he could use it to skin the snake. He dropped the razor into the possibles bag, slung the bag over his shoulder, and crawled back to the snake.

Already flies buzzed around the snake's bloody head. Glass was more respectful. He had once seen a severed snake head implant itself on the nose of a fatally curious dog. Remembering the unfortunate dog, he laid a long stick across the snake's head and pressed down on it with his left leg. He couldn't lift his right arm without setting off intense pain in his shoulder, but the hand functioned normally. He used it to work the razor, sawing the blade to sever the head. He used the stick to flip the head toward the edge of the clearing.

He sliced down the belly beginning at the neck. The razor dulled quickly, reducing its effectiveness with each inch. He managed to cut the length of the snake, nearly five feet to the vent. With the snake laid open he pulled out the entrails, throwing them aside. Beginning again at the neck, he used the razor to peel the scaly

**107**

skin away from the muscle. The meat now glistened before him, irresistible in the face of his hunger.

He bit into the snake, ripping into the raw flesh as if it were an ear of corn. Finally a piece tore free. He gnawed at the springy meat, though his teeth did little to break it down. Oblivious to anything but his hunger, he made the mistake of swallowing. The large chunk of raw meat felt like a stone as it passed through his wounded throat. The pain made him gag. He coughed, and for an instant he thought the chunk of meat might choke him. Finally it passed down his gullet.

He learned his lesson. He spent the rest of the daylight hours carving small bits of meat with the razor, pounding them between two rocks to break down the fibrous flesh, and then mixing each bite with a mouthful of spring water. It was an arduous way to eat, and Glass still felt hungry when he reached the tail. It was worrisome, since he doubted that his next meal would be delivered to him so easily.

In the last moments of daylight he examined the rattles at the tip of the tail. There were ten, one added in each year of the snake's life. Glass had never seen a snake with ten rattles. *A long time, ten years.* Glass thought about the snake, surviving, thriving for a decade on the strength of its brutal attributes. And then a single mistake, a moment of exposure in an environment without tolerance, dead and devoured almost before its blood ceased to pump. He cut the rattles from the remains of the snake and fingered them like a rosary. After a while he dropped them into his possibles bag. When he looked at them, he wanted to remember.

It was dark. Glass pulled his blanket around him, hunched his back, and fell asleep.

He awoke thirsty and hungry from a fitful sleep. Every wound ached.

*Three hundred and fifty miles to Fort Kiowa.* He knew he couldn't allow himself to think about it, not in its totality. *A mile at a time.* He set the Grand as his first goal. He'd been unconscious when the brigade veered off the main river up the spring creek, but from Bridger and Fitzgerald's discussions he assumed it lay near.

Glass pulled the Hudson Bay blanket from his shoulders. With the razor, he cut three long strips from the wool cloth. He wrapped the first around his left knee — his good knee. He would need a pad if he was going to crawl. The other two strips he wrapped around his palms, leaving the fingers free. He rolled up the rest of the blanket and looped the long strap of the possibles bag around both ends. He checked to make sure the bag was tied firmly shut, then situated the bag and blanket across his back. The strap he wore around both shoulders, leaving his hands free.

Glass took a long drink from the creek and began to crawl. Actually, it wasn't a crawl so much as a scooting sort of drag. He could use his right arm for balance, but it would not support his weight. His right leg he could only string along behind him. He had worked to loosen the muscles by bending and straightening the leg, but it remained as rigid as a flagpole.

He fell into the best rhythm he could manage. With his right hand as a sort of outrigger, he kept his weight on his left side, leaning forward on his left arm, pulling up his left knee, then dragging his stiff right leg behind him. Over and over, yard after yard. He stopped several times to adjust the blanket and the possibles bag. His hurky-jerk motion kept loosening the ties of his pack. Eventually he found the right series of knots to keep the bundle in place.

For a while the wool strips on his knee and palms worked fairly well, though they required frequent adjustment. He had failed to consider the effect of dragging his right leg. His moccasin provided protection to the lower part of his foot, but did not cover his ankle. Within a hundred yards he had developed an abrasion, and stopped to cut a strip of blanket for the area in contact with the ground.

It took him almost two hours to crawl down the creek to the Grand.

By the time he arrived at the river, his legs and arms ached from the awkward, unaccustomed motion. He stared down at the old tracks of the brigade and wondered by what providence the Indians had not seen them.

Though he would never see it, the explanation lay clearly on the opposite bank. Had he crossed the river, he would have found the enormous prints of a bear spread throughout a patch of service berries. Just as clear were the tracks of the five Indian ponies. In an irony that Glass would never appreciate, it was a grizzly bear that saved him from the Indians. Like Fitzgerald,

**110**

the bear had discovered the berry patch near the Grand. The animal was gorging itself when the five Arikara warriors rode up the river. In fact it was the scent of the bear that had made the pinto skittish. Confused by the sight and smell of five mounted Indians, the bear lumbered into the brush. The hunters charged after it, never to notice the tracks on the opposite bank.

Once Glass emerged from the protective shelter of the pines, the horizon broadened in a landscape broken only by rolling buttes and scattered clumps of cottonwoods. Thick willows along the river impeded his ability to crawl forward, but did little to block the penetrating heat of the late morning sun. He felt the rivulets of sweat across his back and chest and the sting of salt when it seeped into his wounds. He took one last drink from the cool spring creek. He gazed upriver between swallows, giving one last consideration to the idea of direct pursuit. *Not yet.*

The frustrating necessity of delay was like water on the hot iron of his determination — hardening it, making it unmalleable. He vowed to survive, if for no other reason than to visit vengeance on the men who betrayed him.

Glass crawled for three more hours that day. He guessed he had covered two miles. The Grand's banks varied, with alternating stretches of sand, grass, and rock. Had he been able to stand, there were frequent stretches of shallow water, and Glass could have crossed the river frequently to take advantage of the easiest terrain.

But crossing was not an option for Glass, whose crawling relegated him to the north bank. The rocks created particular difficulty. By the time he stopped, the woolen pads were in tatters. The wool succeeded in keeping abrasions from forming, but it could not stop the bruising. His knee and his palms were black-and-blue, tender to the touch. The muscle in his left arm began to cramp, and once again he felt the quivering weakness from a lack of food. As he anticipated, no easy source of meat fell into his path. For the time being, his subsistence would have to come from plants.

From his time with the Pawnee, Glass possessed a broad familiarity with the plants of the plains. Cattails grew in plentiful clumps wherever the terrain flattened to create marshy backwaters, their furry brown heads capping slender green stalks as high as four feet. Glass used a stave to dig up the root stalks, peeled away the outer skin, and ate the tender shoots. While cattails grew thickly in the marsh, so too did mosquitoes. They buzzed incessantly around the exposed skin on his head, neck, and arms. He ignored them for a while as he dug hungrily among the cattails. Eventually, he gnawed the edge off his hunger, or at least fed his hunger sufficiently that he worried more about the stinging bites of the mosquitoes. He crawled another hundred yards down the river. There was no escaping the mosquitoes at that hour, but their numbers diminished away from the stagnant water of the marsh.

For three days he crawled down the Grand River. Cattails continued to be plentiful, and Glass found a variety of other plants that he knew to be edible —

112

onions, dandelions, even willow leaves. Twice he happened upon berries, stopping each time to gorge himself, picking until his fingers were purple from the juice.

Yet he did not find what his body craved. It had been twelve days since the attack by the grizzly. Before he was abandoned, Glass had swallowed a few sips of broth on a couple occasions. Otherwise, the rattler had been his only real food. Berries and roots might sustain him for a few days. To heal, though, to regain his feet, Glass knew he needed the rich nourishment that only meat could provide. The snake had been a bit of random luck, unlikely to be repeated.

Still, he thought, there was no luck at all in standing still. The next morning he would crawl forward again. If luck wouldn't find him, he would do his best to make his own.

# CHAPTER
# NINE

## *September 8, 1823*

He smelled the buffalo carcass before he saw it. He heard it too. Or at least he heard the clouds of flies that swirled around the heaping mass of hide and bone. Sinews held the skeleton mostly intact, although scavengers had picked it clean of any meat. The massive, bushy head and swooping black horns lent the animal its only measure of dignity, though this too had been undermined by the birds that had picked away the eyes.

Looking at the beast, Glass felt no revulsion, only disappointment that others had beaten him to this potential source of nourishment. A variety of tracks surrounded the area. Glass guessed that the carcass was four or five days old. He stared at the pile of bones. For an instant he imagined his own skeleton — scattered across the bleak ground on some forgotten corner of prairie, his flesh eaten away, carrion for the magpies and coyotes. He thought about a line from Scripture, "dust to dust." *Is this what it means?*

His thoughts turned quickly to more practical considerations. He had seen starving Indians boil hides into a gluey, edible mass. He would willingly have attempted the same, except he had no vessel to contain boiling water. He had another thought. The carcass lay next to a head-sized rock. He picked it up with his left hand and threw it clumsily against the line of smaller ribs. One of the bones snapped, and Glass reached for one of the pieces. The marrow he sought was dry. *I need a thicker bone.*

One of the buffalo's forelegs lay apart from the rest, bare bone down to the hoof. He laid it against a flat stone and began to beat on it with the other rock. Finally a crack appeared, and then the bone broke.

He was right — the thicker bone still contained the greenish marrow. In hindsight, he should have known not to eat it by the smell, but his hunger robbed him of reason. He ignored the bitter taste, sucking the liquid from the bone, then digging for more with the piece of broken rib. *Better to take the risk than to die of starvation.* At least the marrow was easy to swallow. Frenzied by the idea of food, by the very mechanics of eating, he spent the better part of an hour breaking bones and scraping their contents.

About then the first cramp hit. It began as a hollow aching deep inside his bowels. He felt suddenly incapable of supporting his own weight and rolled to his side. The pressure in his head became so intense that Glass was aware of the very fissures in his skull. He began to sweat profusely. Like sunlight through glass, the pain in his abdomen became quickly more focused, burning. Nausea rose in his stomach like a great and inevitable tide. He began to retch, the indignity of the convulsions secondary to the excruciating pain as the bile passed his wounded throat.

For two hours he lay there. His stomach emptied quickly but did not cease to convulse. Between bouts of retching he was perfectly still, as if through lack of motion he could hide from the sickness and pain.

When the first round of sickness was over, he crawled away from the carcass, eager now to escape the sickeningly sweet smell. The motion reignited both the pain in his head and the nausea in his stomach. Thirty yards from the buffalo he crawled into a thick stand of willows, curled onto his side, and lapsed into a state that resembled unconsciousness more than sleep.

For a day and a night his body purged itself of the rancid marrow. The focused pain of his wounds from the grizzly now combined with a diffuse and permeating weakness. Glass came to visualize his strength as the sand in an hourglass. Minute by minute he felt his vitality ebbing away. Like an hourglass, he knew, a moment would arrive when the last grain of sand would tumble down the aperture, leaving the upper chamber void.

He could not shake the image of the buffalo skeleton, of the mighty beast, stripped of its flesh, rotting away on the prairie.

On the morning of the second day after the buffalo, Glass awoke hungry, ravenously hungry. He took it as a sign that the poison had passed from his system. He had tried to continue his laborious crawl downriver, in part because he still hoped to stumble across some other source of food, but more because he sensed the significance of stopping. In two days, he estimated that he had covered no more than a quarter mile. Glass knew that the sickness had cost him more than time and distance. It had sapped him of strength, eaten away at whatever tiny reservoir remained to him.

Without meat in the next few days, Glass assumed that he would die.

His experience with the buffalo carcass and its aftermath would keep him away from anything not freshly killed, no matter how desperate he grew. His first thought was to make a spear, or to kill a cottontail with a stone. But the pain in his right shoulder kept him from raising his arm, let alone thrusting it hard enough to generate a lethal throw. With his left hand, he lacked the accuracy to hit anything.

So hunting was out. That left trapping. With cordage and a knife to carve triggers, Glass knew a variety of ways to trap small game with snares. Lacking even those basics, he decided to try deadfalls. A deadfall was a simple device — a large rock leaning precariously on a stick, rigged to collapse when some unwary prey tripped a trigger.

The willows along the Grand were zigzagged with game trails. Tracks dotted the moist sand near the river. In the tall grass he saw the swirling depressions where deer had bedded down for the night. Glass considered it unlikely that he could trap a deer with a deadfall. For one thing, he doubted he could hoist a rock or tree of sufficient heft. He decided to set his sights on rabbits, which he encountered continuously along the river.

Glass looked for trails near the thick cover preferred by rabbits. He found a cottonwood downed recently by beaver, its leaf-covered branches creating a giant web of obstacles and hiding places. The trails leading to and from the tree were littered with pea-sized scat.

Near the river Glass found three suitable stones: flat enough to provide a broad surface for crushing when the trap was tripped; heavy enough to provide lethal force. The stones he selected were the size of a powder keg and weighed about thirty pounds each. With his crippled arm and leg, it took nearly an hour to push them, one by one, up the bank to the tree.

Next Glass searched for the three sticks he needed to support the deadfalls. The downed cottonwood provided an array of choices. He selected three branches about an inch in diameter and broke them off at a span about the length of his arm. Next he broke the three sticks in two. Snapping the first stick sent a jarring pain through his shoulder and back, so the next two he leaned against the cottonwood and broke with one of his rocks.

When he was finished he had a stick, broken in two, for each trap. Reassembled at the break, the broken stick would support, albeit precariously, the weight of the leaning rock. Where the two pieces of the support stick came together, Glass would wedge a baited trigger stick. When the trigger stick was bumped or tugged, the support stick would collapse like a buckling knee, dropping the lethal weight on the unsuspecting target.

For the trigger sticks, Glass selected three slender willows, cut to a length of about sixteen inches. He had noticed dandelion leaves near the river, and he gathered a large handful to bait the traps, jabbing a number of the tender leaves on each trigger stick.

A narrow trail covered with droppings led into the thickest part of the downed cottonwood. Glass selected this location for the first deadfall and began to assemble the components.

The difficulty with a deadfall lay in striking a balance between stability and fragility. Stability kept the trap from collapsing on its own, though too much would prevent it from collapsing at all; fragility allowed the trap to collapse easily when tripped by its prey, though too much would cause it to collapse on its own. Striking this balance required strength and coordination, and Glass's wounds robbed him of both. His right arm could not support the weight of the rock, so he perched it clumsily against his right leg. Meanwhile, he struggled with his left hand to hold the two pieces of the support stick with the trigger stick wedged in between. Again and again the entire structure collapsed. Twice he decided that he had set the trap too firmly, and knocked it down himself.

After nearly an hour, he finally struck a proper balance point. He found two more suitable locations on the trails near the cottonwood and set the other deadfalls, then retreated away from the cottonwood toward the river.

Glass found a sheltered spot against a cut bank. When he could no longer stand the pangs of hunger, he ate the bitter roots from the dandelions he had plucked for the traps. He drank from the river to wash the taste from his mouth and lay down to sleep. Rabbits were most active at night. He would check the deadfalls in the morning.

Sharp pain in his throat awakened Glass before dawn. The first light of the new day seeped like blood into the eastern horizon. Glass shifted his position in an unsuccessful effort to relieve the pain in his shoulder. As the pain eased he became aware of the chill in the early morning air. He hunched his shoulders and pulled his shredded blanket tightly around his neck. He lay there uncomfortably for an hour, waiting for sufficient light to check the traps.

The bitter taste still lingered in his mouth as he crawled toward the downed cottonwood. He was vaguely aware of the rotten stench of skunk. Both of these sensations evaporated as he imagined a rabbit roasting on a spit above a crackling fire. The nourishment of flesh; he could smell it, taste it.

From fifty yards, Glass could see all three deadfalls. One stood unmoved, but the other two had been tripped — their rocks lay flat on the ground, the support sticks collapsed. Glass could feel his pulse pounding in his throat as he crawled hurriedly forward.

Ten feet from the first trap, he noticed the multitude of new tracks on the narrow game trail, the scattered piles of fresh scat. His breath grew short as he peered around the backside of the rock — nothing protruded. He lifted the rock, still hopeful. The trap was empty. His heart sank in disappointment. *Did I set it too finely? Did it collapse on its own?* He crawled rapidly to the other rock. Nothing protruded from the front. He strained to see around to the blind side of the trap.

He saw a flash of black and white and heard a hiss, barely perceptible.

Pain registered before his mind could grasp what had happened. The deadfall had pinned a skunk by its foreleg, but the animal's capacity to spew forth a noxious spray was very much alive. It felt as if burning lamp oil had been poured into his eyes. He rolled backward in a futile effort to avoid more of the vapor. Completely blind, he half crawled, half rolled toward the river.

He crashed into a deep pool by the bank, desperately seeking to wash away the searing spray. With his face under water, Glass attempted to open his eyes, but the burning was too intense. It took twenty minutes before he could see again, and then only by squinting painfully through bloodred, watery slits. Finally Glass crawled to the bank. The nauseating reek of the skunk's scent clung to his skin and clothing like frost on a windowpane. He had once watched a dog roll in the dirt for a week, trying to rid itself of skunk. Like the dog, he knew the stink would ride him for days.

As the burning in his eyes slowly subsided, Glass took a quick inventory of his wounds. He touched his neck and looked at his fingers. There was no blood, though the internal pain continued when he swallowed or inhaled deeply. He realized that he hadn't tried to speak for several days. Tentatively, he opened his mouth and forced air over his voice box. The action produced sharp pain and a pathetic, squeaking whine. He wondered if he would ever be able to speak normally.

By craning his neck, he could see the parallel cuts that ran from his throat to his shoulder. Bridger's pine tar still coated the area. His entire shoulder ached, but the cuts appeared to be healing. The puncture wounds on his thigh also looked relatively healthy, although his leg still would not support the weight of his body. From touching his scalp he could imagine that it looked horrible, but it no longer bled and it caused no pain.

Aside from his throat, the area that most concerned him was his back. He lacked the agility to inspect the wounds with his hands, and unable to see them, his mind conjured horrible images. He felt strange sensations that he assumed were the repeated breaking of scabs. He knew that Captain Henry had tied sutures, and he occasionally felt scratching from the loose ends of thread.

More than anything he felt the corrosive void of hunger.

He lay on the sandy bank, exhausted and utterly demoralized by this latest turn of events. A clump of yellow flowers stood atop a slender green stalk. The stalk looked like wild onion, but Glass knew better. It was Death Camas. *Is it Providence? Has this been placed here for me?* Glass wondered how the poison would work. Would he drift off peacefully into a never-ending sleep? Or would his body contort in an agonizing death? How different could it be from his current state? At least there would be certainty that the end was coming.

122

As he lay on the riverbank in the early moments of dawn, a fat doe emerged from the willows on the opposite shore. She looked cautiously left and right before stepping forward, haltingly, to drink from the river. She was barely thirty yards away, an easy shot with his rifle. *The Anstadt.*

For the first time that day, he thought about the men who abandoned him. His rage grew as he stared at the doe. Abandonment seemed too benign to describe their treachery. Abandonment was a passive act — running away or leaving something behind. If his keepers had done no more than abandon him, he would at this moment be sighting down the barrel of his gun, about to shoot the deer. He would be using his knife to butcher the animal, and sparking his flint against steel to start a fire and cook it. He looked down at himself, wet from head to toe, wounded, reeking from the skunk, the bitter taste of roots still in his mouth.

What Fitzgerald and Bridger had done was much more than abandonment, much worse. These were not mere passersby on the road to Jericho, looking away and crossing to the other side. Glass felt no entitlement to a Samaritan's care, but he did at least expect that his keepers do no harm.

Fitzgerald and Bridger had acted deliberately, robbed him of the few possessions he might have used to save himself. And in stealing from him this opportunity, they had killed him. Murdered him, as surely as a knife in the heart or a bullet in the brain. Murdered him, except he would not die. Would not die, he vowed, because he would live to kill his killers.

Hugh Glass pushed himself up and continued his crawl down the banks of the Grand.

Glass studied the contour of the land in his immediate vicinity. Fifty yards away, a gentle swale led down on three sides to a broad, dry gully. Sage and low grasses provided moderate cover. The swale reminded him suddenly of the gently rolling hills along the Arkansas River. He remembered a trap he had once seen set by Pawnee children. For the children, it had been a game. For Glass, the exercise was now deadly serious.

He crawled slowly to the bottom of the swale, stopping at the point that seemed like the natural hub. He found a sharp-edged rock and began to dig in the hard-packed, sandy soil.

He dug a pit with a four-inch diameter to the depth of his bicep.

Beginning halfway down, he widened the hole so that it was shaped like a wine bottle with the neck at the top. Glass spread the dirt from the hole to conceal the evidence of recent digging. Breathing heavily from the exertion, he stopped to rest.

Next Glass went in search of a large, flat rock. He found one about forty feet from the hole. He also found three small rocks, which he placed in a triangular pattern around the hole. The flat rock he set on top like a roof over the hole, with a space underneath creating the illusion of a place to hide.

Glass used a branch to camouflage the area around the trap, then crawled slowly away from the hole. In several spots he saw tiny, telltale droppings — a good sign. Fifty yards from the hole he stopped. His knee and palms were raw from crawling. His thigh ached from the motion, and again he felt the awful cracking sensation as the scabbing on his back began to bleed. Stopping provided temporary relief to his wounds, but it also made him aware of his profound fatigue, a low-grade ache that emanated from deep within, then circulated outward. Glass fought the urge to close his eyes and succumb to the beckoning sleep. He knew he could not regain his strength unless he ate.

Glass forced himself into a crawling position. Paying careful attention to his distance, he moved in a wide circle with the pit he had dug as the center point. It took him thirty minutes to complete a circuit. Again his body pleaded with him to stop and rest, but he knew that stopping now would undermine the effectiveness of his trap. He kept crawling, spiraling inward toward the pit in ever-smaller circles. When he encountered a thick clump of brush, he would stop to shake it. Anything inside his circles was driven slowly toward the hidden pit.

An hour later, Glass arrived at his hole. He removed the flat rock from the top and listened. He had seen a Pawnee boy reach his hand into a similar trap and pull it out, screaming, with a rattlesnake attached. The boy's error left a strong impression. He looked around for a suitable branch. He found a long one with a flat end and pounded it several times into the hole.

Having assured himself that anything in his trap was dead, he reached into the hole. One by one, he pulled out four dead mice and two ground squirrels. There was no glory in this method of hunting, but Glass was elated with the results.

The swale provided some measure of concealment, and Glass decided to risk a fire, cursing the lack of his flint and steel. He knew it was possible to create a flame by rubbing two sticks together, but he had never started a fire that way. He suspected that the method, if it worked at all, would take forever.

What he needed was a bow and spindle — a crude machine for making fire. The machine had three parts: a flat piece of wood with a hole where a spindle stick was planted, a round spindle stick about three-quarters of an inch thick and eight inches long, and a bow — like a cellist's — to twirl the spindle.

Glass searched the gully to find the parts. It wasn't hard to locate a flat piece of driftwood and two sticks for the spindle and the bow. *String for the bow.* He had no cord. *The strap on my bag.* He pulled out the razor and sliced the strap from his bag, then tied it to the ends of the stick. Next he used the razor to carve away the edges for a hole in the flat piece of driftwood, careful to make it slightly bigger than the spindle stick.

With the bow and spindle assembled, Glass gathered tinder and fuel.

From his possibles bag, he removed the ball patches, ripping them to fray the edges. He also had saved cattail cotton. He piled the tinder loosely in a shallow pit, then added dry grass. To the few pieces of dry wood in the area he added buffalo dung, bone dry from long weeks in the sun.

With the makings of the fire in place, Glass grabbed the components of the bow and spindle. He filled the hole in the flat piece of wood with tinder, set the spindle stick in the hole, and looped the bowstring around it. He held the spindle stick against the palm of his right hand, still protected by the woolen pad he used to crawl. With his left hand he worked the bow. The back-and-forth motion spun the spindle in the hole on the flat driftwood, creating friction and heat.

The fault in his machine became immediately apparent as he spun the spindle with the bow stick. One end of the spindle rubbed in the hole on the flat driftwood — the end where he wanted to create the fire. The other end, though, spun against the flesh of his hand. Glass remembered that the Pawnee used a palm-size piece of wood to hold the top end of the spindle. He searched again to find the right piece of wood. He located an appropriate chunk and used the razor to carve away a hole for the top of the spindle stick.

He was clumsy with his left hand, and it took several attempts to find the right rhythm, moving the bow in a steady motion without losing his grip on the spindle stick. Soon, though, he had the spindle twirling smoothly. After several minutes, smoke began to rise from the hole. Suddenly the tinder burst into flames. He grabbed cattail cotton and set it to the lick of flame, protecting it with a cupped hand. When the cotton caught fire, he transferred the flame to the tinder in the small pit. He felt the wind whip across his back, and panicked for an instant that it would extinguish the flame, but the tinder caught, then the dry grass. In a few minutes he was feeding the buffalo chips into a small blaze.

There wasn't much meat left by the time he skinned the tiny rodents and removed their entrails. Still, it was fresh. If his trapping technique was time-consuming, at least it had the benefit of simplicity.

Glass was still ravenous as he picked at the tiny rib cage of the last rodent. He resolved to stop earlier the next day. Perhaps dig pits in two locations. The thought of slower progress irritated him. How long could he avoid Arikara on the banks of the well-traveled Grand? *Don't do that. Don't look too far ahead. The goal each day is tomorrow morning.*

With his dinner cooked, the fire no longer merited its risk. He covered it with sand and went to sleep.

# CHAPTER
# TEN

## *September 15, 1823*

Twin buttes framed the valley in front of Glass, forcing the Grand River through a narrow channel between. Glass remembered the buttes from the trip upriver with Captain Henry. As he crawled farther east along the Grand, distinctive features became increasingly rare. Even the cottonwoods seemed to have been swallowed by the sea of prairie grass.

Henry and the fur brigade had camped near the buttes, and Glass intended to stop in the same spot, hoping that something useful might have been left behind. In any event, he remembered that the high bank near the buttes made good shelter. Great stacks of black thunderheads sat ominously on the western horizon. The storm would be overhead in a couple of hours, and he wanted to dig in before it hit.

Glass crawled along the river to the campsite. A ring of blackened stones marked a recent fire. He remembered that the fur brigade had camped with no fire, and wondered who had followed behind them. He stopped, removed the possibles bag and blanket from his back, and took a long drink from the river. Behind him, the cut bank created the shelter he remembered.

He scanned up and down the river, watchful for signs of Indians, disappointed that the vegetation looked sparse. He felt the familiar rumble of hunger, and wondered if there was enough cover to dig an effective mouse pit. *Is it worth the effort?* He weighed the benefits of shelter against the benefits of food. Rodents had sustained him now for a week. Still, Glass knew he was treading water — not drowning, but making no progress toward a safer shore.

A light breeze heralded the approaching clouds, cool across the sweat on his back. Glass turned from the river and crawled up the high bank to check on the storm.

What lay beyond the rim of the bank took his breath away. Thousands of buffalo grazed in the vale below the butte, blackening the plain for a solid mile. A great bull stood sentry no more than fifty yards in front of him. The animal stood close to seven feet at the hump. The shaggy shawl of tawny fur on top of its black body accentuated the powerful head and shoulders, making the horns seem almost redundant. The bull snorted and sniffed at the air, frustrated by the swirling breeze. Behind the bull, a cow wallowed on her back, lifting a cloud of dust. A dozen other cows and calves grazed obliviously nearby.

Glass had glimpsed his first buffalo on the Texas plains. Since then he had seen them, in herds great and herds small, on a hundred different occasions. Yet the sight of the animals never failed to fill him with awe, awe for their infinite numbers, awe for the prairie that sustained them.

A hundred yards downstream from Glass, a pack of eight wolves also watched the great bull and the outliers he guarded. The alpha male sat on his haunches near a clump of sage. All afternoon he had waited patiently for the moment that just arrived, the moment when a gap emerged between the outliers and the rest of the herd. A gap. A fatal weakness. The big wolf raised himself suddenly to all fours.

The alpha male stood tall but narrow. His legs seemed ungainly, knobby and somehow oddly proportioned to his coal-black body. His two pups wrestled playfully near the river. Some of the wolves lay sleeping, placid as barnyard hounds. Taken together, the animals seemed more like pets than predators, though they all perked to life at the sudden movement from the big male.

It wasn't until the wolves began to move that their lethal strength became obvious. The strength was not derivative of muscularity or grace. Rather it flowed from a single-minded intelligence that made their movements deliberate, relentless. The individual animals converged into a lethal unit, cohering in the collective strength of the pack.

The alpha male trotted toward the gap between the outliers and the herd, breaking into a full run after a few yards. The pack fanned out behind him with a precision and unity of purpose that struck Glass as almost military. The pack poured into the gap. Even the pups seemed to grasp the purpose of their enterprise. Buffalo on the edge of the main herd retreated, pushing their calves in front of them before turning outward, shoulder to shoulder in a line against the wolves. The gap widened with the movement of the main herd, stranding the bull and a dozen other buffalo outside its perimeter.

The great bull charged, catching one wolf with its horn and tossing the yelping animal twenty feet. The wolves snarled and growled, snapping with brutal fangs at exposed flanks. Most of the outliers broke for the main herd, realizing instinctively that their safety lay in numbers.

The alpha male nipped at the tender haunch of a calf. Confused, the calf broke away from the herd, toward the steep bank by the river. Collectively aware of the deadly error, the pack fell instantly behind its prey. Bawling as it ran, the calf dashed wildly ahead. It tumbled over the bank, snapping its leg in the fall. The calf struggled to regain its feet. Its broken leg dangled in an odd direction and then collapsed completely when the calf tried to plant it. The calf fell to the ground and the pack was on it. Fangs planted themselves in every part of its body. The alpha male sunk its teeth into the tender throat and ripped.

The calf's last stand took place no more than seventy-five yards down the bank from Glass. He watched with a mixture of fascination and fear, glad that his vantage point lay downwind. The pack focused its complete attention on the calf. The alpha male and his mate ate first, their bloody snouts buried in the soft underbelly. They let the pups eat, but not the others. Occasionally another wolf would slink up to the fallen prey, only to be sent scrambling by a snap or snarl from the big black male.

Glass stared at the calf and the wolves, his mind turning quickly. The calf had been dropped in the spring. After a summer of fattening on the prairie, it weighed close to a hundred and fifty pounds. *A hundred and fifty pounds of fresh meat.* After two weeks of catching his food by the mouthful, Glass could scarcely imagine such bounty. Initially, Glass had hoped that the pack might leave enough for him to scavenge. As he continued to watch, though, the bounty diminished at an alarming rate. Satiated, the alpha male and his mate eventually wandered casually away from the carcass with a severed hind quarter in tow for the pups. The four other wolves fell on the carcass.

In growing desperation, Glass considered the options. If he waited too long, he doubted whether anything would be left. He weighed the prospect of continuing to live off mice and roots. Even if he could find enough to sustain himself, the task took too much time. He doubted he had covered thirty miles since beginning his crawl. At his current pace, he would be lucky to reach Fort Kiowa before cold set in. And of course, every day of exposure on the river was another day for Indians to stumble upon him.

He desperately needed the certain strength that the buffalo meat would give him. He did not know by what Providence the calf had been placed in his path. *This is my chance.* If he wanted his share of the calf, he would have to fight for it. And he needed to do it now.

He scanned the area for the makings of some weapon. Nothing presented itself beyond rocks, driftwood, and sage. *A club?* He wondered for a moment if he could beat back the wolves. It seemed implausible. He couldn't swing hard enough to inflict much of a blow. And from his knees, he forfeited any advantage of height. *Sage.* He remembered the brief but impressive flames created by dry sage branches. *A torch?*

Seeing no other option, he scurried around him for the makings of a fire. The spring floods had tossed the trunk of a large cottonwood against the cut bank, creating a natural windbreak. Glass scooped a shallow pit in the sand next to the trunk.

He took out his bow and spindle, grateful that he at least had the means for quickly creating a flame. From the possibles bag he removed the last of the patches and a large clump of cattail cotton. Glass looked downriver at the wolf pack, still ripping at the calf. *Damn it!*

He looked around him for fuel. The river had left little of the cottonwood beyond the trunk. He found a clump of dead sage and snapped off five large branches, piling them next to the fire pit.

Glass set the bow and spindle in the sheltered pit, carefully placing the tinder. He began to work the bow, slowly at first, then faster as he found his rhythm. In a few minutes he had a low fire burning in the pit by the cottonwood.

He looked downriver toward the wolves. The alpha male, his mate, and their two pups huddled together about twenty yards beyond the calf. Having taken first dibs at the calf, they now were content to gnaw casually at the tasty marrow of the hindquarter. Glass hoped they would stay out of the coming battle. That left four wolves on the carcass itself.

The Loup Pawnee, as their name implied, revered the wolf for its strength and above all for its cunning. Glass had been with Pawnee hunting parties that shot wolves; their hides were an important part of many ceremonies. But he had never done anything like what he prepared to do at that moment: crawl into a pack of wolves and challenge them for food, armed only with a torch of sage.

The five sage branches twisted like giant, arthritic hands. Smaller twigs extended from the main branches at frequent intervals, most of them covered with spindly strands of bark and brittle, blue-green leaves. He grabbed one of the branches and set it to the fire. It caught immediately, a foot-high flame soon roaring from its top. *It's burning too fast.* Glass wondered if the flame would last the distance between him and the wolves, let alone provide a weapon in whatever struggle that lay before him. He decided to hedge his bet. Rather than lighting all of the sage now, he would carry most of the branches unlit, backup ammunition to be added to the torch as needed.

Glass looked again at the wolves. They suddenly seemed larger. He hesitated for an instant. No turning back, he decided. *This is my chance.* With the burning sage branch in one hand and the four backup branches in the other, Glass crawled down the bank toward the wolves. At fifty yards, the alpha male and his mate looked up from the hindquarter to stare at this strange animal approaching the buffalo calf. They viewed Glass as a curiosity, not a challenge. After all, they had eaten their fill.

At twenty yards, the wind shifted and the four animals on the carcass caught scent of the smoke. They all turned. Glass stopped, face-to-face now with four wolves. From a distance, it was easy to see the wolves as mere dogs. Up close, they bore no relation to their domestic cousins. A white wolf showed its bloody teeth and took a half step toward Glass, a deep growl pouring from its throat. It lowered its shoulder, a move that seemed somehow both defensive and offensive at the same time.

The white wolf fought conflicting instincts — one defensive of its prey, the other afraid of fire. A second wolf, this one missing most of one ear, fell in beside the first. The other two continued to rip at the buffalo carcass, appreciative, it seemed, of the exclusive attention to the calf. The burning branch in Glass's right hand began to flicker. The white wolf took another step toward Glass, who remembered suddenly the sickening sensation of the bear's teeth, ripping at his flesh. *What have I done?*

Suddenly there was a flash of bright light, a brief pause, and then the deep bass of thunder rolling down the valley. A raindrop struck Glass's face and wind whipped at the flame. He felt a sickening churn in his stomach. *God no — not now!* He had to act quickly. The white wolf was poised to attack. *Could they really*

**136**

*smell fear?* He had to do the unexpected. He had to attack them.

He grabbed the four sage branches from his right hand and added them to the burning branch in his left. Flames leapt up, hungrily swallowing the dry fuel. It took both hands now to hold the branches together, which meant he could no longer use his left hand for balance. Excruciating pain extended outward from his wounded right thigh as weight shifted to his leg, and he almost fell. He managed to stay upright as he lurched, hobbling forward on his knees in his best approximation of a charge. He let loose the loudest sound he could muster, which came out as a sort of eerie wail. Forward he moved, swinging the burning torch like a fiery sword.

He thrust the torch toward the wolf with one ear. Flames singed the animal's face and it jumped backward with a yelp. The white wolf leapt at Glass's flank, sinking its teeth into his shoulder. Glass pivoted, craning his neck to keep the wolf off his throat. Only a few inches separated Glass's face from the wolf's, and he could smell the animal's bloody breath. Glass struggled again to keep his balance. He swung his arms around to bring the flames in contact with the wolf, burning the animal's belly and groin. The wolf released its grip on his shoulder, retreating a step.

Glass heard a snarl behind him and ducked instinctively. The one-eared wolf came tumbling over his head, missing his strike at Glass's neck, but knocking Glass to his side. He groaned at the impact of the fall, which reignited pain in his back, throat, and shoulder. The bundled torch hit the ground, spilling on the sandy soil. Glass grasped at the branches, desperate to pick them up before they extinguished. At the same time, he struggled to regain the upright position on his knees.

The two wolves circled slowly, waiting for their moment, more cautious now that they had tasted the flame. *I can't let them get behind me.* Lightning struck again, followed rapidly this time by the boom of thunder. The storm was nearly over him. Rain would pour down at any minute. *There's no time.* Even without the rain, the flames on the torch were burning low.

The white wolf and the wolf with one ear closed. They too seemed to sense that the battle was nearing its climax. Glass feigned at them with the torch. They slowed, but did not retreat. Glass had worked himself into a position only a few feet from the calf. The two wolves feeding on the carcass succeeded in tearing off a hindquarter, and retreated from the commotion of the battling wolves and the strange creature with the fire. For the first time, Glass noticed the clumps of dry sage around the carcass. *Would they burn?*

Eyes fixed on the two wolves, Glass set his torch to the sage. There had been no rain for weeks. The brush was dry as tinder and caught fire easily. In an instant, flames rose two feet above the sage next to the carcass. Glass lit two other clumps. Soon, the carcass lay in the middle of three burning bushes. Like Moses, Glass planted himself with his knees on the carcass, waving the remnants of his torch. Lightning struck and thunder boomed. Wind whipped the flames around the brush. Rain fell now, though not yet enough to douse the sage.

The effect was impressive. The white wolf and the wolf with one ear looked around. The alpha male, his mate, and the pups loped across the prairie. With full bellies and a breaking storm, they headed for the shelter of their nearby den. The two other wolves from the carcass also followed, struggling to pull the calf's hindquarter across the prairie.

The white wolf crouched, poised, it seemed, to attack again. But suddenly the wolf with one ear turned and ran after the pack. The white wolf stopped to contemplate the changing odds. He knew well his place in the pack: Others led and he followed. Others picked out the game to be killed, he helped to run it down. Others ate first, he contented himself with the remainder. The wolf had never seen an animal like the one that appeared today, but he understood precisely where it fit in the pecking order. Another clap of thunder erupted overhead, and the rain began to pour down. The white wolf took one last look at the buffalo, the man, and the smoking sage, then he turned and loped after the others.

Glass watched the wolves disappear above the rim of the cut bank. Around him, smoke rose as the rain doused the sage. Another minute and he would be defenseless. He marveled at his fortune as he glanced quickly at the bite on his shoulder. Blood trickled from two puncture wounds, but they were not deep.

The calf lay in the grotesque throes of its failed efforts to escape the wolves. Brutally efficient fangs had ripped the carcass open. Fresh blood pooled beneath the open throat, an eerily brilliant crimson against the muted tans of the sand in the gully. The wolves had focused their attention on the rich entrails that Glass himself craved. He rolled the calf from its side to its back, noting with brief disappointment that nothing remained of the liver. Gone too were the gallbladder, the lungs, and the heart. But a small bit of intestine hung from the animal. Glass removed the razor from his possibles bag, followed the snaking organ into the body cavity with his left hand, and cut a two-foot length at the stomach. Barely able to control himself at the immediacy of food, he put the cut end to his mouth and guzzled.

If the wolf pack had availed itself of the choicer organs, it also had done Glass the favor of nearly skinning its prey. Glass moved to the throat, where with the aid of the razor he could pull back the supple skin. The calf was well fed. Delicate white fat clung to the muscle of its plump neck. The trappers called this fat "fleece" and considered it a delicacy. He cut chunks and stuffed them into his mouth, barely chewing before he swallowed. Each swallow revived the excruciating fire in his throat, but hunger trumped the pain. He gorged himself in the pouring rain, arriving finally at some minimal threshold that allowed him to consider other dangers.

Glass climbed again to the rim of the cut bank, scanning the horizon in all directions. Scattered clumps of buffalo grazed obliviously, but there was no sign of wolf or Indian. The rain and thunder had ended, blowing past as rapidly as they appeared. Angled rays of afternoon sunlight succeeded in breaking through the great thunderheads, streaming forth in iridescent rays extending from heaven to earth.

Glass settled back to consider his fortune. The wolves had taken their share, but an enormous resource lay below him. Glass suffered no illusions about his situation. But he would not starve.

Glass camped for three days on the cut bank next to the calf. For the first few hours he didn't even set a fire, gorging uncontrollably on thin slices of the gloriously fresh meat. Finally he paused long enough to start a low blaze for roasting and drying, concealing the flames as much as possible by setting them near to the bank.

He built racks from the green branches of a nearby stand of willows. Hour after hour he carved away at the carcass with the dull razor, hanging meat on the racks while he steadily fed the fires. In three days he dried fifteen pounds of jerky, enough to sustain him for two weeks if need be. Longer if he could supplement along the way.

The wolves did leave one choice cut — the tongue. He relished this delicacy like a king. The ribs and remaining leg bones he roasted on the fire one by one, cracking them for their rich, fresh marrow.

Glass removed the hide with the dull razor. A task that should have taken minutes took hours, an interval during which he thought bitterly about the two men who stole his knife. He had neither the time nor the tools to work the fur properly, but he did cut a crude parfleche before the skin dried into stiff rawhide. He needed the bag to carry the jerky.

On the third day, Glass went searching for a long branch to use as a crutch. In the fight with the wolves, he had been surprised at the weight that his wounded leg could support. He had exercised the leg over the past two days, stretching and testing it. With the aid of a crutch, Glass believed he could now walk upright, a prospect he relished after three weeks of crawling like a gimpy dog. He found a cottonwood branch of the appropriate length and shape. He cut a long strip from the Hudson Bay blanket, wrapping it around the top of the crutch as a pad.

The blanket had been reduced, strip by strip, to a piece of cloth no more than one foot wide by two feet long. Glass used the razor to cut an opening in the middle of the cloth, large enough so that he could poke his head through. The resulting garment wasn't big enough to call a capote, but at least it would cover his shoulders and keep the parfleche from digging against his skin.

There was a chill in the air again on that last night by the buttes. The last shreds of the slaughtered calf hung drying on the racks above the crimson coals. The fire cast a comforting glow on his camp, a tiny oasis of light amid the black of the moonless plain. Glass sucked the marrow from the last of the ribs. As he tossed the bone on the fire, he realized suddenly that he was not hungry. He savored the seeping warmth of the fire, a luxury he would not enjoy again in the foreseeable future.

Three days of food had worked to repair his wounded body. He bent his right leg to test it. The muscles were tight and sore, but functional. His shoulder too had improved. Strength had not returned to his arm, but some flexibility had. It still scared him to touch his throat. The remnants of the stitches protruded, although the skin had fused. He wondered if he should attempt to cut them away with the razor, but had been afraid to try. Aside from his effort to yell at the wolves, he had not tested his voice for days. He would not do so now. His voice had little to do with his survival in the coming weeks. If it were changed, so be it. He did appreciate the fact that he now could swallow with less pain.

Glass knew that the buffalo calf had turned his fortune. Still, it was easy to temper the assessment of where he stood. He had lived to fight another day. But he was alone and without weapons. Between him and Fort Brazeau lay three hundred miles of open prairie. Two Indian tribes — one possibly hostile and the other certainly so — followed the same river that he depended on to navigate the open space. And of course, as Glass knew painfully well, Indians were not the only hazard before him.

He knew he should sleep. With the new crutch, he hoped to make ten or even fifteen miles the next day. Still, something drew him to linger in the fleeting moment of contentment — sated, rested, and warm.

Glass reached into the possibles bag and pulled out the bear claw. He turned it slowly in the low light of the fire, fascinated again at the dried blood on the tip — his blood, he now realized. He began to carve at the thick base of the claw with the razor, etching a narrow groove that he carefully worked to deepen. From his bag he also removed the hawk's-feet necklace. He wrapped the string of the necklace around the groove he had carved at the base of the claw, tying it into a tight knot. Finally, he tied the ends behind his neck.

He liked the idea that the claw that inflicted his wounds now hung, inanimate, around his neck. *Lucky charm*, he thought, then fell asleep.

# CHAPTER
# ELEVEN

## *September 16, 1823*

*Goddamn it!* John Fitzgerald stood staring at the river in front of him, or more accurately, at the bend in the river.

Jim Bridger walked up beside him. "What's it doing, turning east?" Without warning, Fitzgerald backhanded the boy across the mouth. Bridger sprawled backward, landing on his backside with a stunned look on his face. "What'd you do that for?"

"You think I can't see that the river turns east? When I need you to scout, I'll ask you! Otherwise, keep your eyes open and your goddamned mouth shut!"

Bridger was right, of course. For more than a hundred miles, the river they followed had run predominantly north, the exact bearing they sought to follow. Fitzgerald wasn't even sure of the river's name, but he knew that everything flowed eventually into the Missouri. If the river had continued its northern course, Fitzgerald believed it might intersect within a day's march of Fort Union. Fitzgerald even held out some hope that they were actually on the Yellowstone, though Bridger maintained that they were too far east.

In any event, Fitzgerald had hoped to stick to the river until they hit the Missouri. In truth, he had no

145

instinct for the geography of the vast wasteland before him. There had been little feature to the land since they struck out from the headwaters of the Upper Grand. The horizon stretched out for miles in front of them, a sea of muted grass and swelling hills, each exactly like the last.

Sticking to the river made for straightforward navigation, and it assured an easy supply of water. Still, Fitzgerald had no desire to turn east — the new direction of the river for as far as their eyes could see. Time remained their enemy. The longer they wandered separate from Henry and the brigade, the greater the odds for calamity.

They stood there for several minutes while Fitzgerald stared and stewed.

Finally Bridger took a deep breath and said, "We should cut northwest."

Fitzgerald started to rebuke him, except that he was utterly at a loss about what to do. He pointed to the dry grassland that stretched to the horizon. "I suppose you know where to find water out there?"

"Nope. But we don't need much in this weather." Bridger sensed Fitzgerald's indecision, and felt a corresponding increase in the strength of his own opinion. Unlike Fitzgerald, he *did* have an instinct across open country. He always had, an internal compass that seemed to shepherd him in unmarked terrain. "I think we're no more than two days from the Missouri — and maybe that close to the Fort."

Fitzgerald fought back the urge to strike Bridger again. In fact, he thought again about killing the boy.

He would have done it back on the Grand, had he not felt dependent upon the extra rifle. Two shooters weren't many, but two were better than one alone.

"Listen, boy. You and I need to reach a little understanding before we join up with the others." Bridger had anticipated this conversation ever since they abandoned Glass. He looked down, already ashamed of what he knew was coming.

"We did our best for old Glass, stayed with him longer than most would've. Seventy dollars isn't enough to get scalped by the Rees," Fitzgerald said, using the short name for the Arikara.

Bridger said nothing, so Fitzgerald continued. "Glass was dead from the minute that grizzly finished with him. Only thing we didn't do was bury him." Still Bridger looked away. Fitzgerald's anger began to rise again.

"You know what, Bridger? I don't give a tinker's damn what you think about what we did. But I'll tell you this — you spill your guts and I'll carve your throat from ear to ear."

# CHAPTER
# TWELVE

## *September 17, 1823*

Captain Andrew Henry did not pause to appreciate the raw splendor of the valley spread before him. From his vantage point on a high bluff above the confluence of the Missouri and Yellowstone rivers, Henry and his seven companions commanded a vast horizon demarcated by a blunt plateau. In front of the plateau flowed gentle buttes, spilling like flaxen waves between the steep bench and the Missouri. Though the near bank had been stripped of its timber, thick cottonwoods still held the far bank, fighting against autumn for temporary possession of their greenery.

Nor did Henry stop to contemplate the philosophical significance of two rivers joining. He did not imagine the high mountain meadows where the waters began their journey as pure as liquid diamond. He did not even linger to appreciate the practical import of the fort's location, neatly collecting commerce from two great highways of water.

Captain Henry's thoughts concerned not what he did see, but rather what he did not: He did not see horses. He saw the scattered motion of men and the smoke of a large fire, but not a single horse. *Not even a damn mule*. He fired his rifle into the air, as much in frustration as in greeting. The men in the camp stopped their activities, searching for the source of the shot. Two guns answered in return. Henry and his seven men trudged down the valley toward Fort Union.

It had been eight weeks since Henry left Fort Union, rushing to Ashley's aid at the Arikara village. Henry left two instructions behind: Trap the surrounding streams and guard the horses at all costs. Captain Henry's luck, it appeared, would never change.

Pig lifted his rifle from his right shoulder, where it seemed to have augured a permanent indentation in his flesh. He started to move the heavy gun to his left shoulder, but there the strap of his possibles bag had worn its own abrasion. He finally resigned himself to simply carrying the gun in front of him, a decision that reminded him of the aching pain in his arms.

Pig thought of the comfortable straw tick in back of the cooper's shop in St. Louis, and he arrived once again at the conclusion that joining Captain Henry had been a horrible mistake.

In the first twenty years of his life, Pig had never once walked more than two miles. In the past six weeks, not a single day had passed when he had walked fewer than twenty miles, and often the men covered thirty or even more. Two days earlier, Pig had worn through the bottoms of his third pair of moccasins. Gaping holes admitted frosty dew in the morning. Rocks cut jagged scrapes. Worst of all, had he had stepped squarely on a prickly pear cactus. He had failed in repeated efforts to pick out the tines with his skinning knife, and now a festering toe made him wince with every step.

Not to mention the fact that he had never been hungrier in his life.

He longed for the simple pleasure of dunking a biscuit in gravy, or sinking his teeth into a fat chicken leg. He remembered fondly the heaping tin plate of food provided thrice daily by the cooper's wife. Now his breakfast consisted of cold jerky — and not much of that. They barely stopped for lunch, which also consisted of cold jerky. With the captain skittish about gunshots, even dinners consisted primarily of cold jerky. And on the occasions when they did have fresh game, Pig struggled to eat it, hacking at slabs of wild game or wrestling to break bones for their marrow. Food on the frontier required so damn much work. The effort it took to eat left him famished.

Pig questioned his decision to go west with each rumble of his stomach, with every painful step. The riches of the frontier remained as elusive as ever. Pig had not set a beaver trap for six months. As they walked into the camp, horses were not the only thing absent. *Where are the pelts?* A few beaver plews hung on willow frames against the timber walls of the fort, along with a mishmash of buffalo, elk, and wolf. But this was hardly the bonanza to which they had hoped to return.

A man named Stubby Bill stepped forward and started to extend his hand to Henry in greeting.

Henry ignored the hand. "Where the hell are the horses?"

Stubby Bill's hand hung there for a moment, lonely and uncomfortable.

Finally he let it drop. "Blackfeet stole 'em, Captain."

"You ever hear of posting a guard?"

"We posted guards, Captain, but they came out of nowhere and stampeded the herd."

"You go after them?"

Stubby Bill shook his head slowly. "We ain't done so well against the Blackfeet." It was a subtle reminder, but also effective. Captain Henry sighed deeply. "How many horses left?"

"Seven . . . well, five and two mules. Murphy's got all of them with a trapping party on Beaver Creek."

"Doesn't look like there's been much trapping going on."

"We've been at it, Captain, but everything near the Fort is trapped out. Without more horses we can't cover any ground."


Jim Bridger lay curled beneath a threadbare blanket. There would be heavy frost on the ground in the morning, and the boy felt the damp chill as it seeped into the deepest marrow of his bones. They slept again with no fire. In fits and starts, his discomfort surrendered to his fatigue and he slept.

In his dream he stood near the edge of a great chasm. The sky was the purple-black of late evening. Darkness prevailed, but enough light remained to illuminate objects in a faint glow. The apparition appeared at first as the vaguest of shapes, still distant. It approached him slowly, inevitably. Its contours took form as it drew closer, a twisted and limping body. Bridger wanted to flee, but the chasm behind him made escape impossible.

At ten paces he could see the horrible face. It was unnatural, its features distorted like a mask. Scars crisscrossed the cheeks and forehead. The nose and ears were placed haphazardly, with no relation to balance or symmetry. The face was framed by a tangled mane and beard, furthering the impression that the being before him was something no longer human.

As the specter moved closer still, its eyes began to burn, locked onto Bridger in a hateful gaze he could not break.

The specter raised its arm in a reaper's arc and drove a knife deep into Bridger's chest. The knife cleaved his sternum cleanly, shocking the boy with the piercing strength of the blow. The boy staggered backward, caught a final glimpse of the burning eyes, and fell.

He stared at the knife in his chest as the chasm swallowed him. He recognized with little surprise the silver cap on the pommel. It was Glass's knife. In some ways it was a relief to die, he thought, easier than living with his guilt.

Bridger felt a sharp thud in his ribs. He opened his eyes with a start to find Fitzgerald standing above him. "Time to move, boy."

# CHAPTER
# THIRTEEN

## *October 5, 1823*

The burnt remains of the Arikara village reminded Hugh Glass of skeletons. It was eerie to walk among them. This place that teemed so recently with the vibrant life of five hundred families now sat dead as a graveyard, a blackened monument on the high bluff above the Missouri.

The village lay eight miles north of the confluence with the Grand, while Fort Brazeau lay seventy miles south. Glass had two reasons for the diversion up the Missouri. He had run out of jerky from the buffalo calf and found himself once again reliant upon roots and berries. Glass remembered the flush cornfields surrounding the Arikara villages and hoped to scavenge from them.

He also knew that the village would provide the makings of a raft.

With a raft, he could float lazily downstream to Fort Brazeau. As he walked slowly through the village, he realized there would be no problem finding building materials. Between the huts and the palisades, there were thousands of suitable logs.

Glass stopped to peer into a big lodge near the center of the village, clearly some type of communal building.

He saw a flash of motion in the dark interior. He stumbled back a step, his heart racing. He stopped, peering into the lodge as his eyes adjusted to the light. No longer needing the crutch, he had sharpened the end of the cottonwood branch to make a crude spear. He held it in a ready position.

A small dog, a pup, whimpered in the middle of the lodge. Relieved and excited at the prospect of fresh meat, Glass took a slow step forward. He turned the spear to bring the blunt end forward. If he could lure the dog closer, a quick whack would smash the animal's skull. *No need to damage the meat.* Sensing the danger, the dog bolted toward dark recesses at the back of the open room.

Glass moved quickly in pursuit, stopping in shock when the dog jumped into the arms of an ancient squaw. The old woman huddled on a pallet, curled into a tight ball on a tattered blanket. She held the puppy like a baby. With her face buried against the animal, only her white hair was visible in the shadows. She cried out and began to wail hysterically. After a few moments, the wailing took on a pattern, a frightening and foreboding chant. *Her death chant?*

The arms and shoulders gripping the little dog were nothing more than leathery old skin hung loosely on bone. As Glass's eyes adjusted, he saw the waste and filth scattered about her. A large earthen pot contained water, but there was no sign of food. *Why hasn't she gathered corn?* Glass had gathered a few ears as he walked into the village. The Sioux and the deer had taken most of the crop, but certainly remnants remained. *Is she lame?*

He reached into his parfleche and pulled out an ear of corn. He shucked it and bent down to offer it to the old woman. Glass held out the corn for a long time as the woman continued her wailing chant. After a while the puppy sniffed at the corn, then began to lick it. Glass reached out and touched the old woman on the head, gently stroking the white hair. Finally the woman stopped chanting and turned her face toward the light that streamed in from the door.

Glass gasped. Her eyes were perfectly white, completely blind. Now Glass understood why the old woman had been left behind when the Arikara fled in the middle of the night.

Glass took the old woman's hand and gently wrapped it round the corn. She mumbled something that he could not understand and pushed the corn to her mouth. Glass saw that she had no teeth, pressing the raw corn between her gums. The sweet juice seemed to awaken her hunger, and she gnawed ineffectively at the cob. *She needs broth.*

He looked around the hut. A rusty kettle sat next to the fire pit in the center of the room. He looked at the water in the large earthen pot. It was brackish and sediment floated on the surface. He picked up the pot and carried it outside. He dumped the water and refilled it from a small creek that flowed through the village.

Glass spotted another dog by the creek, and this one he did not spare.

Soon he had a fire burning in the center of the hut. Part of the dog he roasted on a spit over the fire and part he boiled in the kettle. He threw corn into the pot with the dog meat and continued his search through the village. Fire had not affected many of the earthen huts, and Glass was pleased to find several lengths of cordage for a raft. He also found a tin cup and a ladle made from a buffalo horn.

When he returned to the big lodge he found the blind old woman as he had left her, still sucking at the cob of corn. He walked to the kettle and filled the tin cup with broth, setting it next to her on the pallet. The pup, unsettled at the smell of his brethren roasting on the fire, huddled at the woman's feet. The woman could smell the meat too. She grasped the cup and gulped the broth the first moment the temperature would allow. Glass filled the cup again, this time adding tiny bits of meat that he cut with the razor. He filled the cup three times before the old woman stopped eating and fell asleep. He adjusted the blanket to cover her bony shoulders.

Glass moved to the fire and began to eat the roasted dog. The Pawnee considered dog a delicacy, harvesting an occasional canine the way white men butchered a spring pig. Glass certainly preferred buffalo, but in his present state, dog would do just fine. He pulled corn from the pot and ate that too, saving the broth and the boiled meat for the squaw.

He had eaten for about an hour when the old woman cried out. Glass moved quickly to her side. She said something over and over. "*He tuwe he . . . He tuwe*

**156**

*he . . ."* She spoke this time not in the fearful tone of her death chant, but in a quiet voice, a voice seeking urgently to communicate an important thought. The words meant nothing to Glass. Not knowing what else to do, he took the woman's hand. She squeezed it weakly and pulled it to her cheek. They sat like that for a while. Her blind eyes closed and she drifted off to sleep.

In the morning she was dead.

Glass spent the better part of the morning building a crude pyre overlooking the Missouri. When it was finished, he returned to the big hut and wrapped the old woman in her blanket. He carried her to the pyre, the dog trailing pitifully behind them in an odd cortege. Like his wounded leg, Glass's shoulder had healed nicely in the weeks since the battle with the wolves. Still, he winced as he hoisted the body up on the pyre. He felt the familiar, disconcerting twinges along his spine. His back continued to worry him. With luck, he would be at Fort Brazeau in a few days. Someone there could tend to him properly.

He stood for a moment at the pyre, old conventions calling from a distant past. He wondered for a moment what words had been spoken at his mother's funeral, what words had been spoken for Elizabeth. He pictured a mound of fresh-turned earth next to an open grave. The notion of burial had always struck him as stifling and cold. He liked the Indian way better, setting the bodies up high, as if passing them to the heavens.

The dog growled suddenly and Glass whipped around. Four mounted Indians rode slowly toward him from the village at a distance of only seventy yards. From their clothing and hair, Glass recognized them immediately as Sioux. He panicked for an instant, calculating the distance to the thick trees of the bluff. He thought back to his first encounter with the Pawnee, and decided to hold his ground.

It had been little more than a month since the trappers and the Sioux had been allies in the siege against the Arikara. Glass remembered that the Sioux had quit the fight in disgust over Colonel Leavenworth's tactics, a sentiment shared by the men of the Rocky Mountain Fur Company. *Do remnants of that alliance still stand?* So he stood there, affecting as much confidence as he could muster, and watched the Indians approach.

They were young; three were barely more than teens. The fourth was slightly older, perhaps in his mid-twenties. The younger braves approached warily, weapons ready, as if moving toward a strange animal. The older Sioux rode a half-length ahead of the others. He carried a London fusil, but he held the gun casually, the barrel resting across the neck of an enormous buckskin stallion. A brand etched the animal's haunch, "U.S." *One of Leavenworth's.* In another setting, Glass might have found humor in the colonel's misfortune.

The older Sioux reined his horse five feet in front of Glass, studying him from head to foot. Then the Sioux looked beyond him to the pyre. He struggled to understand the relationship between this mangled, filthy white man and the dead Arikara squaw. From a distance they had watched him struggle to place her body on the scaffolding. It made no sense.

The Indian swung his leg across the big stallion and slipped easily to the ground. He walked up to Glass, his dark eyes penetrating. Glass felt his stomach roil, though he met the gaze unflinchingly.

The Indian accomplished effortlessly what Glass was compelled to pretend — an air of complete confidence. His name was Yellow Horse. He was tall, over six feet, with square shoulders and perfect posture that accentuated a powerful neck and chest. In his tightly braided hair he wore three eagle feathers, notched to signify enemies killed in battle. Two decorative bands ran down the doeskin tunic on his chest. Glass noticed the intricacy of the work, hundreds of interwoven porcupine quills dyed brilliantly in vermillion and indigo.

As the two men stood face-to-face, the Indian reached out, slowly extending his hand to Glass's necklace, examining the enormous bear claw as he turned it in his fingers. He let the claw drop, his eyes moving to trace the scars around Glass's skull and throat. The Indian nudged Glass's shoulder to turn him, examining the wounds beneath his tattered shirt. He said something to the other three as he looked at Glass's back. Glass heard the other braves dismount and approach, then talk excitedly as they pushed and probed at his back. *What's happening?*

The source of the Indians' fascination was the deep, parallel wounds extending the length of Glass's back. The Indians had seen many wounds, but never this.

The deep gashes were animated. They were crawling with maggots.

One of the Indians managed to pinch a twisting white worm between his fingers. He held it for Glass to see. Glass cried out in horror, tearing at the remnants of his shirt, reaching ineffectively toward the wounds he could not touch, and then falling to his hands and knees, retching at the sickening thought of this hideous invasion.

They put Glass on a horse behind one of the young braves and rode away from the Arikara village. The old woman's dog started to follow behind the horses. One of the Indians stopped, dismounted, and coaxed the dog close. With the dull side of a tomahawk, he bashed the dog's skull, grabbed the animal by the hind legs, and rode to catch the others.

The Sioux camp lay just south of the Grand. The arrival of the four braves with a white man sparked immediate excitement, and scores of Indians trailed behind them like a parade as they rode through the teepees.

Yellow Horse led the procession to a low teepee set away from the camp. Wild designs covered the teepee: lightning bolts spewing from black clouds, buffalo arranged geometrically around a sun, vaguely human figures dancing around a fire. Yellow Horse called out a greeting, and after a few moments, an ancient, gnarled Indian emerged from a flap on the teepee. He squinted in the bright sun, although even without squinting, his eyes were barely visible beneath deep wrinkles. Black paint covered the upper half of his face, and he had tied a dead, withered raven behind his right ear. He was naked from the chest up despite the chill of the October day, and below the waist he wore only a loincloth. The skin hanging loosely from his sunken chest was painted in alternating stripes of black and red.

Yellow Horse dismounted, and signaled Glass to do the same. Glass stepped down stiffly, his wounds aching anew from the unaccustomed bouncing of the ride. Yellow Horse told the medicine man about the strange white man they found in the remains of the Arikara village, how they had watched as he set loose the spirit of the old squaw. He told the medicine man that the white man had shown no fear as they approached him, though he had no weapons but a sharpened stick. He told about the bear-claw necklace and the wounds on the man's throat and back.

The medicine man said nothing during Yellow Horse's long explanation, though his eyes peered intently through the furrowed mask of his face. The assembled Indians huddled close to listen, a murmur rising at the description of the maggots in the wounded back.

When Yellow Horse finished, the medicine man stepped up to Glass.

The top of the shrunken man's head barely rose to Glass's chin, which put the old Sioux at a perfect angle to examine the bear claw. He poked at the tip with his thumb, as if to verify its authenticity. His palsied hands trembled slightly as they reached to touch the pinkish scars extending from Glass's right shoulder to his throat.

Finally he turned Glass around to examine his back. He reached up to the collar of the threadbare shirt and ripped.

The cloth offered little resistance. The Indians pushed close to see for themselves what Yellow Horse had described. They broke instantly into excited chatter in the strange language. Glass again felt his stomach turn at the thought of the spectacle that sparked such fervor.

The medicine man said something and the Indians fell instantly silent.

He turned and disappeared behind the flap on his teepee. When he emerged a few minutes later, his arms were full of assorted gourds and beaded bags. He returned to Glass and motioned him to lie facedown on the ground. Next to Glass, he spread out a beautiful white pelt. On the pelt he laid out an array of medicines. Glass had no idea what the vessels contained. *I don't care.* Only one thing mattered. *Get them off me.*

The medicine man said something to one of the young braves, who ran off, returning in a few minutes with a black pot full of water. Meanwhile, the medicine man sniffed at the largest of the gourds, adding ingredients from the assortment of bags. He broke into a low chant as he worked, the only sound to rise above the respectful silence of the villagers.

The principal ingredient of the big gourd was buffalo urine, taken from the bladder of a large bull in a hunt

162

the past summer. To the urine he added alder root and gunpowder. The resulting astringent was as potent as turpentine.

The medicine man handed Glass a short stick, six inches in length. It took a moment before Glass understood its purpose. He took a deep breath and placed the stick between his teeth.

Glass braced himself and the medicine man poured.

The astringent ignited the most intense pain that Glass had ever felt, like molten iron in a mold of human flesh. At first the pain was specific, as the liquid seeped into each of the five cuts, inch by excruciating inch. Soon though, the pointed fire spread into a broader wave of agony, pulsating with the rapid beat of his heart. Glass sunk his teeth into the soft wood of the stick. He tried to imagine the cathartic effect of the treatment, but he could not transcend the immediacy of the pain.

The astringent had the desired effect on the maggots. Dozens of the wriggling white forms struggled to the surface. After a few minutes, the medicine man used a large ladle of water to wash the worms and the burning liquid from Glass's back. Glass panted as the pain slowly receded. He had just begun to catch his breath when the medicine man poured again from the big gourd.

The medicine man applied four doses of the astringent. When he had washed the final traces away, he packed the wounds in a steaming poultice of pine and larch. Yellow Horse helped Glass into the medicine man's teepee. A squaw brought freshly cooked venison.

He ignored his stinging back long enough to gorge himself, then laid down on a buffalo robe and fell into a deep sleep.

He passed in and out of sleep for almost two straight days. In his moments of wakefulness, he found next to him a replenished supply of food and water. The medicine man tended his back, twice changing the poultice. After the jolting pain of the astringent, the humid warmth of the poultice was like the soothing touch of a maternal hand.

The first light of early morning lit the teepee in a faint glow when Glass awoke on the morning of the third day, the silence broken only by the occasional rustling of horses and the cooing of mourning doves. The medicine man lay sleeping, a buffalo robe pulled over his bony chest. Next to Glass lay a pile of neatly folded, buckskin clothing — breeches, beaded moccasins, and a simple doeskin tunic. He raised himself slowly and dressed.

The Pawnee considered the Sioux their mortal enemies. Glass had even fought against a band of Sioux hunters in a small skirmish during his days on the Kansas plains. He had a new perception now. How could he be anything but appreciative for the Samaritan actions of Yellow Horse and the medicine man? The medicine man stirred, raising himself to a sitting position when he saw Glass. He said something that Glass could not understand.

Yellow Horse showed up a few minutes later. He seemed pleased that Glass was up and about. The two Indians examined his back and seemed to speak approvingly at what they found. When they finished, Glass pointed to his back, raised his eyebrows questioningly to ask, "Does it look okay?" Yellow Horse pursed his lips and nodded his head.

They met later that day in Yellow Horse's teepee. Through a hodgepodge of sign language and drawings in the sand, Glass attempted to communicate where he came from and where he wanted to go. Yellow Horse seemed to understand "Fort Brazeau," which Glass confirmed when the Indian drew a map showing the precise placement of the fort at the confluence of the Missouri with the White River. Glass nodded his head furiously. Yellow Horse said something to the braves assembled in the teepee. Glass could not understand, and went to sleep that night wondering if he should simply strike out on his own.

He awoke the next morning to the sound of horses outside the medicine man's teepee. When he emerged, he found Yellow Horse and the three young braves from the Arikara village. They were mounted, and one of the braves held the bridle of a riderless pinto.

Yellow Horse said something and pointed to the pinto. The sun had just crested the horizon as they began the ride south toward Fort Brazeau.

# CHAPTER
# FOURTEEN

## *October 6, 1823*

Jim Bridger's sense of direction did not fail him. He had been right when he urged Fitzgerald to cut overland and away from the eastern turn of the Little Missouri River. The western horizon swallowed the last sliver of sun when the two men fired a rifle shot to signal their approach to Fort Union. Captain Henry sent out a rider to greet them.

The men of the Rocky Mountain Fur Company treated Fitzgerald's and Bridger's entry into the fort with somber respect. Fitzgerald bore Glass's rifle like the proud ensign of their fallen comrade. Jean Poutrine crossed himself as the Anstadt paraded past, and a few of the men removed their hats. Inevitable or not, the men found it unsettling to confront Glass's death.

They gathered in the bunkhouse to hear Fitzgerald's account. Bridger had to marvel at his skill, at the subtlety and deftness with which he lied. "Not much to tell," said Fitzgerald. "We all knew where it was going. I won't pretend to have been his friend, but I respect a man who fights like he fought.

"We buried him deep . . . covered him with enough rock to keep him protected. Truth is, Captain, I wanted to get moving right away — but Bridger said we ought to make a cross for the grave." Bridger looked up, horrified at this last bit of embellishment. Twenty admiring faces stared back at him, a few nodding in solemn approval. *God — not respect!* What he had craved was now his, and it was more than he could bear. Whatever the consequences, he had to purge the awful burden of their lie — his lie.

He felt Fitzgerald's icy stare from the corner of his eye. *I don't care.* He opened his mouth to speak, but before he could find the right words, Captain Henry said, "I knew you'd pull your weight, Bridger." More approving nods from the men of the brigade. *What have I done?* He cast his eyes to the ground.

# CHAPTER
# FIFTEEN

## *October 9, 1823*

Fort Brazeau's claim to the appellation of "fort" was tenuous at best. Perhaps the motivation for the name had been vanity — a desire to institutionalize a family name. Or perhaps the hope had been to deter attack through sheer force of nomenclature. Either way, the name exceeded its grasp.

Fort Brazeau consisted of a single log cabin, a crude dock, and a hitching post. The cabin's narrow slits for shooting represented the only evidence that any consideration had been given to the martial aspects of the building, and they did more to impede light than arrows.

Scattered teepees spotted the clearing around the fort, a few pitched temporarily by Indians visiting to trade, a few pitched permanently by resident Yankton Sioux drunks. Anyone traveling on the river put in for the night. They usually camped under the stars, although for two bits the prosperous could share space on a straw tick in the cabin.

Inside, the cabin was part sundry shop and part saloon. Dimly lit, the main sensations were olfactory: day-old smoke, the greasy musk of fresh hides, open barrels of salted codfish. Barring drunken conversation, the primary sounds came from the constant buzz of flies and occasional buzz of snoring from a sleeping loft among the rafters.

The fort's namesake, Kiowa Brazeau, peered at the five approaching riders through thick spectacles that made his eyes appear unnaturally large. It was with considerable relief that he made out the face of Yellow Horse. Kiowa had worried about the disposition of the Sioux.

William Ashley had just spent the better part of a month at Fort Brazeau, planning the future of his Rocky Mountain Fur Company in the wake of the debacle at the Arikara villages. The Sioux had been allies with the whites in the battle against the Arikara. Or, more accurately, the Sioux had been allies until they had grown weary of Colonel Leavenworth's listless tactics. Halfway through Leavenworth's siege, the Sioux abruptly departed (though not before stealing horses from both Ashley and the U.S. Army). Ashley viewed the Sioux desertion as treachery. Kiowa harbored quiet sympathy for the attitude of the Sioux, though he saw no need to offend the founder of the Rocky Mountain Fur Company. After all, Ashley and his men had been Kiowa's best customers ever, purchasing virtually his entire inventory of supplies.

Ultimately, though, Fort Brazeau's meager economy depended on trade with the local tribes. The Sioux took on added significance since the dramatic change in relations with the Arikara. Kiowa worried that the Sioux's disdain for Leavenworth might extend to him and his trading post. The arrival of Yellow Horse and three other Sioux braves was a good sign, particularly when it became clear that they were delivering a white man who had apparently been in their care.

A small crowd of resident Indians and transiting voyageurs gathered to greet the newcomers. They stared in particular at the white man with the horrible scars on his face and scalp. Brazeau spoke to Yellow Horse in fluent Sioux, and Yellow Horse explained what he knew of the white man. Glass became the uncomfortable focus of dozens of gazing eyes. Those who spoke Sioux listened to Yellow Horse's description of finding Glass, alone with no weapons, grievously wounded by a bear. The rest were left to wonder, though it was obvious that the white man had a story to tell.

Kiowa listened to Yellow Horse's story before addressing himself to the white man. "Who are you?" The white man seemed to struggle with his words. Thinking he did not understand, Brazeau switched to French:

"*Qui êtes-vous?*"

Glass swallowed and gently cleared his throat. He remembered Kiowa from the Rocky Mountain Fur Company's brief layover on its way upriver. Kiowa obviously didn't remember him. It occurred to Glass that his appearance had changed significantly, although he still had not had a good glimpse of his own face since the attack. "Hugh Glass." It pained him to speak, and his voice came out as a kind of pitiful, screeching whine. "Ashley man."

"You just missed Monsieur Ashley. He sent Jed Stuart west with fifteen men, then headed back to St. Louis to raise another brigade." Kiowa waited a minute, thinking that if he paused the wounded man might offer more information.

When the man showed no signs of saying anything further, a one-eyed Scotsman gave voice to the group's impatience. In a dim-witted brogue he asked, "What happened to you?"

Glass spoke slowly and with as much economy as possible. "Grizzly attacked me on the Upper Grand." He hated the pathetic whine of his voice, but he continued. "Captain Henry left me with two men." He paused again, placing his hand to comfort his wounded throat. "They ran off and stole my kit."

"Sioux bring you all the way here?" asked the Scot.

Seeing the pain in Glass's face, Kiowa answered for him. "Yellow Horse found him alone at the Arikara villages. Correct me if I'm wrong, Monsieur Glass, but I'll wager you made it down the Grand on your own."

Glass nodded.

The one-eyed Scotsman started to ask another question, but Kiowa cut him off. "Monsieur Glass can save his tale for later. I'd say he deserves a chance to eat and sleep." The eyeglasses lent Kiowa's face an intelligent and avuncular air. He grabbed Glass by the shoulder and led him into the cabin. Inside, he placed Glass at a long table and said something in Sioux to his wife. She produced a heaping plate of stew from a giant, cast iron pot. Glass inhaled the food, then two more large helpings.

Kiowa sat across the table from him, watching patiently through the dim light and shooing away the gawkers.

As he finished eating, Glass turned to Kiowa with a sudden thought.

"I can't pay."

"I didn't expect that you'd be carrying a lot of cash. An Ashley man can draw credit at my fort." Glass nodded his head in acknowledgment. Kiowa continued, "I can equip you and get you on the next boat to St. Louis."

Glass shook his head violently. "I'm not going to St. Louis." Kiowa was taken aback. "Well, just where do you plan on going?"

"Fort Union."

"Fort Union! It's October! Even if you make it past the Rees to the Mandan villages, it'll be December by the time you get there. And that's still three hundred miles from Fort Union. You going to walk up the Missouri in the middle of winter?"

Glass didn't answer. His throat hurt. Besides, he wasn't looking for permission. He took a sip of water from a large tin cup, thanked Kiowa for the food, and started to climb the rickety ladder to the sleeping loft. He stopped part way, climbed back down and walked outside.

Glass found Yellow Horse camped away from the Fort on the banks of the White River. He and the other Sioux had tended their horses, done a little trading, and would leave in the morning. Yellow Horse avoided the fort as much as possible. Kiowa and his Sioux wife had always treated him honestly, but the whole establishment depressed him. He felt disdain and even shame for the filthy Indians who camped around the fort, prostituting their wives and daughters for the next drink of whiskey. There was something to fear in an evil that could make men leave their old lives behind and live in such disgrace.

Beyond Fort Brazeau's effect on the resident Indians, other aspects of the post left him profoundly disquieted. He marveled at the intricacy and quality of the goods produced by the whites, from their guns and axes to their fine cloth and needles. Yet he also felt a lurking trepidation about a people who could make such things, harnessing powers that he did not understand. And what about the stories of the whites' great villages in the East, villages with people as numerous as the buffalo. He doubted these stories could be true, though each year the trickle of traders increased. Now came the fight with the Arikara and the soldiers. True, it was the Arikara that the whites sought to punish, a tribe for which he himself held no goodwill. And true, the white soldiers had been cowards and fools. He struggled to understand his unease. Taken bit by bit, none of his forebodings seemed over-whelming. Yet Yellow Horse sensed that these scattered strands came together somehow, braided in a warning that he could not yet fully perceive.

Yellow Horse stood when Glass walked into the camp, a low fire illuminating their faces. Glass had thought about trying to pay the Sioux for their care, but something told him that Yellow Horse would take offense. He thought about some small gift — a pigtail of tobacco or a knife. Such trifles seemed inadequate expressions of his gratitude. Instead he walked up to Yellow Horse, removed his bear-claw necklace, and placed it around the Indian's neck.

Yellow Horse stared at him for a moment. Glass stared back, nodded his head, then turned and walked back toward the cabin.

When Glass climbed again to the sleeping loft, he found two voyageurs already asleep on the large straw tick. In a corner under the eaves, a ratty hide had been spread in the cramped space. Glass eased himself down and found sleep almost instantly.

A loud conversation in French woke Glass the next morning, rising to the loft from the open room below. Jolly laughter interspersed the discussion, and Glass noticed he was alone in the loft. He lay there for a while, enjoying the luxury of shelter and warmth. He rolled from his stomach to his back.

The medicine man's brutal treatment had worked. If his back was not yet fully healed, the wounds at least had been purged of their vile infection. He stretched his limbs one by one, as if examining the complex components of a newly purchased machine. His leg could bear the full weight of his body, although he still walked with a pronounced limp. And though his strength had not returned, his arm and shoulder could function normally. He assumed that the recoil of a rifle would cause sharp pain, but he was confident in his ability to handle a gun.

A *gun*. He appreciated Kiowa's willingness to equip him. What he wanted, though, was *his* gun. His gun and a reckoning from the men who stole it. Reaching Fort Brazeau seemed markedly anticlimactic. True, it was a milestone. Yet for Glass the fort did not mark a finish line to cross with elation, but rather a starting line to cross with resolve. With new equipment and his increasingly healthy body, he now had advantages that he had lacked in the past six weeks. Still, his goal lay far away.

As he lay on his back in the loft, he noticed a bucket of water on a table. The door opened below and a cracked mirror on the wall caught the morning light. Glass rose from the floor and walked slowly to the mirror.

He wasn't exactly shocked at the image staring back at him. He expected to look different. Still, it was strange finally to see the wounds that for weeks he could only imagine. Three parallel claw marks cut deep lines through the heavy beard on his cheek. They reminded Glass of war paint. No wonder the Sioux had been respectful. Pinkish scar tissue ringed his scalp line, and several gashes marked the top of his head. Where hair did grow, he noticed that gray now mixed with the brown he knew before — particularly in his beard. He paid particular attention to his throat. Again, parallel swaths marked the path of the claws. Knobby scars marked the points where the sutures had been tied.

Glass lifted his doeskin blouse in an effort to look at his back, but the dark mirror showed little more than the outline of the long wounds. The mental image of the maggots still haunted him. Glass left the mirror and climbed down from the loft.

A dozen men gathered in the room below, crowding the long table and spilling beyond. The conversation stopped as Glass descended the ladder from the loft.

Kiowa greeted him, switching easily to English. The Frenchman's facility with language was an asset for a trader amid the frontier Babel.

"Good morning, Monsieur Glass. We were just talking about you." Glass nodded his head in acknowledgment but said nothing.

"You're in luck," continued Kiowa. "I may have found you a ride upriver." Glass's interest was immediate.

"Meet Antoine Langevin." A short man with a long mustache stood up formally from the table, reaching to shake Glass's hand. Glass was surprised by the power of the small man's grip.

"Langevin arrived last night from upriver. Like you, Monsieur Glass, he arrived with something of a story to tell. Monsieur Langevin came all the way from the Mandan villages. He tells me that our wandering tribe, the Arikara, has established a new village on land only a mile south of the Mandans."

Langevin said something in French that Glass did not understand. "I'm getting to that, Langevin," said Kiowa, irritated at the interruption.

"I thought our friend might appreciate a bit of historical context." Kiowa continued with his explanation. "As you can imagine, our friends the Mandans are nervous that their new neighbors are bringing trouble

**176**

with them. As a condition of occupying Mandan territory, the Mandans have exacted a promise that the Arikara will cease their attacks on whites."

Kiowa removed his spectacles, wiping the lenses with his long shirttail before returning them to the perch on his ruddy nose. "Which brings me to my own circumstances. My little fort depends on river traffic. I need trappers and traders like yourself moving up and down the Missouri. I appreciated the lengthy visit by Monsieur Ashley and his men, but this fighting with the Arikara will drive me out of business.

"I've asked Langevin to lead a deputation up the Missouri. They'll take gifts and reestablish ties with the Arikara. If they succeed, we'll send word to St. Louis that the Missouri is open for business.

"There's room for six men and supplies on Langevin's *bâtard*. This is Toussaint Charbonneau." Kiowa pointed to another man at the table. Glass knew the name, and stared with interest at the husband of Sacagewea. "Toussaint translated for Lewis and Clark. He speaks Mandan, Arikara, and anything else you might need on the way."

"And I speak English," said Charbonneau, which sounded like, *end ah speek eegleesh*. Kiowa's English was almost without accent, but Charbonneau's carried the thick melody of his native tongue. Glass reached for Charbonneau's hand.

Kiowa continued with the introductions. "This is Andrew MacDonald." He pointed to the one-eyed Scot from the day before. Glass noticed that in addition to the missing eye, the Scot was missing a significant portion from the tip of his nose. "There's a good chance he's the dumbest man I ever met," said Kiowa. "But he can paddle all day without stopping. We call him 'Professeur.'" Professeur cocked his head to bring Kiowa within range of his good eye, which squinted in dim recognition at the mention of his name, although the irony clearly eluded him.

"Finally — there is Dominique Cattoire." Kiowa pointed to a voyageur smoking a thin clay pipe. Dominique rose, shook Glass's hand and said, "*Enchanté.*"

"Dominique's brother is Louis Cattoire, king of the *putains*. He's going too, if we pry him and his *andouille* out of the whore's tent. We call Louis 'La Vierge.'" The men around the table laughed.

"Which brings me to you. They're rowing upriver, so they need to travel light. They need a hunter to provide meat for the camp. I suspect you are pretty good at finding food. Probably even better once we get you a rifle."

Glass nodded his head in response.

"There's another reason our deputation can use an extra rifle," continued Kiowa. "Dominique heard rumors that an Arikara chief named Elk's Tongue has broken away from the main tribe. He's leading a small band of warriors and their families somewhere between Mandan and the Grand. We don't know where they're at, but he's vowed to avenge the attack on the Ree village."

Glass thought about the blackened remnants of the Arikara village and nodded in response.

**178**

"Are you in?"

Part of Glass did not want the encumbrance of fellow travelers. His plan had been to make his way up the Missouri alone, on foot. He intended to leave that day, and hated the idea of waiting. Still, he recognized the opportunity. Numbers meant safety, if the men were any good. The men of Kiowa's deputation seemed seasoned, and Glass knew there were no finer boatmen than the scrappy voyageurs. He also knew that his body was still healing, and his progress would be slow if he walked. Paddling the *bâtard* upstream would be slow too. But riding while the others paddled would give him another month to mend.

Glass put his hand to his throat. "I'm in."

Langevin said something to Kiowa in French. Kiowa listened and then turned to Glass. "Langevin says he needs today to make repairs to the *bâtard*. You'll leave tomorrow at dawn. Eat some food and then let's get you provisioned."

Kiowa kept his wares along a wall at the far end of the cabin. A plank over two empty barrels served as the counter. Glass focused first on a long arm. There were five weapons to choose from. Three were rusted northwest muskets of ancient vintage, clearly meant for trade with the Indians. Between the two rifles, the choice at first seemed obvious. One was a classic Kentucky long rifle, beautifully crafted with a burnished walnut finish. The other was a weathered Model 1803 U.S. Infantry rifle whose stock had been broken and repaired with rawhide. Glass picked up the two rifles and carried them outside, accompanied by

Kiowa. Glass had an important decision to make, and he wanted to examine the weapons in full light.

Kiowa looked on expectantly as Glass examined the long Kentucky rifle. "That's a beautiful weapon," said Kiowa. "The Germans can't cook for shit but they know how to make a gun."

Glass agreed. He had always admired the elegant lines of Kentucky rifles. But there were two problems. First, Glass noticed with disappointment the rifle's small caliber, which he correctly gauged as .32. Second, the gun's great length made it heavy to carry and cumbersome to load. This was an ideal gun for a gentleman farmer, squirrel hunting in Virginia. Glass needed something different.

He handed the Kentucky rifle to Kiowa and picked up the Model 1803, the same gun carried by many of the soldiers in Lewis and Clark's Corps of Discovery. Glass first examined the repair work on the broken stock. Wet rawhide had been tightly stitched around the break, then allowed to dry. The rawhide had hardened and shrunk as it dried, creating a rock-sturdy cast. The stock was ugly, but it felt solid. Next Glass examined the lock and trigger works. There was fresh grease and no sign of rust. He ran his hand slowly down the half stock, then continued the length of the short barrel. He put his finger into the fat hole of the muzzle, noting approvingly the heft of its .53 caliber.

"You like the big gun, eh?" Glass nodded in reply.

"A big gun is good," said Kiowa. "Give it a try." Kiowa smiled wryly. "Gun like that, you could kill a bear!"

180

Kiowa handed Glass a powder horn and a measure. Glass poured a full charge of 200 grains and dumped it into the muzzle. Kiowa handed him a big .53 ball and a greased patch from his vest pocket. Glass wrapped the ball in the patch and tapped it into the muzzle. He pulled out the ramrod and set the ball firmly in the breech. He poured powder in the pan and pulled the hammer to full cock, searching for a target.

Fifty yards away a squirrel sat placidly in the crotch of a big cottonwood.

Glass sighted on the squirrel and pulled the trigger. The briefest of instants separated the ignition in the pan and the primary explosion deep in the barrel. Smoke filled the air, momentarily obscuring the target from sight. Glass winced at the stiff punch of the recoil against his shoulder.

As the smoke cleared, Kiowa ambled slowly to the foot of the cottonwood. He stooped to pick up the tattered remains of the squirrel, which now consisted of very little beyond a bushy tail. He walked back to Glass and tossed the tail at Glass's feet. "I think that gun is not so good for squirrels."

This time Glass smiled back. "I'll take it."

They returned to the cabin and Glass picked out the rest of his supplies. He chose a .53 pistol to complement the rifle. A ball mold, lead, powder, and flints. A tomahawk and a large skinning knife. A thick leather belt to hold his weapons. Two red cotton shirts to wear beneath the doeskin tunic. A large Hudson's Bay capote. A wool cap and mittens. Five pounds of salt and three pigtails of tobacco. Needle and thread.

Cordage. To carry his newfound bounty, he picked a fringed leather possibles bag with intricate quill beading. He noticed that the voyageurs all wore small sacks at the waist for their pipe and tobacco. He took one of those too, a handy spot for his new flint and steel.

When Glass finished, he felt rich as a king. After six weeks with nothing but the clothes on his back, Glass felt immensely prepared for whatever battles lay before him. Kiowa calculated the bill, which totaled one hundred twenty-five dollars. Glass wrote a note to William Ashley:

October 10, 1823
Dear Mr. Ashley:
My kit was stolen by two men of our brigade with whom I will settle my own account. Mr. Brazeau has extended me credit against the name of the Rocky Mountain Fur Co. I have taken the liberty of advancing the attached goods against my pay. I intend to recover my property and I pledge to repay my debt to you.
Your most obedient servant,
Hugh Glass

"I'll send your letter with the invoice," said Kiowa.

Glass ate a hearty dinner that evening with Kiowa and four of his five new companions. The fifth, Louis "La Vierge" Cattoire, had yet to emerge from the whore's tent. His brother Dominique reported that La Vierge had alternated between bouts of inebriation and fornication since the moment of their arrival at Fort

Brazeau. Except when it directly involved Glass, the voyageurs did most of their talking in French. Glass recognized scattered words and phrases from his time on Campeche, though not enough to follow the conversation.

"Make sure your brother's ready in the morning," said Langevin. "I need his paddle."

"He'll be ready."

"And remember the task at hand," said Kiowa. "Don't be laying up with the Mandans all winter. I need confirmation that the Arikara won't attack traders on the river. If I haven't heard from you by New Year's, I can't get word to St. Louis in time to effect planning for the spring."

"I know my job," said Langevin. "I'll get you the information you need."

"Speaking of information" — Kiowa switched seamlessly from French to English — "we'd all like to know exactly what happened to you, Monsieur Glass." At this, even the dim eye of Professeur flickered with interest.

Glass looked around the table. "There's not much to tell." Kiowa translated as Glass spoke, and the voyageurs laughed when they heard what Glass had said.

Kiowa laughed too, then said: "With all due respect, *mon ami*, your face tells a story by itself — but we'd like to hear the particulars."

Settling in for what they expected to be an entertaining tale, the voyageurs packed fresh tobacco into their long pipes. Kiowa removed an ornate silver

**183**

snuffbox from his vest pocket and put a pinch to his nose.

Glass put his hand to his throat, still embarrassed by his whining voice.

"Big grizzly attacked me on the Grand. Captain Henry left John Fitzgerald and Jim Bridger behind to bury me when I died. They robbed me instead. I aim to recover what's mine and see justice done."

Glass finished. Kiowa translated. A long silence followed, pregnant with expectation.

Finally Professeur asked in his thick brogue, "Ain't he gonna tell us anymore?"

"No offense, monsieur," said Toussaint Charbonneau, "but you're not much of a *raconteur*."

Glass stared back, but offered no further detail.

Kiowa spoke up. "It's your business if you want to keep the details of your fight with the bear, but I won't let you leave without telling me about the Grand."

Kiowa understood early in his career that his trade dealt not only in goods, but also in information. People came to his trading post not just for the things they could buy, but also for the things they could learn. Kiowa's fort sat at the confluence of the Missouri and the White River, so the White he knew well. So too the Cheyenne River to his north. He had learned what he could about the Grand from a number of Indians, but details remained sparse.

Kiowa said something in Sioux to his wife, who retrieved for him a well-worn book which they both handled as if it were the family Bible. The book wore a long title on its tattered cover. Kiowa adjusted his

**184**

spectacles and read the title aloud: "*History of the Expedition . . .*"

Glass finished it: "*. . . Under the Command of Captains Lewis and Clark.*" Kiowa looked up excitedly. "*Ah bon!* Our wounded traveler is a man of letters!"

Glass too was excited, forgetting for a while the pain of speaking.

"Edited by Paul Allen. Published in Philadelphia, 1814."

"Then you're also familiar with Captain Clark's map?"

Glass nodded. He remembered well the electricity that accompanied the long-awaited publication of the memoirs and map. Like the maps that shaped his boyhood dreams, Glass first saw *History of the Expedition* in the Philadelphia offices of Rawsthorne & Sons.

Kiowa set the book on its spine and it fell open to Clark's map, entitled "*A Map of Lewis and Clark's Track, Across the Western Portion of North America From the Mississippi to the Pacific Ocean.*" To prepare for their expedition, Clark had trained intensively in cartography and its tools. His map was the marvel of its day, surpassing in detail and accuracy anything produced before it. The map showed clearly the major tributaries feeding the Missouri from St. Louis to the Three Forks.

Though the map portrayed accurately the rivers that flowed into the Missouri, detail usually ended near the point of confluence. Little was known about the course and source of these streams. There were a few exceptions: By 1814, the map could incorporate discoveries in the Yellowstone Basin by Drouillard and Colter. It showed the trace of Zebulon Pike through the southern Rockies. Kiowa had sketched in the Platte, including a rough estimate of its north and south forks. And on the Yellowstone, Manuel Lisa's abandoned fort was marked at the mouth of the Bighorn.

Glass pored eagerly over the document. What interested him was not Clark's map itself, which he knew well from his long hours at Rawsthorne & Sons and his more recent studies in St. Louis. What interested Glass were the details added by Kiowa, the penciled etchings of a decade's accreted knowledge.

The recurrent theme was water, and the names told the stories of the places. Some memorialized fights — War Creek, Lance Creek, Bear in the Lodge Creek. Others described the local flora and fauna — Antelope Creek, Beaver Creek, Pine Creek, the Rosebud. Some detailed the character of water itself — Deep Creek, Rapid Creek, the Platte, Sulphur Creek, Sweet Water. A few hinted at something more mystical — Medicine Lodge Creek, Castle Creek, Keya Paha.

Kiowa peppered Glass with questions. How many days had they walked up the Grand before striking the upper fork? Where did creeks flow into the river? What landmarks distinguished the path? What signs of beaver and other game? How much wood? How far to the Twin Buttes? What signs of Indians? Which tribes? Kiowa used a sharp pencil to sketch in the new details.

Glass took as well as gave. Though the rough map was etched in his memory, the details assumed new urgency as he contemplated traversing the land alone. How many miles from the Mandan villages to Fort Union? What were the principal tributaries above Mandan, and how many miles between them? What was the terrain? When did the Missouri freeze over? Where could he save time by cutting across the bends in the river? Glass copied key portions of Clark's map for his own future reference. He focused on the expanse between the Mandan villages and Fort Union, tracing both the Yellowstone and the Missouri rivers for several hundred miles above Fort Union.

The others drifted away from the table as Kiowa and Glass continued into the night, the dim oil lamp casting wild shadows on the log walls. Hungry at the rare opportunity for intelligent conversation, Kiowa would not release Glass from his grasp. Kiowa marveled at Glass's tale of walking from the Gulf of Mexico to St. Louis. He brought out fresh paper and made Glass draw a crude map of the Texas and Kansas plains.

"A man like you could do well at my post. Travelers are hungry for the type of information you possess."

Glass shook his head.

"Truly, *mon ami*. Why don't you lay up for the winter? I'll hire you on."

Kiowa would gladly have paid, just for the company.

Glass shook his head again, more firmly this time. "I have my own affairs to attend."

"Bit of a silly venture, isn't it? For a man of your skills? Traipsing across Louisiana in the dead of winter. Chase down your betrayers in the spring, if you're still inclined."

The warmth of the earlier conversation seemed to drain from the room, as if a door had been opened on a frigid winter day. Glass's eyes flashed and Kiowa regretted immediately his comment.

"It's not an issue on which I asked your counsel."

"No, monsieur. No, it was not."

There remained barely two hours before sunlight when Glass, exhausted, finally climbed up the ladder to the loft. Still, the anticipation of debarkation allowed him little sleep.

Glass awoke to a potpourri of shouted obscenities. One of the speakers was a man, screaming in French. Glass did not understand the individual words, but context made their general meaning clear.

The speaker was "La Vierge" Cattoire, having just been rudely roused from the depths of a drunken slumber by his brother Dominique. Weary of his sibling's antics and unable to awaken him with the standard kick in the ribs, Dominique tried another tactic: He made water on his brother's face. It was this act of considerable disrespect that triggered the rantings from La Vierge. Dominique's actions also angered the squaw with whom La Vierge had spent the night. She tolerated many forms of indecency in her teepee. Some she even encouraged. But Dominique's indiscriminate pissing had soiled her best blanket, and that made her mad. She yelled with the piercing screech of an offended magpie.

By the time Glass emerged from the cabin, the yelling match had degenerated into a fistfight. Like an ancient Greek wrestler, La Vierge stood facing his brother without a stitch of clothing. La Vierge had the advantage of size over his elder brother, but he bore the disadvantage of three consecutive days of heavy drinking, not to mention a rather abrupt and distasteful awakening. His vision had not cleared and his balance was off, though these handicaps did not temper his willingness to engage. Familiar with La Vierge's fighting style, Dominique stood firm, waiting for the inevitable attack. With a guttural roar, La Vierge lowered his head and barreled forward.

La Vierge put the full momentum of his charge behind the looping swing he aimed at his brother's head. Had he connected, he might well have planted Dominique's nose in the back of his brain. As it was, Dominique parried casually to the side.

Missing his target completely, La Vierge's swing threw him completely off balance. Dominique kicked him hard across the back of his knees, sweeping his feet from under him. La Vierge landed square on his back, knocking the wind from his lungs. He writhed pathetically for a moment, gasping for air. As soon as he could breathe again, he resumed his swearing and struggled for his feet. Dominique kicked him hard in the solar plexus, returning La Vierge to his quest for air.

"I told you to be ready, you miserable pinhead! We leave in half an hour." To underscore his point, Dominique kicked La Vierge in the mouth, splitting his upper and lower lips.

The fight over, the assembled crowd broke up. Glass walked down to the river. Langevin's *bâtard* floated at the dock, the swift current of the Missouri tugging against its mooring rope. As its name implied, the *bâtard* lay between the normal sizes of voyageur cargo canoes. Though smaller than the big *canots de maître*, the *bâtard* was sizable, almost thirty feet in length.

With the downstream current of the Missouri to propel them, Langevin and Professeur had been able to steer the *bâtard* by themselves, along with a full load of furs obtained in trade with the Mandans. Fully loaded, the *bâtard* would have required ten men to paddle upstream. Langevin's cargo would be light — a few gifts to bestow upon the Mandan and Arikara. Still, with only four men to paddle, their progress would be arduous.

Toussaint Charbonneau sat atop a barrel on the dock, casually eating an apple, while Professeur loaded the canoe under Langevin's supervision. To distribute the weight of their cargo, they laid two long poles on the floor of the canoe from bow to stern. On these poles Professeur placed the cargo, neatly arranged in four small bales. Professeur appeared to speak no French (at times, the Scotsman appeared to speak no English). Langevin compensated for Professeur's lack of comprehension by speaking more loudly. The increased volume aided Professeur very little, though Langevin's constant gesticulating provided a wealth of clues.

Professeur's blind eye contributed to his dim appearance. He lost the eye in a Montreal saloon, when a notorious brawler named "Oyster Joe" nearly shucked it from the Scotsman's skull. Professeur had managed

**190**

to pop the eye back in place, but it no longer functioned. The unblinking orb was fixed permanently at a skewed angle, as if watching for an attack from his flank. Professeur had never gotten around to making a patch.

There was little fanfare to their departure. Dominique and La Vierge arrived at the dock, each with a rifle and a small bag of possessions. La Vierge squinted at the glare of the morning sun on the river. Mud caked his long hair, and blood from the split lips painted his chin and the front of his blouse. Still, he hopped spryly into bowsman's position at the front of the *bâtard*, and a glint filled his eyes that had nothing to do with the angle of the sun. Dominique took the position of the steersman in the stern. La Vierge said something and both brothers laughed.

Langevin and Professeur sat next to each other in the wide middle of the canoe, each paddling to one side. One cargo bale sat before them, one behind. Charbonneau and Glass arranged themselves around the cargo, with Charbonneau toward the bow and Glass toward the stern.

The four voyageurs picked up their paddles, bringing the bow into the swift current. They dug deep and the *bâtard* moved upstream.

La Vierge began to sing as he paddled, and the voyageurs joined in:

> *Le laboureur aime sa charrue,*
> *Le chasseur son fusil, son chien;*
> *Le musicien aime sa musique;*

*Moi, mon canot — c'est mon bien!*
His cart is beloved of the ploughman,
The hunter loves his gun, his hound;
The musician is a music lover;
To my canoe I'm bound!

"*Bon voyage, mes amis!*" yelled Kiowa. "Don't lay up with the Mandans!" Glass turned to look behind him. He stared for a moment at Kiowa Brazeau, standing and waving from the dock at his little fort. Then Glass turned to look upriver and did not look back.

It was October 11, 1823. For more than a month he had moved away from his quarry. A strategic retreat — but retreat none the less. Beginning today, Glass resolved to retreat no more.

# PART TWO

# CHAPTER
# SIXTEEN

## *November 29, 1823*

Four paddles hit the water in perfect unison. The slender blades cut the surface, pushed to a depth of eighteen inches, then dug hard. The *bâtard* slogged forward with the stroke, bucking against the heavy flow of the current. When the stroke ended, the paddles lifted from the water. For an instant it appeared that the river would steal back their progress, but before it could rob them completely, the paddles hit the water again.

A paper-thin layer of ice had covered the still water when they embarked at dawn. Now, a few hours later, Glass leaned back against a thwart, basking appreciatively in the midmorning sun and enjoying the nostalgic, buoyant sensation of floating on water.

On their first day out of Fort Brazeau, Glass actually tried to handle a paddle. After all, he reasoned, he was a sailor by training. The voyageurs laughed when he picked up the oar, strengthening his determination. His folly became obvious immediately. The voyageurs paddled at the remarkable rate of sixty strokes a minute, regular as a fine Swiss watch. Glass could not have kept pace even if his shoulder had been fully healed. He flailed at the water for several minutes before something soft and wet hit him in the back of the head. He turned to see Dominique, a mocking grin filling his face. "For you, Mr. Pork Eater!" *For yew, meeSTER pork eeTAIR!* For the rest of their voyage, Glass manned not a paddle but an enormous sponge, constantly bailing water as it pooled on the bottom of the canoe.

It was a full-time job, since the *bâtard* leaked steadily. The canoe reminded Glass of a floating quilt. Its patchwork skin of birch bark was sewn together with *wattope*, the fine root of a pine tree. The seams were sealed with pine tar, reapplied constantly as leaks appeared. As birch had become more difficult to find, the voyageurs were forced to use other materials in their patching and plugging. Rawhide had been employed in several spots, stitched on and then slathered in gum. Glass was amazed at the fragility of the craft. A stiff kick would easily puncture the skin, and one of La Vierge's main tasks as steersman was the avoidance of lethal, floating debris. At least they benefited from the relatively docile flow of the fall season. The spring floods could send entire trees crashing downstream.

There was an upside to the *bâtard*'s shortcomings. If the vessel was frail, it was also light, an important consideration as they labored against the current. Glass came quickly to understand the odd affection of voyageurs for their craft. It was a marriage of sorts, a partnership between the men who propelled the boat and the boat that propelled the men. Each relied upon the other. The voyageurs spent half their time complaining bitterly about the manifold ails of the craft, and half their time nursing them tenderly.

They took great pride in the appearance of the *bâtard*, dressing it in jaunty plumes and bright paint. On the high prow they had painted a stag's head, its antlers tilted challengingly toward the flowing water. (On the stern, La Vierge had painted the animal's ass.)

"Good landing up ahead," said La Vierge from his vantage point on the prow.

Langevin peered upriver, where a gentle current brushed lightly against a sandy bank; then he glanced up to judge the position of the sun. "Okay, I'd say that's a pipe. *Allumez.*"

So vaunted was the pipe in voyageur culture that they used it to measure distance. A "pipe" stood for the typical interval between their short breaks for smoking. On a downstream run, a pipe might represent ten miles; on flat water, five; but on the tough pull up the Missouri, they felt lucky to make two.

Their days fell quickly into a pattern. They ate breakfast in the purple-blue glow before dawn, fueling their bodies with leftover game and fried dough, chasing away the morning chill with tin cups of scalding hot tea. They were on the water as soon as the light allowed them to see, eager to squeeze motion from every hour of the day. They made five or six pipes a day. Around noon they stopped long enough to eat jerky and a handful of dried apples, but they didn't cook again until supper. They put ashore with the setting sun after a dozen hours on the water. Glass usually had an hour or so of dimming light to find game. The men waited with anticipation for the single shot that signaled his success. Rarely did he return to camp without meat.

La Vierge jumped into the knee-deep water near the bank, careful to keep the *bâtard*'s fragile bottom from scraping against the sand. He waded ashore, securing the cordelle to a large piece of driftwood. Langevin, Professeur, and Dominique jumped out next, rifles in hand, scanning the tree line. Glass and Professeur covered the others from the canoe as they waded ashore, then followed. The day before, Glass found an abandoned campsite, including the stone rings of ten teepees. They had no way of knowing if it was Elk Tongue's band, but the discovery put them on edge.

The men pulled pipes and tobacco from the *sacs au feu* at their waists, passing a flame from a tiny fire set by Dominique. The two brothers sat on their butts in the sand. In their positions as bowsman and steersman, Dominique and La Vierge stood to paddle. As a consequence, they sat to smoke. The others stood, happy for the opportunity to stretch the kinks from their legs.

The colder weather settled into Glass's wounds the way a storm creeps its way up a mountain valley. He awoke each morning stiff and sore, his condition made worse by the long hours at his cramped perch in the *bâtard*. Glass took full advantage of the break, pacing up and down the sandbar to coax circulation through his aching limbs.

He regarded his travel companions as he walked back toward them. The voyageurs were remarkably similar in dress, almost, thought Glass, as if they all had been issued a formal uniform. They wore red woolen caps with sides that could be turned down to cover their ears and a tassel trailing off the top. (La Vierge dressed his cap with a jaunty ostrich feather.) For shirts they wore long cotton blouses in white, red, or navy, tucked in at the waist. Each voyageur tied a parti-colored sash around his waist, its ends left to dangle down one leg or the other. Over the sash hung the *sac au feu*, keeping their pipes and a few other essentials close at hand. They wore doeskin breeches, supple enough to allow the comfortable folding of legs in a canoe. Below each knee they tied a bandanna, adding more dandy dash to their attire. On their feet they wore moccasins with no socks.

With the exception of Charbonneau, who was gloomy as January rain, the voyageurs approached each waking moment with an infallibly cloudless optimism. They laughed at the slimmest opportunity. They showed little tolerance for silence, filling the day with unceasing and passionate discussion of women, water, and wild Indians. They fired constant insults back and forth. Indeed, to pass up an opportunity for a good joke was viewed as a character flaw, a sign of weakness. Glass wished he understood more French, if only for the entertainment value of following the banter that kept them all so jolly.

In the rare moments when conversation lagged, someone would break out in zestful song, an instant cue for the others to join in. What they lacked in musical ability, they compensated in unbridled enthusiasm. All in all, thought Glass, an agreeable way of life.

During this break, Langevin interrupted their brief rest with a rare moment of seriousness. "We need to start setting a sentry at night," he said. "Two men each night, half shifts."

Charbonneau blew a long stream of smoke from his lungs. "I told you at Fort Brazeau — I translate. I don't stand watch."

"Well, I'm not pulling extra watch so he can sleep," stated La Vierge flatly.

"Me either," said Dominique.

Even Professeur looked distressed.

They all looked to Langevin expectantly, but he refused to allow the dispute to intrude on his enjoyment of the pipe. When he finished, he simply stood and said, "*Allons-y*. We're wasting daylight."

Five days later they arrived at the confluence of the river and a small creek. The crystal water of the stream discolored quickly when it mixed with the muddy flow of the Missouri. Langevin stared at the stream, wondering what to do.

"Let's camp, Langevin," said Charbonneau. "I'm sick of drinking mud."

"I hate to agree with him," said La Vierge, "but Charbonneau's right. All this bad water is giving me the shits."

Langevin too liked the prospect of clear drinking water. What bothered him was the location of the stream — on the western bank of the Missouri. He assumed that Elk Tongue's band was west of the river. Since Glass found the recent Indian campsite, the deputation had hung scrupulously to the eastern bank, especially when deciding where to stop for the night. Langevin looked west, where the horizon swallowed the last crimson sliver of sun. He looked east, but there were no landings before the next bend in the river. "Okay. We don't have much choice."

They paddled to the bank. Professeur and La Vierge unloaded the packs, and with the canoe empty, the voyageurs carried it ashore. There they flipped the boat on its side, creating a rough shelter that opened toward the river.

Glass waded ashore, nervously scanning the landing. The sandbar ran a hundred yards downstream to natural jetty-mounded boulders overgrown with thick willows and brush. Driftwood and other debris caught behind the jetty, obstructing the river and forcing it away from the gentle bank. Beyond the sandbar, more willows led to a stand of cottonwoods, increasingly rare as they paddled north.

"I'm hungry," said Charbonneau. "Get us some good supper, Mr. Hunter."

*Geet US some goood suPEUR, MeeSTER HunTEUR.*

"No hunting tonight," said Glass. Charbonneau started to object, but Glass cut him off. "We've got plenty of jerky. You can go a night without fresh meat, Charbonneau."

"He's right," agreed Langevin.

So they ate jerky along with fried mush, cooked in an iron skillet over a low fire. The fire drew them close. A bitter wind had diminished with the setting sun, but they could see their breath. The clear sky meant a cold night and a hard frost by morning.

Langevin, Dominique, and La Vierge lit their clay pipes and sat back to enjoy a smoke. Glass had not smoked since the grizzly attack; the burning sensation hurt his throat. Professeur scraped mush from the skillet. Charbonneau had walked away from the camp a half hour before.

Dominique sang quietly to himself, as if daydreaming out loud:

> I have culled that lovely rosebud,
> I have culled that lovely rosebud,
> I have culled petal by petal,
> Filled my apron with its scent . . .

"It's a good thing you can sing about it, brother," remarked La Vierge. "I bet you haven't culled any rosebuds for a year. They ought to call you the Virgin."

"Better to go thirsty than to drink out of every mud hole on the Missouri."

"Such a man of standards. So discriminating."

"I don't see a need to apologize for having standards. Unlike you, for example, I am quite fond of women with teeth."

"I'm not asking them to chew my food."

"You'd lay down with a pig if it wore a calico skirt."

"Well, I guess that makes you the pride of the Cattoire family. I'm sure Maman would be very proud to know that you only sleep with the fancy whores in St. Louis."

"Maman, no. Papa — maybe." They both laughed loudly, then solemnly crossed themselves.

"Keep your voices down," hissed Langevin. "You know how sound carries on the water."

"Why are you so cross tonight, Langevin?" asked La Vierge. "It's bad enough putting up with Charbonneau. I've had more fun at funerals."

"We'll be having a funeral if you two keep yelling."

La Vierge refused to let Langevin spoil a good conversation. "Do you know that squaw back at Fort Kiowa had *three* nipples."

"What good are three nipples?" asked Dominique.

"Your problem is that you lack imagination."

"Imagination, eh? If you had a little bit less imagination maybe it wouldn't hurt so bad when you piss."

La Vierge pondered a reply, but in truth, he had grown weary of conversation with his brother. Langevin clearly was not in a talking mood. Charbonneau was off in the woods. He looked at Professeur, with whom he'd never known anyone to have a conversation.

Finally La Vierge looked at Glass. It occurred to him suddenly that they had not really spoken with Glass since leaving Fort Kiowa. There had been scattered exchanges, most concerning Glass's success in putting fresh game in their pot. But no real conversation, certainly none of the ambling forays on which La Vierge liked to embark.

La Vierge felt suddenly guilty for his lack of social graces. He knew little about Glass beyond the fact that he had come up short in a scrape with a bear. More importantly, thought La Vierge, Glass knew little about *him* — and he must certainly want to know more. Besides, it was a good opportunity to practice his English, a language in which La Vierge considered himself an accomplished speaker.

"Hey, Pork Eater." When Glass looked up he asked, "From where do you come?"

The question — and the sudden use of English — took Glass by surprise.

He cleared his throat. "Philadelphia."

La Vierge nodded his head, waiting for a reciprocal inquiry from Glass.

None came.

Finally La Vierge said, "My brother and I, we are from Contrecoeur." Glass nodded his head, but said nothing. Clearly, decided La Vierge, this American would need to be coaxed along.

"You know how it is that we all come to be voyageurs?" *Yew NO how eet EES zat wi all come to bee voyaGEURS?*

Glass shook his head no. Dominique rolled his eyes, recognizing the prelude to his brother's tired stories.

"Contrecoeur is on the great St. Lawrence River. There was a time, a hundred years ago, when all the men in our village were poor farmers. All day they worked in the fields, but the dirt was bad, the weather too cold — they never made a good crop.

**204**

"One day a beautiful maiden named Isabelle was working in a field by the river. Suddenly from the water came a stallion — big and strong, black like coal. He stood in the river, staring at the girl. And she was very afraid. The stallion, he sees that she is about to run away, so he kicks at the water — and a trout goes flying to the girl. It lands there in the dirt at her feet . . ." La Vierge couldn't find the English word he wanted, so he made a flip-flop motion with his hands.

"Isabelle, she sees this *petit cadeau*, and she is very happy. She picks it up and she takes to her family for dinner. She tells her papa and her brothers about this horse, but they think she is making a joke. They laugh and they tell her to get more fish from her new friend.

"Isabelle goes back to the field, and each day now she sees the black stallion again. Each day he comes a little closer, and each day he gives to her a gift. One day an apple, one day some flowers. Each day she tells her family about this horse who comes from the river. And each day they laugh at her story.

"Finally there comes a day when the stallion walks all the way up to Isabelle. She climbs on his back, and the stallion runs to the river. They disappear into the current — and they are never seen again."

The fire cast dancing shadows behind La Vierge as he spoke. And the rush of the river was like a hissing affirmation of his tale.

"That night, when Isabelle doesn't come home, her father and her brothers go looking for her in the fields. They find the tracks of Isabelle and they find the tracks of the stallion. They see that Isabelle has mounted the horse, and they see that the horse has run into the river. They search up and down the river, but they cannot find the girl.

"The next day, all the men of the village take to their canoes and join the search. And they take a vow — they will abandon their farms and stay on the river until they find the poor Isabelle. But they never find her. And so you see, Monsieur Glass, since that day we are voyageurs. Still this day we keep up the search for the poor Isabelle."

"Where's Charbonneau?" asked Langevin.

"Where's Charbonneau!" retorted La Vierge. "I tell you the story of a lost maiden and you're thinking about a lost old man?"

Langevin said nothing in reply. "He's *malade comme un chien*," said La Vierge with a smile. "I'll call to him — make sure he's safe." He cupped his hand to his mouth and yelled into the willows. "Don't worry, Charbonneau — we're sending out Professeur to help you wipe your ass!"

Touissaint Charbonneau sat on his haunches, his naked ass pointing discreetly toward a bush. He had been in that position for some time. Long enough, in fact, that he had begun to develop a cramp in his thigh. He hadn't been right since Fort Brazeau. No doubt he'd been poisoned by Kiowa's shitty food. He could hear La Vierge taunting him from the camp. He was starting to hate that bastard. A twig snapped.

Charbonneau bolted upright. One hand reached for his pistol and the other tugged at his deerskin trousers. Neither hand accomplished its task. The pistol slipped to the dark ground. His pants slipped to his ankles. When he lurched again for the pistol, his pants tripped him. He sprawled on the ground, scraping his knee on a large rock. He grunted in pain while from the corner of his eye he watched a large elk lope through the timber.

"*Merde!* Charbonneau returned to his business, grimacing at the sharp new pain in his leg.

By the time he made his way back to camp, Charbonneau's normal pique had been ratcheted up a notch. He stared at Professeur, who sat reclining against a large log. The big Scot wore a beard of mush.

"It's disgusting the way he eats," said Charbonneau.

La Vierge looked up from his pipe. "I don't know, Charbonneau. The way the fire lights up the porridge on his chin — it kind of reminds me of the Northern Lights." Langevin and Dominique laughed, which further irritated Charbonneau. Professeur continued to chew, oblivious to the humor at his expense.

Charbonneau spoke again in French: "Hey, you idiot Scot bastard, do you understand a word of what I'm saying?" Professeur continued to work on the mush, placid as a cow with its cud.

Charbonneau smiled thinly. He appreciated the opportunity for such wholly naked cattiness. "What happened to his eye, anyway?"

No one jumped at the opportunity for conversation with Charbonneau.

Finally Langevin said, "Poked out in a brawl in Montreal."

"It looks like all hell. Makes me nervous, having the damn thing staring at me all day."

"Blind eye can't stare," said La Vierge. He had come to like Professeur, or at least to appreciate the Scot's ability with a paddle. Whatever he thought of Professeur, he was certain that he did not like Charbonneau. The old man's grousing commentary had grown stale by the first bend in the river.

"Well, it sure seems to stare," insisted Charbonneau. "Always looks like he's peeking around the corner. Never blinks, either. I don't see how the damn thing doesn't dry up."

"What if it could see — it's not like you're much to look at, Charbonneau," said La Vierge.

"He could at least put a patch over it. I'm tempted to tack one on there myself."

"Why don't you? Be nice if you had something to do."

"I'm not your damned engagé!" hissed Charbonneau. "You'll be glad I'm along when the Arikara come looking for your flea-bit scalp!" The translator had worked himself into a frothy lather, spittle forming in the corner of his mouth as he talked. "I was blazing trails with Lewis and Clark when you were still messing your pants."

"Jesus Christ, old man! If I hear one more of your damned Lewis and Clark stories, I swear I'm going to put a bullet in my brain — or better yet, your brain! Everyone would appreciate that."

"Ça suffit!" Langevin finally interjected. "Enough! I'd put you both out of my misery if I didn't need you!"

Charbonneau gave a triumphant sneer.

"But you listen, Charbonneau," said Langevin. "There's none of us that wears just one hat. We're too few. You'll take your turn with the dirty work just like everyone else. And you can start with the second watch tonight."

It was La Vierge's turn to sneer. Charbonneau stalked away from the fire, muttering something about the bitterroot as he laid out his bedroll under the *bâtard*.

"Who says he gets the *bâtard* tonight?" complained La Vierge. Langevin started to say something, but Dominique beat him to the punch. "Let it go."

# CHAPTER
# SEVENTEEN

## *December 5, 1823*

Professeur woke the next morning to two urgent sensations: He was cold, and he needed to piss. His thick wool blanket failed to cover his ankles, not even when he curled his long frame and lay on his side. He lifted his head so that his good eye could see, and found that frost had settled on the blanket in the night.

The first hint of a new day glowed faintly beneath the eastern horizon, but a bright half-moon still dominated the sky. All the men but Charbonneau lay sleeping, radiating like spokes around the last embers of the fire.

Professeur stood slowly, his legs stiff from the cold. At least the wind had died down. He threw a log on the fire and walked toward the willows. He had taken a dozen steps when he nearly tripped on a body. It was Charbonneau.

Professeur's first thought was that Charbonneau was dead, killed on his watch. He started to yell an alarm when Charbonneu bolted upright, fumbling for his rifle, eyes wide as he struggled to orient himself. *Asleep on watch*, thought Professeur. *Langevin won't like that.*

Professeur's pressing need became more urgent, and he hurried past Charbonneau toward the willows.

Like many of the things he encountered each day, Professeur was confused by what happened next. He felt an odd sensation and looked down to find the shaft of an arrow protruding from his stomach. For a moment he wondered if La Vierge had played some kind of joke. Then a second arrow appeared, then a third. Professeur stared in horrified fascination at the feathers on the slender shafts. Suddenly he could not feel his legs and he realized he was falling backward. He heard his body make heavy contact with the frozen ground. In the brief moments before he died, he wondered, *Why doesn't it hurt?*

Charbonneau turned at the sound of Professeur falling. The big Scot lay flat on his back with three arrows in his chest. Charbonneau heard a hissing sound and felt a burning sensation as an arrow grazed his shoulder. *"Merde!"* He dropped instinctively to the ground and scanned the dark willows for the shooter. The move saved his life. Forty yards away, the flash of guns erupted in the inky predawn light.

For an instant, the shots revealed the positions of their attackers. Charbonneau guessed that there were eight guns at least, plus a number of Indians with bows. He cocked his rifle, drew a bead on the nearest target and fired. A dark form slumped. More arrows flew out of the willows. He spun around and broke for the camp, twenty yards behind him.

Charbonneau's expletive woke the camp. The Arikara volley ignited chaos. Musket balls and arrows rained into the half-sleeping men like iron hailstones. Langevin cried out as a bullet ricocheted off his short rib. Dominique felt a shot rip the muscle of his calf. Glass opened his eyes in time to watch an arrow bury itself in the sand, five inches in front of his face.

The men scrambled for the paltry cover of the beached canoe as two Arikara braves broke from the willows. They hurtled toward the camp, their piercing war cries filling the air. Glass and La Vierge paused long enough to aim their rifles. They fired almost in sync at a range of no more than a dozen yards. With no time to coordinate or even to think, they had both aimed at the same target — a large Arikara with a buffalo horn helmet. He crashed to the ground as both shots penetrated his chest. The other brave ran full force toward La Vierge, the arc of his battle-ax descending toward the voyageur's head. La Vierge brought his rifle up with both hands to block the blow.

The Indian's ax locked with the barrel of La Vierge's rifle, the force knocking both of them to the ground. The Arikara found his feet first. His back to Glass, he raised the ax to strike at La Vierge again. Glass used both hands to drive his rifle butt into the back of the Indian's head. He felt the sickening sensation of breaking bone as the metal butt-plate connected. Stunned, the Arikara dropped to his knees in front of La Vierge, who by this time had scrambled to his feet. La Vierge swung his rifle like a club, catching the Indian full force across the side of his skull. The brave toppled sideways, and Glass and La Vierge tumbled behind the canoe.

212

Dominique raised himself long enough to fire toward the willows.

Langevin handed Glass his rifle, the other hand pressed against the bullet hole on his side. "You shoot — I'll load."

Glass raised to fire, finding and hitting his target with cool precision.

"How bad are you hit?" he asked Langevin.

"Not bad. Òu se trouve Professeur?"

"Dead by the willows," said Charbonneau matter-of-factly as he rose to fire.

Shots continued to pour from the willows as they hunkered behind the canoe. The report of the guns mixed with the sound of the bullets and arrows smashing through the thin skin of the bâtard.

"You son of a bitch, Charbonneau!" screamed La Vierge. "You fell asleep, didn't you?" Charbonneau ignored him, focused instead on pouring powder into the muzzle of his rifle.

"It doesn't matter now!" said Dominique. "Let's get the damn canoe in the water and get out of here!"

"Listen to me!" ordered Langevin. "Charbonneau, La Vierge, Dominique — the three of you carry the boat to the water. Take another shot first, then reload your rifle and lay it here." He pointed to the ground between him and Glass. "Glass and I will cover you with a last round of shots, then join you. Cover us from the boat with your pistols."

Glass understood most of what Langevin had said from context. He looked around the tense faces. No one had a better idea. They had to get off the beach. La

Vierge popped above the lip of the canoe to fire his rifle, followed by Dominique and Charbonneau. Glass raised himself to take another shot as the others reloaded. By exposing themselves they prompted heavier fire from the Arikara. Bullet-size holes kept punching through the birch bark, but the voyageurs managed — at least for the moment — to deter an all-out rush.

Dominique tossed two paddles on the stack with the rifles. "Make sure you bring these!"

La Vierge threw his rifle between Glass and Langevin and braced himself against the middle thwart of the *bâtard*. "Let's go!" Charbonneau slid to the front of the canoe, Dominique to the rear.

Langevin shouted, "On my count! *Un, deux, trois!*" They lifted the *bâtard* above their heads in a single motion and made for the water, ten yards away. They heard excited shouts and the firing again intensified. Arikara warriors began emerging from concealed positions.

Glass and Dominique aimed their shots. With the canoe gone, the only cover came from pressing flat against the ground. They were only about fifty yards from the willows. Glass could see clearly the boyish face of an Arikara, squinting as he drew a short bow. Glass fired and the boy pitched backward. He reached for Dominique's rifle. Langevin's gun exploded next to him as Glass pulled the hammer of Dominique's to full cock. Glass found another target and squeezed the trigger. There was a spark in the pan, but the main charge failed to ignite. "Damn it!"

Langevin reached for Charbonneau's rifle while Glass refilled the pan on Dominique's. Langevin started to fire, but Glass put his hand on his shoulder. "Hold one shot!" They scooped up the rifles and paddles and broke for the river.

Ahead of Glass and Langevin, the three men with the *bâtard* covered the short distance to the river. In their haste to escape, they practically threw the canoe into the water. Charbonneau crashed into the river behind it and scrambled to climb in. "You're tipping it!" yelled La Vierge. Charbonneau's weight on the edge of the craft rocked it wildly — but it stayed upright. He flipped his legs over the lip and flattened himself on the floor of the boat, already taking on water from the seeping bullet holes. Charbonneau's momentum pushed the *bâtard* away from the shoreline. The current caught the stern and spun the boat around, propelling the craft away from shore. The long cordelle trailed behind it like a snake. The brothers saw Charbonneau's eyes, peering above the gunwale. Mini-geysers from bullets erupted in the water around them.

"Grab the rope!" shouted Dominique. Both brothers dove for the line, desperate to keep the canoe from floating away. La Vierge caught the cordelle in both hands, struggling to gain his feet in the thigh-deep water. He pulled back with all his strength as the slack disappeared from the line. Dominique slogged heavily through the water to come to his aid. His foot crashed hard into a submerged rock. He grunted in pain as the current swept his feet from beneath him. He found himself completely submerged. He recovered and stood up, two yards from La Vierge.

"I can't hold it!" yelled La Vierge. Dominique started to reach for the taut line, when suddenly La Vierge let go. Dominique watched in horror as the cordelle skidded across the water, trailing after the drifting *bâtard*. He started to swim after it when he noticed the stunned look on La Vierge's face.

"Dominique . . ." stammered La Vierge, "I think I'm shot." Dominique sloshed to his brother's side. Blood streamed into the river from a gaping hole in his upper back.

Glass and Langevin reached the river at the same moment that the bullet crashed into La Vierge. They watched in horror as he recoiled at the impact of the shot, dropping the cordelle. For a moment they thought that Dominique could grab the line, but he ignored it, turning instead to his brother.

"Get the boat!" barked Langevin.

Dominique paid no attention. In frustration Langevin screamed, "Charbonneau!"

"I can't stop it!" yelled Charbonneau. In an instant the boat was fifty feet from shore. With no paddle, it was true that Charbonneau could do nothing to slow the boat. It was certainly true that he had no intention of trying.

Glass turned to Langevin. Langevin started to say something when a musket ball buried itself in the back of his head. He was dead before his body hit the water. Glass looked back at the willows. At least a dozen Arikara poured toward the shoreline. Gripping a rifle in

216

each hand, Glass dove toward Dominique and La Vierge. They had to swim for it.

Dominique supported La Vierge, struggling to keep his brother's head above the water. Looking at La Vierge, Glass could not tell for sure if he was alive or dead. Distraught and nearly hysterical, Dominique yelled something incomprehensible in French.

"Swim for it!" yelled Glass. He grabbed Dominique by the collar and pulled him deeper into the river, losing his grip on one of the rifles in the process. The current caught the three men and dragged them downstream. Bullets continued to rain into the water, and Glass looked back to see the Arikara lining the shoreline.

Glass struggled to keep one hand gripped on La Vierge and one hand gripped on the remaining rifle while kicking furiously to stay afloat. Dominique kicked too, and they managed to clear the jetty. La Vierge's face kept bobbing beneath the water. Both men battled to keep the wounded man afloat. Dominique started to yell something, which was drowned out when a rapid swamped his own face. The same rapid nearly caused Glass to lose his grip on his rifle. Dominique began to kick toward the shoreline.

"Not yet!" Glass implored. "Further downstream!" Dominique ignored him. His feet brushed the bottom in chest-deep water, and he flailed toward the shallows. Glass looked behind them. The rocks of the jetty created a significant barrier on land. The shoreline below the jetty consisted of a high-cut bank. Still, it wouldn't take the Arikara more than a few minutes to maneuver their way around it.

"We're too close!" yelled Glass. Again Dominique ignored him. Glass contemplated swimming on alone, but instead helped Dominique drag La Vierge ashore. They lay him on his back, reclined against the steep curve of the bank. His eyes flickered open, but when he coughed, blood spit forth from his mouth. Glass rolled him to his side to inspect the wound.

The bullet had entered La Vierge's back below his left shoulder blade.

Glass saw no way that it could have missed his heart. Dominique came silently to the same conclusion. Glass checked the rifle. For the moment, the wet charge rendered it useless. He looked at his belt. The hatchet still hung in its place, but his pistol was lost. Glass looked at Dominique. *What do you want to do?*

They heard a soft sound and turned to see La Vierge, the faintest smile at the corner of his mouth. His lips began to move, and Dominique took his brother's hand and held his ear close to understand. In a faint whisper, La Vierge was singing:

*Tu es mon compagnon de voyage . . .*

Dominique recognized instantly the familiar song, though never before had it seemed so completely despondent. His eyes welled with tears, and he sang along in a gentle voice:

**218**

*Tu es mon compagnon de voyage.*
*Je veux mourir dans mon canot.*
*Sur le tombeau, près du rivage,*
*Vous renverserez mon canot.*
You are my voyageur companion.
I'll gladly die in my canoe.
And on the grave beside the canyon,
You'll overturn my canoe.

Glass looked toward the jetty, seventy-five yards upriver. Two Arikara appeared on the rocks. They pointed guns and began to yell.

Glass put his hand on Dominique's shoulder. He started to say, "They're coming," but the report of two rifles said it for him. The bullets thudded against the bank.

"Dominique, we can't stay here."

"I won't leave him," he said in his thick accent.

"Then we've all got to try the river again."

"No." Dominique shook his head emphatically. "We can't swim with him."

Glass looked again toward the jetty. The Arikara swarmed over now.

*There's no time!*

"Dominique." Glass's tone was urgent now. "If we stay here, we'll all die." More guns cracked.

For an excruciating moment, Dominique said nothing, gently stroking his brother's ashen cheek. La Vierge stared peacefully ahead, a dim light glinting in his eyes. Finally Dominique turned to Glass. "I won't leave him." More guns.

Glass fought a collision of instincts. He needed time, time to think through his action, time to justify it — but there was none. Rifle in hand, he dove into the river.

Dominique heard a whining sound and felt a bullet bury itself in his shoulder. He thought about the horrible stories he had heard of Indian mutilations. He looked down at La Vierge. "I won't let them cut us up." He grabbed his brother under the arms and dragged him into the river. Another bullet crashed into his back. "Don't worry, little brother," he whispered, leaning back into the current's welcoming arms. "It's all downstream from here."

# CHAPTER
# EIGHTEEN

## *December 6, 1823*

Glass squatted naked next to the small fire, as close to the flame as he could bear. He cupped his hands to capture the heat. He held them close, waiting until the last instant before he was certain his skin would blister, then pressed the hot flesh against his shoulders or thighs. The heat seeped in for a moment, but failed to penetrate the chill instilled in him by the icy waters of the Missouri.

His clothing hung on crude racks around three sides of the fire. The buckskins remained soggy, though he noted with relief that his cotton shirt was mostly dry.

He had floated nearly a mile downstream before climbing out into the thickest stand of brush he could find. He burrowed into the center of the bramble on a trail cut by rabbits, hopeful that no larger animal would follow. Within the tangle of willows and driftwood, he found himself once again taking somber inventory of his wounds and his possessions.

By comparison to the recent past, Glass felt considerable relief. He had a number of bruises and abrasions from the fight on the banks and the flight down the river. He even discovered a wound on his arm where it appeared that a bullet had grazed him. His old wounds ached in the cold, but did not appear otherwise aggravated. Except for the possibility that he would freeze to death, a possibility that seemed very real, he had managed to survive the Arikara attack. For an instant he saw again the image of Dominique and La Vierge, huddled on the cut bank. He pushed the thought from his mind.

As for his possessions, the most significant loss was his pistol. His rifle was soaked but serviceable. He had his knife and his possibles bag with flint and steel. He had his hatchet, which he used to shave kindling into a shallow pit. He hoped his powder was dry. He uncapped his powder horn and poured a dab on the ground. He set a flame to it from the fire and the powder ignited with a smell like rotten eggs.

His satchel was gone, with his spare shirt, blanket, and mittens. The satchel also contained his hand-sketched map, carefully marking the tributaries and landmarks of the upper Missouri. It mattered little since he remembered them by heart. Relatively speaking, he felt well equipped.

Though still damp, he decided to put on his cotton shirt. At least the weight of the cloth helped take the chill off his aching shoulder. Glass tended the fire for the rest of the day. He worried about the smoke it created, but he worried more about catching his death of cold. He tended his rifle to take his mind off the chill, drying it completely and applying grease from a small container in his possibles bag. By night-time his clothing and rifle were ready.

He considered moving only at night. Somewhere nearby lurked the same Arikara that attacked the camp. He hated just sitting there, even if his position was well concealed. But there was no moon to light a path along the rough bank of the Missouri. He had no choice but to wait until morning.

As daylight faded, Glass took the clothes from the willow rack and dressed himself. Next he scooped a shallow, square pit near the fire. He used two sticks to remove scorching-hot stones from a ring around the flames, arranged them in the pit, then covered them with a thin layer of dirt. He added as much wood to the fire as he dared, then lay down on top of the seething stones. Between the mostly dry buckskins, the stones, the fire, and sheer exhaustion, he crossed a minimal threshold for warmth that permitted his body to sleep.

For two days Glass crept up the Missouri. For a while he wrestled with the question of whether he had inherited responsibility for Langevin's mission with the Arikara. He finally decided that he had not. Glass's commitment to Brazeau had been to provide game for the deputation, a task he had dutifully performed. He had no idea whether Elk Tongue's band represented the intentions of the other Arikara. It mattered little. The ambush underscored the vulnerability of slogging upriver by boat. Even if he received assurances from some faction of the Arikara, he had no intention of returning to Fort Brazeau. His own business was more pressing.

Glass guessed, correctly, that the Mandan village lay nearby. Though the Mandan were known as peaceful, he worried about the effect of their new alliance with the Arikara. *Would the Arikara be present in the Mandan village? How might the attack on the voyageurs have been portrayed?* Glass saw no reason to find out. He knew that a small trading post called Fort Talbot lay ten miles up the Missouri from the Mandan village. He decided to skirt the Mandans altogether, aiming instead for Fort Talbot. The few supplies he wanted, a blanket and a pair of mittens, he could find at the fort.

On the evening of the second day after the attack, Glass decided that he could no longer avoid the risk of hunting. He was ravenous, and a hide would also give him something to trade. He found fresh elk tracks near the river and followed them through a grove of cottonwoods into a large clearing, flanking the river for half a mile. A small stream parceled the clearing in two. Grazing near the stream, Glass could see a large bull along with two cows and three fat calves. Glass worked his way slowly through the clearing. He was almost within range when something spooked the elk. All six stood staring in the direction of Glass. Glass started to shoot when he realized that the elk weren't looking at him — they were looking behind him.

Glass looked over his shoulder to find three mounted Indians emerging from the cottonwoods, a quarter mile back. Even at that distance, Glass could make out the spiked hairstyle worn by Arikara braves. He could see the Indians pointing as they kicked their horses and galloped toward him.

He desperately looked around him for any source of cover. The closest trees stood more than two hundred yards in front of him. He would never cover the ground in time. Nor could he make it to the river — he was cut off. He could stand and shoot, but even if he hit his target, he could never reload in time to hit all three riders, probably not even two. In desperation he ran for the distant trees, ignoring the pain that shot up his leg.

Glass had barely covered thirty yards when he pulled up in dread — another mounted Indian stepped from the cover of the cottonwoods in *front* of him. He looked back. The charging Arikara had covered half the distance between them. He looked again toward the new rider — now aiming down the barrel of his gun. The new rider fired. Glass winced in anticipation of the shot, but it flew high over his head. He turned back toward the Arikara. One of their horses was down! The Indian in front of him had shot at the other three! Now the shooter galloped toward him, as Glass realized he was Mandan.

Glass had no idea why, but the Mandan appeared to be coming to his aid. Glass spun to face his attackers. The two remaining Arikara had closed to within a hundred and fifty yards. Glass cocked his rifle and aimed. At first he tried to line his sights on one of the riders, but both Arikara hunched low behind their ponies' heads. He moved his aim to one of the horses, picking the hollow spot just below the neck.

He squeezed the trigger and the rifle spit forth his shot. The horse screamed and its legs seemed to fold in front of it. Dust flew as it ploughed to an abrupt stop, its rider flying over the dead animal's head.

Glass heard the pounding of hooves and looked up at the Mandan, who motioned him to jump on the horse. He leapt up, looking back to see the remaining Arikara rider rein his mount, firing a shot that missed. The Mandan kicked his horse and they broke for the trees. He turned the horse when they reached the cottonwoods. Both men dismounted to reload their rifles.

"Rees," said the Indian, pointing in their direction. "No good."

Glass nodded as he rammed a new charge home.

"Mandan," said the Indian, pointing to himself. "Good friendly." Glass aimed at the Arikara, but the sole remaining rider had retreated out of range. The two mountless Indians flanked him on either side. The loss of two horses had stolen their appetite for pursuit.

The Mandan called himself Mandeh-Pahchu. He had been tracking the elk when he had stumbled across Glass and the Arikara. Mandeh-Pahchu had a good idea where the scarred white man came from. Only the day before, the translator Charbonneau had arrived in the Mandan village. Well known to the Mandans from his time with Lewis and Clark, Charbonneau related the story of the Arikara attack on the voyageurs. Mato-Tope, a Mandan chief, had been furious with Elk Tongue and his renegade band. Like the trader Kiowa Brazeau, Chief Mato-Tope wanted the Missouri open for business. Though he understood Elk Tongue's anger, clearly the voyageurs meant no harm. In fact, according to Charbonneau, they had come bearing gifts and an offer of peace.

Mato-Tope had feared exactly this type of incident when the Arikara came seeking a new home. The Mandan relied increasingly on commerce with the white man. There had been no traffic from the south since Leavenworth's attack on the Arikara. Now word of this newest incident would keep the river closed.

Word of Chief Mato-Tope's anger spread quickly through the Mandan village. The young Mandeh-Pahchu saw the rescue of Glass as an opportunity to gain favor with the chief. Mato-Tope had a beautiful daughter for whose affection Mandeh-Pahchu had been competing. He pictured himself parading through the village with his new trophy, delivering the white man to Mato-Tope, the entire village looking on as he recounted his tale. The white man, though, seemed to suspect the detour. He doggedly repeated a single phrase: "Fort Talbot."

From his vantage point on the back of his horse, Glass regarded Mandeh-Pahchu with keen interest. Though he had heard many stories, he had never seen a Mandan in the flesh. The young brave wore his hair like a crown — a preening mane to which he obviously devoted considerable attention. A long ponytail wrapped in strips of rabbit skin trailed down his back. On the top of his head his hair hung loose, flowing like water over the sides, plastered down with grease and cut bluntly at the jaw line. In the center of his forehead a forelock had also been greased and combed. There were other gaudy adornments. Large pewter earrings tugged at three gaping holes where his right ear had been pierced. A choker of white beads contrasted sharply against the copper skin of his neck.

Reluctantly, Mandeh-Pahchu decided to take the white man to Fort Talbot. It was close, barely three hours' ride. Besides, perhaps he could learn something at the fort. There had been rumors of an incident with the Arikara at Fort Talbot. Perhaps the fort would want to pass a message to Mato-Tope. It was a big responsibility, passing messages. Between the story about the white man and the important message he would no doubt be carrying, Mato-Tope would be pleased. His daughter could not help but be impressed.

It was almost midnight when the onyx profile of Fort Talbot loomed up suddenly against the featureless night. The fort cast no light onto the plain, and Glass was surprised to find himself only a hundred yards from the log ramparts.

They saw a flash of fire and at the same instant heard the sharp crack of a rifle from the fort. A musket ball whined inches above their heads.

The horse jumped and Mandeh-Pahchu struggled to control it. Glass mustered his voice, calling out angrily, "Hold your fire! We're friendly!"

A voice answered suspiciously from the blockhouse. "Who are you?"

Glass saw a glimmer of light off the barrel of a rifle and the dark form of a man's head and shoulders.

"I'm Hugh Glass with the Rocky Mountain Fur Company." He wished that he could still project strength with his voice. As it was, he could barely make himself heard across even this short distance.

"Who's the savage?"

"He's a Mandan — he just saved me from three Arikara warriors." The man on the tower yelled something and Glass heard fragments of a conversation. Three more men with rifles appeared on the blockhouse. Glass heard noise behind the heavy gate. A small wicket opened and they felt themselves again under scrutiny. From the wicket a gruff new voice demanded, "Ride up where we can see you better."

Mandeh-Pahchu nudged the horse forward, reining in front of the gate. Glass dismounted and said, "Any particular reason you're so trigger-happy?"

The gruff voice said, "My partner was murdered by Rees in front of this gate last week."

"Well, neither one of us is Arikara."

"Wouldn't know that, sneaking around in the dark."

In contrast to Fort Brazeau, Fort Talbot felt like a place under siege. Its log walls rose twelve feet around a rectangular perimeter, perhaps a hundred feet on the long sides and no more than seventy on the short ones. Two crude blockhouses stood on diagonally opposite corners, built so that their innermost corner touched the outermost corner of the fort. From this abutted position they commanded all four walls. One of the blockhouses — the one above them — had a crude roof, evidently built to protect a large-bore swivel gun from the elements. The other had the beginnings of a roof that had never been completed. A rough corral backed up to the fort on one side, though no stock grazed within.

Glass waited while the eyes behind the wicket continued their scrutiny. "What's your business?" asked the gruff voice.

"I'm bound for Fort Union. I need a few provisions."

"Well we ain't got much to provide."

"I don't need food or powder. Just a blanket and mittens and I'll be on my way."

"Don't appear that you've got much to trade."

"I can sign a draft for a generous price on behalf of William Ashley. The Rocky Mountain Fur Company will be sending a party downriver in the spring. They'll make good on the draft." There followed a long pause. Glass added, "And they'll look favorably on a post that gives aid to one of their men."

Another pause, then the wicket closed. They heard the movement of a heavy timber and the gate began to yawn on its hinge. The gruff voice attached itself to a runt of a man who appeared to be in charge. He stood there with a rifle and two pistols at his belt. "Just you. No red niggers in my fort."

Glass looked at Mandeh-Pahchu, wondering how much the Mandan understood. Glass started to say something, then stopped, proceeding inside as the gate slammed closed behind him.

Two ramshackle structures stood inside the walls. From one of them, the faint glow of light seeped through the greased hides that served as windows. The other building was dark and Glass assumed they used it for storage. The rear walls of the buildings served as the back wall of the fort. Their fronts faced a tiny courtyard, dominated by the stench of dung. The source of the odor stood hitched to a post — two mangy mules, presumably the only animals that the Arikara had been unable to steal. In addition to the animals, the courtyard held a large machine for pressing pelts, an anvil on a cottonwood stump, and a teetering pile of firewood. Five men stood inside, soon joined by the man from the blockhouse. The dim light illuminated Glass's scarred face, and Glass felt their curious stares.

"Come inside if you want."

Glass followed the men into the lit structure, crowding into a cramped room configured as a bunkhouse. A smoky fire burned in a crude clay fireplace against the back wall. The only redeeming quality of the sour-smelling room was its warmth, a heat generated as much by the proximity of other men as by the fire.

The runty man started to say something more when his body contorted in a deep, wet cough. A similar cough appeared to afflict most of the men, and Glass feared the source. When the runty man finally stopped hacking, he said again, "We ain't got any food to spare."

"I told you I don't need your food," said Glass. "Let's settle on the price of a blanket and mittens and I'll be gone." Glass pointed to a table in the corner. "Throw in that skinning knife."

The runty man puffed his chest as if offended. "We ain't meaning to be stingy, mister. But the Rees got us holed up in here. Stole all our stock. Last week, five braves come riding up to the gate like they want to trade. We open the gate and they start shooting. Killed my partner in cold blood."

Glass said nothing, so the man continued. "We haven't been able to get out to hunt or cut wood. So you'll understand if we're frugal with our supplies." He kept looking at Glass for affirmation, but Glass offered none.

Finally Glass said, "Shooting at a white man and a Mandan won't fix your problem with the Rees."

The shooter spoke up, a filthy man with no front teeth: "All I seen was some Indian slinking around in the middle of the night. How was I to know you're riding double?"

"You might make a habit of being able to see your target before you shoot."

The runty man spoke again. "I'll tell my men when to shoot, mister. The Rees and the Mandans ain't never looked no different to me. Besides, they're forting up together now. One big thieving tribe. I'd rather shoot the wrong one than trust the wrong one."

Words began to spill from the runty man like water from a broken dam, and he pointed a bony finger as he spoke. "I built this fort with my own hands — and I got a license to trade here from the governor of Missouri. We ain't ever leaving and we'll shoot anything red that falls in our sights. I don't care if we have to kill every damn one of those murdering, thieving bastards."

"Who exactly do you plan on trading with?" asked Glass.

"We'll make our way, mister. This is prime property. The army'll come up here before long and set these savages straight. There'll be plenty of white men trading up and down this river — you said it yourself."

Glass stepped into the night and the gate slammed behind him. He exhaled deeply, watching as his breath condensed in the cold night air, then drifted away on the hint of a frozen breeze. He saw Mandeh-Pahchu on his horse by the river. The Indian turned at the sound of the gate and rode forward.

Glass took the new skinning knife and cut a slit in the blanket, poking his head through and wearing it as a capote. He put his hands into the furry mittens, staring at the Mandan and wondering what to say. What was there to say, really? *I have my own business to attend.* He couldn't right every wrong in his path.

Finally he handed the skinning knife to Mandeh-Pahchu. "Thank you," said Glass. The Mandan looked at the knife and then looked at Glass, searching his eyes. Then he watched as Glass turned and walked away, up the Missouri and into the night.

# CHAPTER
# NINETEEN

## *December 8, 1823*

John Fitzgerald walked to his sentry post, just down the river from Fort Union. Pig stood there, his heaving chest sending great clouds of his breath into the frigid night air. "My watch," said Fitzgerald, practically friendly in his tone.

"Since when are you so cheery about standing watch?" asked Pig, then ambled toward camp, looking forward to the four hours of sleep before breakfast.

Fitzgerald cut a thick plug of tobacco. The rich flavor filled his mouth and calmed his nerves. He waited a long time before he spit. The night air bit at his lungs when he breathed, but Fitzgerald didn't mind the cold. The cold was a function of a perfectly clear sky — and Fitzgerald needed a clear sky. A three-quarter moon cast bright light on the river. Enough light, he hoped, to steer a clear channel.

Half an hour after the change of guard, Fitzgerald walked to the thick willows where he had cached his plunder: a pack of beaver pelts to trade downstream, twenty pounds of jerky in a jute sack, three horns of powder, a hundred lead balls, a small cooking pot, two wool blankets, and, of course, the Anstadt. He piled the supplies next to the water's edge, then turned upstream to get the canoe.

As he crept along the riverbank he wondered if Captain Henry would bother sending anyone after him. *Stupid bastard.* Fitzgerald had never met a man more likely to catch the tail end of a lightning bolt. Under Henry's star-crossed leadership, the men of the Rocky Mountain Fur Company never stood more than a short step from calamity. *It's a wonder we're not all dead.* They were down to three horses, which limited the reach of their trapping parties to a few local waters, long since played out. Henry's numerous efforts to trade with the local tribes for new mounts (or, in many cases, to buy back their own stolen mounts) met with uniform failure. Finding food each day for thirty men had become a problem. The hunting parties had not seen buffalo for weeks, and their primary subsistence now consisted of stringy antelope.

The final straw came the week before, when Fitzgerald heard a whispered rumor from Stubby Bill. "Captain's thinking about moving us up the Yellowstone — occupy what's left of Lisa's old fort on the Big Horn." In 1807, a cagey trader named Manuel Lisa established a trading post at the junction of the Yellowstone and Big Horn rivers. Lisa named the structure Fort Manuel, and used it as a base for trade and exploration of both rivers. Lisa maintained particularly good relations with the Crow and the Flathead, who used the guns they bought from Lisa to wage war on the Blackfeet. The Blackfeet, in turn, became bitter enemies of the whites.

Encouraged by his modest commercial success, in 1809 Lisa founded the St. Louis Missouri Fur Company. One of the new venture's investors was Andrew Henry. Henry led a party of a hundred trappers on his ill-fated venture to the Three Forks. On his way up the Yellowstone, Henry had stopped at Fort Manuel. He remembered the strategic location, ample game, and timber. Henry knew that Fort Manuel had been abandoned for more than a dozen years, but he hoped to salvage the beginnings of a new post.

Fitzgerald did not know the distance to the Big Horn, but he knew it lay in the opposite direction from where he wanted to go. While frontier life had been more agreeable than he expected when he fled St. Louis, he had long since grown weary of the bad food, the cold, and the general discomfort of forting up with thirty smelly men. Not to mention the considerable chance of getting killed. He missed the taste of cheap whiskey and the smell of cheap perfume. And, with seventy dollars in gold coins — the bounty for tending Glass — he thought constantly about gambling. After a year and a half, things should have quieted down for him in St. Louis — perhaps even farther south. He intended to find out.

Two dugout canoes lay upside down on the long beach below the fort.

Fitzgerald had examined them thoroughly a few days before, determined that the smaller of the two was better made. Besides, though the downstream current would carry him, he needed a vessel small enough to manage on his own. He quietly flipped the canoe, set its two paddles inside, and pulled it across the sandbar to the water's edge.

*Now the other.* In planning his desertion, Fitzgerald had worried about how to immobilize the second canoe. He considered boring a hole through the log skin before arriving at a more straightforward solution. He returned to the second canoe, reaching underneath to grab its paddles. *Canoe's no good without a paddle.*

Fitzgerald pushed his canoe into the water, jumped aboard, and paddled twice to set the boat in the current. The water grabbed the canoe and propelled it downstream. He stopped after a few minutes to pick up his stolen provisions, then put the boat in the current again. In a matter of minutes Fort Union disappeared behind him.

Captain Henry sat alone in the musty confines of his quarters, the only private room at Fort Union. Beyond privacy, a rare commodity at the fort, there was little to commend the space. The only heat and light came from an open doorway to the adjoining room. Henry sat in the cold and dark, wondering what to do.

Fitzgerald himself was no great loss. Henry had distrusted the man since the first day in St. Louis. They could do without the canoe — it wasn't as if he'd stolen their remaining horses. The loss of a fur pack was maddening, but hardly fatal.

The loss was not the man who was gone, but rather its effect on the men who stayed. Fitzgerald's desertion was a statement — a statement loud and clear — of the other men's unspoken thoughts: The Rocky Mountain

Fur Company was a failure. *He* was a failure. *Now what?*

Henry heard the latch open on the bunkhouse door. Short, heavy footsteps scuffed across the dirt floor toward his quarters, then Stubby Bill stood in the doorway.

"Murphy and the trapping party's coming in," reported Stubby.

"They got any plews?"

"No, Captain."

"None at all?"

"No, Captain. Well, you see, Captain — it's a little worse than just that."

"Well?"

"They ain't got no horses, either."

Captain Henry took a moment to absorb the news. "Anything else?"

Stubby thought a minute and then said, "Yes, Captain. Anderson is dead."

The captain said nothing further. Stubby waited until the silence made him uncomfortable, then he left.

Captain Henry sat there for a few more minutes in the cold darkness before making his decision. They would abandon Fort Union.

# CHAPTER
# TWENTY

## *December 15, 1823*

The hollow formed a near perfect bowl on the floor of the plains. On three sides, low hills rose to shelter the depression from the relentless winds of more open ground. The hollow funneled moisture toward its center, where a stand of hawthorn trees stood vigil. The combination of the hills and the trees created considerable shelter.

The little hollow stood barely fifty yards from the Missouri. Hugh Glass sat cross-legged beside a small fire, the flames tickling at the lean carcass of a rabbit suspended on a willow spit.

As he waited for the rabbit to roast, Glass became suddenly aware of the sound of the river. It was an odd thing to notice, he thought. He had clung to the river for weeks. Yet suddenly he heard the waters with the acute sensitivity of new discovery. He turned from the fire to stare at the river. It struck him as strange that the smooth flow of water would create any sound at all. Or that the wind would, for that matter. It occurred to him that it wasn't so much the water or the wind that accounted for the noise, but rather the objects in their path. He turned back to the fire.

Glass felt the familiar soreness in his leg and adjusted his position. His wounds posed constant reminders that, while he was healing, he was not healed. The cold accentuated the ache in both his leg and his shoulder. He assumed now that his voice would never return to normal. And of course his face gave permanent notice of his encounter on the Grand. It wasn't all bad, though. His back no longer caused him pain. Nor did it hurt to eat, something he appreciated as he inhaled the scent of the roasting meat.

Glass had shot the rabbit a few minutes earlier in the fading light of the day. He'd seen no sign of Indians for a week, and when the fat cottontail loped across his path, the prospect of such a tasty dinner had been too much to pass up.

A quarter mile upriver from Glass, John Fitzgerald had been watching for a spot to put ashore when he heard the nearby crack of the rifle. *Shit!* He paddled quickly toward shore to slow his forward drift. He bobbed in an eddy, back-paddling, as he peered through the dimming light to identify the source of the shot.

*Too far north for Arikara. Assiniboine?* Fitzgerald wished he could see better. The flicker of a campfire appeared a few minutes later. He could make out the buckskin form of a man, but could discern no detail. He assumed it was an Indian. Certainly no white man had business this far north, not in December, anyway. *Are there more than one?* Daylight faded rapidly.

Fitzgerald weighed the options. He sure as hell couldn't stay where he was. If he put ashore for the night, it seemed likely that the shooter would discover him in the morning. He thought about creeping up and killing the shooter, except he still wasn't sure whether he faced one man or many. Finally he decided to attempt slipping past. He would wait for the cover of nightfall and hope the distraction of the fire would keep the shooter's eye — and any others — off the water. Meanwhile, the full moon would provide enough light to steer.

Fitzgerald waited almost an hour, quietly pulling the prow of the dugout onto the soft sandbar. The western horizon swallowed the final remnants of daylight, sharpening the glow of the campfire. The shooter's silhouette hunched above the fire, and Fitzgerald assumed that he must be busy tending his dinner. *Now.* Fitzgerald checked the Anstadt and his two pistols, setting them within easy reach. Then he pulled the dugout off the bank and jumped aboard. He paddled twice to push the boat into the current. After that he used the paddle as a rudder, gently placing it on one side or the other. As much as he could, he let the boat drift.

Hugh Glass tugged at the rabbit's hindquarter. The joint was loose, and with a twist he tore off the leg. He sunk his teeth into the succulent meat.

Fitzgerald tried to steer as far away from the shoreline as possible, but the current ran practically beside it. The fire approached now with dizzying speed. Fitzgerald tried to watch the river while simultaneously peering at the back of the man by the fire. He could make out a capote made from a Hudson's Bay blanket

— and what looked like a wool hat. *A wool hat? A white man?* Fitzgerald looked back toward the water. A giant boulder loomed suddenly from the dark water of the river — barely ten feet in front of him!

Fitzgerald thrust his paddle deep into the river, pulling as hard as he could. He lifted the paddle at the end of the stroke and pushed it against the rock. The dugout turned — but not enough. Its side scraped the rock with a rasping grate. Fitzgerald paddled with all his strength. *No point holding back now.*

Glass heard a splash followed by a long scrape. He reached instinctively for his rifle, then turned toward the Missouri, moving quickly away from the light of the fire. He crept rapidly toward the river, his eyes adjusting from the glare of the firelight.

He scanned the water for the source of the sound. He heard the splash of a paddle and could just make out a canoe at a distance of a hundred yards. He raised his rifle, cocking the hammer and sighting on the dark form of a man with a paddle. His finger moved inside the trigger guard . . . He stopped.

Glass saw little point in shooting. Whoever it was, the boatman appeared intent on avoiding contact. In any event, he was headed rapidly in the opposite direction. Whatever his intention, the fleeing boatman appeared to pose little threat to Glass.

Onboard the dugout, Fitzgerald paddled hard until he rounded a bend in the river, a quarter mile from the campfire. He let the dugout drift for almost a mile before guiding the boat to the opposite bank and searching for a suitable landing.

Finally he pulled the dugout from the water and flipped it, spreading his bedroll underneath. He chewed on a piece of jerky while he contemplated again the figure by the fire. *Damn strange spot for a white man in December.*

Fitzgerald carefully lay the rifle and his two pistols beside him before curling beneath his blanket. The bright moon flooded his campsite with pale light. The Anstadt caught the light and held it, the silver fittings gleaming like mirrors in the sun.

Captain Henry finally caught a stretch of good luck. So many good things happened with such rapid succession that he barely knew what to make of it.

For starters, the skies shone blue as indigo for two straight weeks. With the good weather, the brigade covered the two hundred miles between Fort Union and the Big Horn River in six days.

When they arrived, the abandoned fort stood almost as Henry remembered it. The condition of the post far exceeded his expectations. The years of abandonment had worn on the structure, but most of the timber remained solid. The find would save them weeks of hard labor, cutting and hauling logs.

Henry's experience with the local tribes (at least initially) presented another stark contrast to his dismal fortune at Fort Union. He dispatched a party led by Allistair Murphy and showered gifts on his new neighbors, primarily bands of Flathead and Crow. In his relations with the local Indians, Henry discovered that he was the beneficiary of his predecessor's diplomacy. Both tribes seemed relatively happy at the resettlement of the post. At least they were willing to trade.

The Crow, in particular, were flush with horses. Murphy traded for seventy-two of the animals. Streams spilled off the nearby Big Horn Mountains, and Captain Henry set out a plan for the aggressive deployment of his newly mobile trappers.

For two weeks, Henry kept checking his back, as if misfortune must be stalking him from behind. He allowed himself the smallest bit of optimism. *Maybe my luck has changed?* It had not.

Hugh Glass stood before the remnants of Fort Union. The gate itself lay flat on the ground, its hinge carried off when Captain Henry abandoned the post. The indignities of the failed venture continued inside. All of the metal hinges had been removed, salvaged, Glass assumed, for use at their next destination. Logs had been torn from the palisades, apparently used as firewood by the boorish visitors who followed Henry's departure. One of the bunkhouses had a blackened wall from what appeared to be a halfhearted attempt to fire the fort. Dozens of horse tracks had churned the snow in the yard.

*I'm chasing a mirage.* How many days had he walked — crawled toward this moment? He thought back to the clearing by the spring on the Grand River. *What month was that? August? What is it now? December?*

Glass climbed the crude ladder to the blockhouse, scanning the whole valley from the top. A quarter mile away he saw the rusty smudge of a dozen antelope, pawing through the snow to nibble at sage. A big "V" of geese, wings locked to land, settled on the river. Otherwise there were no signs of life. *Where are they?*

He camped for two nights in the fort, unable to simply walk away from the destination he had so long pursued. Yet he knew his true aim was not a place, but two people — two people and two final, vengeful acts.

Glass followed the Yellowstone from Fort Union. He could only guess at Henry's path, but he doubted that the captain would risk a repeat of his failure on the Upper Missouri. That left the Yellowstone.

He had followed the Yellowstone for five days when he crested a high bench above the river. He stopped, awestruck.

Fusing heaven to earth, the Big Horn Mountains stood before him. A few clouds swirled around the highest peaks, furthering the illusion of a wall reaching forever upward. His eyes watered from the glare of the sun against snow, but he could not look away. Nothing in Glass's twenty years on the plains had prepared him for such mountains.

Captain Henry had spoken often of the enormity of the Rockies, but Glass assumed his stories were infused with the standard dose of campfire embellishment. In actuality, Glass thought, Henry's portrait had been woefully inadequate. Henry was a straightforward man, and his descriptions focused on the mountains as obstacles, barriers to be surmounted in the drive to connect a stream of commerce between east and west.

Missing entirely from Henry's description had been any hint of the devout strength that flowed into Glass at the sight of the massive peaks.

Of course he understood Henry's more practical reaction. The terrain of the river valleys was difficult enough. Glass could scarcely imagine the effort required to portage furs over mountains such as those before him now.

His awe of the mountains grew in the days that followed, as the Yellowstone River led him nearer and nearer. Their great mass was a marker, a benchmark fixed against time itself. Others might feel disquiet at the notion of something so much larger than themselves. But for Glass, there was a sense of sacrament that flowed from the mountains like a font, an immortality that made his quotidian pains seem inconsequential.

And so he walked, day after day, toward the mountains at the end of the plain.


Fitzgerald stood outside the crude stockade, enduring the interrogation of the runty, coughing man on the rampart above the gate.

Fitzgerald had practiced the lie during his long days in the canoe. "I'm carrying a message to St. Louis for Captain Henry of the Rocky Mountain Fur Company."

"Rocky Mountain Fur Company?" The runty man snorted. "We just saw another of yours headed the other direction — bad-mannered fellow riding double with a redskin. In fact, if you're from his company, you can make good on his draft."

Fitzgerald felt his stomach contract and his breath drew suddenly short. *The white man on the river!* He struggled to keep his voice calm, nonchalant. "I must have missed him on the river. What was his name?"

"Don't even recall his name. We gave him a couple of things and he left."

"What'd he look like?"

"Well, I do remember that. Scars all over his face, like he'd been chewed on by a wild animal."

*Glass! Alive! Goddamn him!*

Fitzgerald traded two plews for jerky, eager to get back on the water.

No longer content to drift with the current, he paddled to propel the dugout forward. Forward and away. Glass might be headed in the opposite direction, thought Fitzgerald, but he harbored no doubt about the old bastard's intent.

# CHAPTER
# TWENTY-ONE

## *December 31, 1823*

Snow began falling about halfway through the day. The storm clouds approached casually, obscuring the sun so gradually that Henry and his men took little notice.

They had no reason to be concerned. Their refurbished fort stood complete, ready to withstand whatever challenges the elements might present. Besides, Captain Henry had declared the day a celebration. Then he had broken out a surprise that resulted in delirious excitement among his men — alcohol.

Henry was a failure at many things, but he understood the power of incentives. Henry's brew was made from yeast and serviceberries, buried for a month in a barrel to allow fermentation. The resulting concoction tasted like acid. None of the men could drink it without wincing in pain, and none of them passed up the opportunity. The liquid resulted in a profound and almost immediate state of drunkenness.

Henry had a second bonus for his men. He was a decent fiddle player, and for the first time in months, his mood lifted sufficiently to pick up his battered instrument. The shrieking fiddle combined with drunken laughter to create a foundation of jovial chaos in the crowded bunkhouse.

A good part of the merriment centered around Pig, whose obese carcass lay sprawled in front of the fireplace. Pig's capacity for alcohol, it turned out, did not match his girth.

"Looks like he's dead," said Black Harris, kicking him squarely in the belly. Harris's foot disappeared momentarily in the squishy fat around Pig's midsection, but otherwise the kick evoked no response.

"Well if he's dead . . ." said Patrick Robinson, a quiet man who most of the trappers had never heard speak before the application of Henry's moonshine, "we owe him a decent burial."

"Too cold," said another trapper. "But we could make him a proper shroud!" This idea evoked great enthusiasm among the men. Two blankets were produced, along with a needle and heavy thread. Robinson, an able tailor, began the task of tightly sewing the shroud around Pig's great mass. Black Harris delivered a moving sermon, and one by one the men took turns with eulogies.

"He was a good man and a God-fearing man," said one speaker. "We return him to you, oh Lord, in his virgin state . . . never once having been touched by soap."

"If you can manage the lift," said another, "we beseech you to hoist him up to the Great Beyond."

A loud argument diverted attention from Pig's funeral. Allistair Murphy and Stubby Bill had a difference of opinion over who between them was the finer shot with a pistol. Murphy challenged Stubby Bill to a duel, a notion that Captain Henry quickly quashed. However, he did authorize a shooting match.

At first Stubby Bill suggested that they each shoot a tin cup from the other's head. Even in his drunken state, however, it occurred to him that such a contest might create a dangerous mixture of motivations. As a compromise, they ultimately decided to shoot a tin cup from *Pig*'s head. Both Murphy and Stubby Bill considered Pig a friend, so both would have the appropriate incentive for marksmanship. They propped Pig's shroud-encased body in a sitting position against the wall, then placed a cup on his head.

The men cleared a path down the center of the long bunkhouse, with the shooters at one end and Pig at the other. Captain Henry hid a musket ball in one hand; Murphy picked correctly and elected to shoot second. Stubby Bill removed the pistol from his belt, carefully checking the powder in the pan. He adjusted his weight from foot to foot, ultimately situating himself sideways to his target. He bent his shooting arm to form a perfect right angle with the pistol pointing to the roof. His thumb reached up and cocked the pistol with a dramatic snap, the only sound in the tense cabin. After several pendulous moments in this position, he lowered the pistol to its firing position in a slow, graceful arc.

Then he hesitated. The impact of an errant shot became suddenly palpable at the vision — through his pistol sights — of Pig's lumpy mass. Stubby Bill liked Pig. Quite a lot, actually. *This is a bad idea*. He felt a bead of sweat trickle down his short spine. His peripheral vision made him newly aware of the men crowded on either side of him. His breathing became labored, causing his shooting arm to heave up and down. The pistol seemed suddenly heavy. He held his breath to stop the swaying, but then the lack of air made him light-headed and dizzy. *Don't miss now.*

Finally he hoped for the best and squeezed the trigger, closing his eyes with the flash of the powder. The ball crashed into the log wall behind Pig, a full twelve inches above the cup on the fat man's shrouded head. The spectators erupted in laughter. "Nice shot, Stubby!"

Murphy stepped forward. "You think too much." In a single, liquid motion, he drew, aimed, and fired. The shot exploded and the bullet ripped into the base of the tin cup on Pig's head. The cup slammed against the wall before clamoring to the floor next to Pig.

If neither shot killed Pig, the second at least succeeded in rousing him.

The lumpy shroud began a series of wild contortions. The men cheered the shot, then doubled over in unbridled glee at the sight of the writhing shroud. The long blade of a knife thrust suddenly out from the inside of the blanket, hacking open a narrow slit. Two hands appeared, ripping open the shroud. Next emerged Pig's fleshy face, blinking at the light. More laughter and taunts. "Like watching a calf get born!"

The gunfire had sprinkled their celebration with fitting punctuation, and soon all the men began firing their weapons into the ceiling. Black powder smoke filled the room along with hearty cries of "Happy New Year!"

"Hey, Captain," said Murphy. "We ought to fire off the cannon!" Henry had no objection, if for no other reason than to remove the trappers from the bunkhouse before they destroyed it. Clamoring loudly, the men of the Rocky Mountain Fur Company opened the door, stepped into the dark night, and stumbled en masse for the blockade.

They were surprised at the intensity of the storm. The light dusting of the afternoon had degenerated into a full-bore blizzard, swirling winds driving heavy snow. Ten inches or more had accumulated, deeper still where drifts had formed. Had they been cogent, the men would have appreciated the good fortune that held the storm at bay while they constructed shelter. Instead, they focused entirely on the cannon.

The four-pound howitzer was really more of a giant shotgun than cannon, designed not for the ramparts of a fort, but for the bow of a keelboat. It was mounted on a swivel in the corner of the blockhouse, which allowed it to command two of the fort's walls. The iron tube measured barely three feet, with three trunnions for reinforcement (insufficient, as it would turn out).

A big man named Paul Hawker fancied himself the resident cannoneer. He even claimed to have been an artilleryman in the War of 1812. Most of the men doubted this claim, though they admitted that Hawker sounded authoritative when he barked out the drill for loading. Hawker and two other men scrambled up the ladder to the blockhouse. The rest stayed below, content to watch from the relative shelter of the parade ground.

"Cannoneers to your posts!" shouted Hawker. Hawker may have known the drill, but his subordinates clearly did not. They stared blankly, waiting for a civilian explanation of their responsibilities. Under his breath, Hawker pointed to one and said, "You grab the powder and some wadding." Pointing to the other he said, "You go light the lanyard from the fire." Returning to his military bearing, he then shouted, "Commence firing . . . Load!"

Under Hawker's direction, the man with the powder poured thirty drams into a measure, kept in the blockhouse for that purpose. Hawker tipped the brass muzzle of the cannon toward the sky and they dumped in the powder. Next they inserted a fist-size wad of old cloth and used a ramstaff to seat the charge firmly in the breech of the gun.

While they waited for the return of the lanyard, Hawker unwrapped an oilcloth that held the primers — three-inch sections of goose quill, packed with gunpowder and sealed at both ends with a dab of wax. One of these primers he placed in the small vent hole at the breech of the cannon. When the burning lanyard was set to the quill, it melted the wax and ignited the powder in the quill, which in turn set off the main charge in the breech.

The man with the burning lanyard now made his way up the ladder.

The lanyard was a long stick with a hole in the end. A thick piece of rope, treated with saltpeter to make it burn, threaded the hole. Hawker blew on the ember at the tip of the lanyard, the fiery glow casting an ominous red on his face. With the pomp of a West Point cadet, he screamed, "READY!"

The men below looked up at the blockhouse in eager anticipation of a colossal blast. Though he himself held the lanyard, Hawker yelled "FIRE!" and set the spark to the primer.

The ember on the lanyard melted quickly through the wax. The primer sparked with a hiss and then "pop." Compared with the stupendous explosion they expected, the cannon's bark seemed barely louder than the clap of two hands.

"What the hell was that?" came a cry from the yard, along with a sprinkling of catcalls and mocking laughter. "Why don't you just bang on a pot!"

Hawker stared at his cannon, horrified that this moment of testicular exhibition had wilted so prominently. This had to be rectified. "Just warming it up!" he yelled down. Then, urgently, "Cannoneers to your posts!"

His two cannoneers looked at Hawker dubiously now, suddenly mindful of the exposure of their own reputations.

"Move, you idiots!" hissed Hawker. "Triple the charge!" More powder would help. Then again, maybe the problem had been too little wadding. More stuffing, reasoned Hawker, would create more resistance — and a louder explosion. *I'll give them a blast.*

They poured the triple charge down the muzzle. *What to use for wadding?* Hawker ripped off his leather tunic and rammed it down the tube of the cannon. *More.* Hawker looked at his assistant. "Give me your tunics," he said to his crew.

The men stared back, clearly alarmed. "It's cold, Hawker."

"Give me your damn tunics!"

The men reluctantly complied, and Hawker added these new garments to the wadding. The jeering continued as Hawker worked furiously to reload the big gun. By the time he finished, the entire length of the cannon had been filled with buckskin, tightly packed.

"Ready!" yelled Hawker, reaching again for the burning lanyard.

"FIRE!" He set the spark to the primer and the cannon exploded. Actually exploded. The buckskins did indeed create additional resistance — so much so that the weapon blew itself into a thousand, glorious bits.

For a brilliant moment, the fire of the blast lit the night sky, then an enormous cloud of acrid smoke hid the blockhouse from view. The men ducked as shrapnel from the explosion ripped into the log walls of the fort and sunk hissing into the snow. The explosion knocked both of Hawker's crewmen over the edge of the blockhouse and into the yard below. One broke an arm in the fall; the other two ribs. Both might have died had they not managed to land in a deep snowdrift.

As the driving wind cleared the smoke from the blockhouse, all eyes turned upward, searching for their brave artilleryman. No one said anything for a moment, until the captain called out, "Hawker!"

Another long moment passed. The swirling winds pushed the smoke away from the blockhouse. They saw a hand reach over the edge of the rampart. A second hand appeared — and then Hawker's head. His face was black as coal from the blast. His hat had been blown from his head, and blood trickled from both ears. Even with his hands on the blockhouse he tottered from side to side. Most of the men expected him to pitch forward and die. Instead he yelled, "Happy New Year, you dirty sons of bitches!"

A great roar of approval filled the night.

Hugh Glass stumbled in the drift, surprised that the snow could already be so deep. He wore no mitten on his shooting hand, so the fall thrust his bare flesh into the snow. The icy sting made him wince. He pushed his hand under his capote to dry it. The snow had begun as scattered flurries, hardly enough to justify forting up. Glass now realized his mistake.

He looked around, trying to gauge the remaining daylight. The storm drew the horizon in close, as the high mountains in the background disappeared altogether. He could make out a thin ridge line of sandstone and the occasional pine sentinel. Otherwise, even the foothills seemed to fuse with the white-gray formless clouds of the sky. Glass was glad for the sure path of the Yellowstone River. *An hour before sunset?* Glass pulled the mitten from his possibles bag and placed it on his stiff, damp hand. *Nothing to shoot at in this weather anyway.*

It had been five days since Glass struck out from Fort Union. He knew now that Henry and his men had come this way; the path of thirty men was not difficult to follow. From the maps he had studied, Glass remembered Manuel Lisa's abandoned trading post on the Big Horn. *Surely Henry would go no farther — not in this season.* He had a rough idea of the distances. But how much ground had he covered? Glass could only guess.

The temperature dropped precipitously with the arrival of the storm, but it was the wind that worried Glass. The wind seemed to animate the cold, endowing it with an ability to penetrate every seam of his clothing. He felt it first as a biting sting on the exposed flesh of his nose and ears. Wind forced water from the corners of his eyes and his running nose created moisture, compounding the chill. As he trudged through the deepening snow, the sharp bite faded slowly into an aching numbness, leaving once agile fingers as lumps of dysfunctional flesh. He needed to seek shelter while he could still find fuel — and while his fingers could still work the flint and steel.

The opposite bank rose steeply from the river. It would have provided some cover, but there was no way to ford the river. The terrain along his side of the river was featureless and flat, making no concessions to the driving wind. He saw a stand of a dozen cottonwoods about a mile away, barely perceptible through the blowing snow and the growing darkness. *Why did I wait?*

It took twenty minutes to cover the distance. In places the whipping wind had cleared the ground down to the dirt, but in others the drifts rose to his knees. Snow filled his moccasins and he cursed himself for not having fashioned gaiters. His deerskin breeches became wet from the snow and then froze solid, stiff shells encasing his lower legs. By the time he reached the cotton-woods he could no longer feel his toes.

The storm intensified as he scanned the tree stand for the best shelter. The wind seemed to blow from every direction at once, making it difficult to pick a spot. He settled on a downed cottonwood. The upturned roots spread out in a perpendicular arc from the thick base of the trunk, creating a windbreak in two directions. *If only the wind would stop blowing from all four.*

He set down his rifle and immediately began to gather fuel. He found plenty of wood. The problem was tinder. Several inches of snow covered the ground. When he dug beneath it, the leaves were damp and unsuitable. He tried to snap small branches from the cottonwood, but it was still green. Glass scoured the clearing. Daylight seemed to pour away, and he realized with growing concern that it was later than he had thought. By the time he gathered what he needed, he was working in near total darkness.

Glass piled his fuel next to the downed tree, then dug furiously to create a sheltered depression for the fire. He removed his mittens to handle the tinder, but his frozen fingers barely functioned. He cupped his hands against his mouth and blew into them. His

258

breath created a brief tingle of warmth which faded instantly against the onslaught of frigid air. He felt a new blast of bitter wind on his back and neck, penetrating to his skin and then, it seemed, deeper still. *Is the wind shifting?* He paused for an instant, wondering whether he should move to the other side of the cottonwood. The wind receded, and he decided to stay put.

He spread his tinder in the shallow depression, then dug into his *sac au feu* for the flint and steel. On his first attempt to strike the steel, his flint nicked the knuckle on his thumb. The sting extended all the way up his arm like the vibration of a tuning fork. He tried to ignore the pain as he struck again at the steel. Finally a spark landed in the tinder and began to burn. He dropped over the tiny flame, sheltering it with his body while blowing, desperate to breathe his own life into the fire. Suddenly he felt a great swirling rush of wind and his face filled with sand and smoke from the depression. He coughed and rubbed at his eyes and when he could open them, the flame was gone. *Damn it!*

He pounded the flint against the steel. Sparks showered down, but too much of the tinder had already burned. The backs of his hands ached from the exposure. His fingers, meanwhile, had lost all sensation. *Use the powder.*

He arranged the remaining tinder as best he could, this time adding larger pieces of wood. From his horn he poured gunpowder, cursing as it gushed into the depression. He situated his body again to block as much wind as possible, then struck at the steel with his flint.

A flash arose from the depression, burning his hands and singeing his face. He barely noticed the pain, so desperate was he to nurture the flames that now jumped up and down with the swirling wind. He crouched over the fire, spreading his capote to create a greater windbreak. Most of the tinder already had disappeared, but he saw with relief that some of the larger chunks were burning. He added more fuel, and in a few minutes was confident that the fire would continue to burn on its own.

He had just settled back against the downed tree when another great blast of wind nearly extinguished his fire. Again he threw himself over the flames, spreading his capote to block the wind while he blew against the glowing embers. Sheltered again, the flames sprang back to life.

Glass stayed in that position, hunched over the fire with his arms spread wide to hold the capote, for almost half an hour. Snow piled around him, several more inches in the short time he guarded the flames. He could feel the weight of the drifting snow where the capote dragged the ground. He felt something else, and his stomach sank at the realization. *It's shifted.* The wind beat against his back, no longer swirling, but with constant, relentless pressure. The cottonwood provided no shelter. Worse still, it caught the wind and turned it — back against him and into the fire.

He fought against a growing sense of panic, a vicious circle of conflicting fears. The starting point was clear

— without a fire he would freeze to death. At the same time, he could not continue to hold his current position, stooped over the flames, arms spread wide, the blizzard beating at his back. He was exhausted, and the storm could easily rage for hours or even days. He needed shelter, however crude. The wind's direction now seemed consistent enough to bet on the other side of the tree. It couldn't be worse, but Glass doubted he could move without losing the fire. Could he start another fire from scratch? In the dark? With no tinder? He saw no choice but to try.

He set upon a plan. He would rush to the other side of the downed cottonwood, scoop a new depression for the fire, then seek to transfer the flames.

No sense waiting. He grabbed his rifle and as much of his fuel as he could carry. The wind seemed to sense the presence of a new target, blasting him with renewed fury. He ducked his head and waded around the giant roots, cursing as he felt more snow pour into his moccasins.

The opposite side did seem better sheltered from the wind, though the snow was piled just as deep. He dropped his rifle and wood and began to scoop. It took five minutes to scrape an area large enough for a fire. He rushed back to the other side, retracing his footprints in the snow. The clouds made it almost completely dark, and he hoped for the glow of his fire as he came around the base of the tree. *No light — no fire.*

The only sign of his fire was a faint depression in a mound of drifted snow. Glass dug down, foolishly hoping that somehow an ember might have survived. He found nothing, though the heat from the fire had turned the snow into a slushy mix. It soaked his woolen mittens. He felt the frigid chill of moisture on his hands, then an odd mixture of pains that seemed to burn and freeze, all at the same time.

He retreated quickly to the more sheltered side of the tree. The wind seemed to have settled on a course, but also intensified. His face ached and his hands again lost all dexterity. He ignored his feet, which was easy since he felt no sensation below his ankles. With the more consistent direction of the wind, the cottonwood at least created a windbreak. The temperature continued to drop, though, and without a fire, Glass again thought he would die.

There was no time to hunt for tinder, even if there had been enough light to see. He decided to cut kindling with his hatchet, then hope that another shot of gunpowder would be enough to start the blaze. For an instant he worried about conserving his powder. *Least of my problems.* He drove the hatchet into the end of a short log to seat the blade, then pounded up and down to split the wood.

The sound of his own work almost obscured another sound — a dull clap like distant thunder. He froze, his neck craning in search of the source. *A rifle shot? No — too big.* Glass had heard thunder before during snowstorms, but never in temperatures this cold.

He waited several minutes, listening intently. No sound competed with the screaming winds, and Glass became aware again of the excruciating pain in his hands. To wander in the storm on some quest for a strange sound seemed like folly. *Start the damn fire*. He planted the hatchet's blade in the top of another log.

When he had cut a sufficient amount, Glass arranged the kindling in a pile and reached for his powder horn. It scared him how little powder remained. As he poured he wondered if he should conserve some powder for a second attempt. He fumbled, barely able to calibrate the actions of his frozen hands. *No — this is it*. He emptied the powder horn, then reached again for his flint and steel.

He raised his flint to strike the steel, but before he could do so, an enormous roar rolled down the valley of the Yellowstone. This time he knew. The unmistakable blast of a cannon. *Henry!*

Glass stood, reaching for his rifle. The winds again found a target and pounded with a vigor that nearly staggered him. He began to wade through the deep snow toward the Yellowstone. *Hope I'm on the right side of the river*.

Captain Henry was outraged at the loss of the cannon. Though the weapon had little utility in actual combat, its deterrent value was significant. Besides, a real fort had a cannon, and Henry wanted one for his.

With the notable exception of the captain, the loss of the cannon had not dampened spirits at the fort's New Year's celebration. To the contrary, the great explosion seemed to boost the level of revelry. The blizzard drove the men back inside, but the cramped bunkhouse pulsed with a relentless cacophony of unbridled chaos.

Then the cabin door blasted suddenly open — completely open — as if some great external force had built up outside before blowing the portal inward. The elements came in with the open door, frigid fingers grabbing at the men inside, ripping them from the snug comfort of the shelter and fire.

"Close the door, you bloody idiot!" yelled Stubby Bill without looking at the door. Then they all did look. The wind shrieked outside. Snow swirled around the looming presence in the doorway, making it appear to be part of the storm, disgorged in their midst like some rogue element of the wilderness itself.

Jim Bridger stared in horror at the specter. Driven snow was plastered against every surface of its body, encasing it in frozen white. On its face, ice clung to a haggard beard and hung down like crystal daggers from the folded brow of a wool cap. The apparition might have been carved wholly of winter — had not the crimson streaks of raking scars dominated its face, had not its eyes burned as fiery as molten lead. Bridger watched as the eyes scanned the interior of the cabin, deliberate and searching.

Stunned silence filled the room as the men struggled to comprehend the vision before them. Unlike the others, Bridger understood instantly. In his mind he had seen this vision before. His guilt swelled up, churning like a paddle wheel in his stomach. He wanted desperately to flee. *How do you escape something that comes from inside?* The revenant, he knew, searched for him.

Several instants passed before Black Harris finally said, "Jesus Christ. It's Hugh Glass."

264

Glass scanned the stunned faces before him. Disappointment flashed briefly as he failed to locate Fitzgerald among the men — but he did find Bridger. Their eyes would have met, except Bridger turned away. *Just like before.* He noticed the familiar knife that Bridger now wore at his waist. Glass lifted his rifle and cocked it.

The desire to shoot Bridger down nearly overwhelmed him. Having crawled toward this moment for a hundred days, the prospect of vengeance was now immediate, the power to consummate requiring no more than the gentle squeeze of a trigger. Yet a mere bullet seemed too intangible to express his rage, an abstraction at a moment craving the satisfaction of flesh against flesh. Like a starving man set before a feast, he could pause briefly to enjoy the last moment of an aching hunger about to be sated. Glass lowered the rifle and leaned it against the wall.

He walked slowly toward Bridger, the other men clearing a path as he approached. "Where's my knife, Bridger?" Glass stood directly before him. Bridger turned his head to look up at Glass. He felt the familiar disconnect between his desire to explain and his inability to do so.

"Stand up," said Glass. Bridger stood.

Glass's first punch struck him full force in the face. Bridger offered no resistance. He saw the punch coming but did not turn his head or even wince. Glass could feel the cartilage snap in Bridger's nose, saw the torrent of blood set loose. He had imagined the satisfaction of this moment a thousand times, and now it had arrived. He was glad he hadn't shot him — glad that he hadn't robbed himself of the full carnal pleasure of revenge.

Glass's second blow caught Bridger under the chin, knocking him backward against the log wall of the cabin. Again Glass wallowed in the raw satisfaction of the contact. The wall kept Bridger from falling, holding him upright.

Glass closed in tight now, erupting in a spasm of punches against Bridger's face. When the blood became so thick that his punches began to slide off ineffectively, he shifted his blows to Bridger's stomach. Bridger crumpled as he lost his wind, finally falling to the floor. Glass began to kick him, and Bridger could not, or would not fight back. Bridger too had seen the approach of this day. It was his reckoning, and he felt no entitlement to resist.

Finally Pig stepped forward. Even through the haze of alcohol, Pig had pieced together the full implications of the violent event unfolding before him. Clearly, Bridger and Fitzgerald had lied about their time with Glass. Still, it seemed wrong to let Glass walk in and kill their friend and comrade. Pig reached to grab Glass from behind.

But someone grabbed him. Pig turned to find Captain Henry. Pig appealed to the captain: "You gonna let him kill Bridger?"

"I'm not gonna do anything," said the captain. Pig started to protest further, but Henry cut him off. "This is for Glass to decide."

Glass delivered another brutal kick. Though he tried to contain it, Bridger groaned at the impact of the blow. Glass stood above the crumpled form at his feet, panting at the sheer exertion of the beating he had inflicted. He felt his heart pound in his temple as his eyes came to rest again on the knife in Bridger's belt. In his mind he saw Bridger standing at the edge of the clearing on that day — catching the knife that Fitzgerald had thrown to him. *My knife.* He reached down and pulled the long blade from its sheath. The grip of the molded pommel was like the embrace of a familiar hand. He thought of the times he had needed that knife and his hate spiked again. *The moment's arrived.*

How long had he nourished himself with the prospect of this moment?

And now it had arrived, a vengeance more perfect than even his imagination had conjured. He turned the blade in his hand, felt its weight, prepared to drive it home.

He looked down at Bridger, and something unexpected began to happen. The perfection of the moment began to evaporate. Bridger looked back at Glass, and in his eyes, Glass saw not malice, but fear; not resistance, but resignation. *Fight back, damn you!* One twitch of opposition to justify the final strike.

It never came. Glass continued to grip the knife, staring at the boy. *A boy!* As Glass looked down at him, new images suddenly competed with his memory of the stolen knife. He remembered the boy tending his wounds, arguing with Fitzgerald. He saw other images too, like the ashen face of La Vierge on the cut bank of the Missouri.

Glass's breathing began to slow. His temple ceased to pulsate in sync with his heart. He looked around the room, as if suddenly aware of the ring of men surrounding him. He stared for a long time at the knife in his hand, then slipped it in his belt. Turning from the boy, Glass realized he was cold and walked toward the fire, extending his bloodied hands to the warmth of the crackling flames.

# CHAPTER
# TWENTY-TWO

## *February 27, 1824*

A steamship named *Dolley Madison* had arrived in St. Louis the week before. It carried a cargo of goods from Cuba, including sugar, rum, and cigars. William H. Ashley loved cigars, and he wondered briefly why the fat Cuban perched on his lip was failing to impart its usual pleasure. Of course he knew the reason. When he walked each day to the river-front, he didn't go in search of steamships bearing trifles from the Caribbean. No, he went in ravenous anticipation of a fur-laden pirogue from the far west. *Where are they?* There had been no word from Andrew Henry or Jedediah Smith in five months. *Five months!*

Ashley paced the length of his cavernous office at the Rocky Mountain Fur Company. He hadn't been able to sit still all day. He stopped again in front of the enormous map on the wall. The map was ornate, or at least it had been. Ashley had punctured it with more pins than a tailor's dummy, and used a fat pencil to scratch the location of rivers, streams, trading posts, and other assorted landmarks.

His eyes traced the path up the Missouri and he tried again to fight off the sensation of impending ruin. He paused, staring at a spot on the river just west of St. Louis, where one of his flatboats had sunk with ten thousand dollars' worth of supplies. He paused at the pin marking the Arikara villages, where sixteen of his men had been murdered and robbed, and where even the power of the U.S. Army had been unable to clear a path for his venture. He paused at a bend in the Missouri above the Mandan villages, where two years before Henry had lost a herd of seventy horses to the Assiniboine. He followed the Missouri past Fort Union to the Great Falls, where an attack by the Blackfeet had later sent Henry retreating down the river.

He looked down at a letter in his hand, the latest inquiry from one of his investors. The letter demanded an update on the "status of the venture on the Missouri." *I have no idea.* And, of course, every penny of Ashley's own fortune rode with Andrew Henry and Jedediah Smith.

Ashley felt an overwhelming desire to act, to strike out, to do something, *to do anything* — yet there was nothing more he could do. He already had managed to secure a loan for a new keelboat and provisions. The keelboat floated at a dock on the river and his provisions sat stacked in a warehouse. His recruitment for a new fur brigade was oversubscribed. He'd spent weeks culling forty men from a hundred who applied. In April he would personally lead his men up the Missouri. *More than a month away!*

And where would he go? When Ashley dispatched Henry and Smith last August, their loose understanding was to rendezvous in the field — location to be determined through messengers. *Messengers!*

His eyes returned to the map. He used his finger to trace the scrawled line that represented the Grand River. He remembered drawing that line, and how he had guessed at the course of the river. *Was I right?* Did the Grand provide a direct line toward Fort Union? Or did it veer in some other direction? How long had it taken Henry and his men to reach the fort? Long enough, it appeared, that they had not been able to conduct a fall hunt. *Are they even alive?*

Captain Andrew Henry, Hugh Glass, and Black Harris sat next to the dying coals of the fire in the bunkhouse of the fort on the Big Horn. Henry stood and walked outside the cabin, returning with an armful of wood. He set a log on the coals and the three men watched as flames reached eagerly for the fresh fuel.

"I need a messenger to go back to St. Louis," said Henry. "I should have sent one before, but I wanted to wait till we were set up on the Big Horn."

Glass seized immediately at the opportunity. "I'll go, Captain." Fitzgerald and the Anstadt were somewhere down the Missouri. Besides, a month in Henry's company had been more than sufficient to remind Glass of the cloudy weather that the captain could not shake.

"Good. I'll give you three men and horses. I assume you agree that we ought to stay off the Missouri?"

Glass nodded. "I think we ought to try the Powder down to the Platte. Then it's a straight shot to Fort Atkinson."

"Why not the Grand?"

"More chance of Rees on the Grand. Besides, if we're lucky we might bump into Jed Smith on the Powder."

The next day, Pig heard from a trapper named Red Archibald that Hugh Glass was returning to St. Louis, carrying a message to William H. Ashley from the captain. He immediately sought out Captain Henry and volunteered to go along. As much as he feared a journey away from the relative comfort of the fort, the prospect of staying was worse. Pig was not cut out for life as a trapper and he knew it. He thought about his former life as a cooper's apprentice. He missed his old life and its rudimentary comforts more than he imagined possible.

Red was going too. And a friend of his, a bow-legged Englishman named William Chapman. Red and Chapman had been plotting to desert when the rumor spread about messengers to St. Louis. Captain Henry was even paying a bounty to the volunteers. Accompanying Glass would save them the trouble of sneaking off. They could leave early and get paid for the privilege. Chapman and Red could scarcely believe their good fortune. "You remember the saloon at Fort Atkinson?" asked Red.

Chapman laughed. He remembered it well, the last taste of decent whiskey on their way up the Missouri.

John Fitzgerald heard none of the bawdy din in the saloon at Fort Atkinson. He was too focused on his cards, picking them up, one by one as they were dealt, from the stained felt top of the table: Ace . . . *Maybe my luck is changing* . . . Five . . . Seven . . . Four . . . then —

Ace. *Yes.* He looked around the table. The smarmy lieutenant with the big pile of coins threw three cards on the table and said, "I'll take three and bet five dollars."

The sutler threw down all of his cards. "I'm out."

A strapping boatman threw down a single card and pushed five dollars to the center of the table.

Fitzgerald threw down three cards as he calculated his competition.

The boatman was an idiot, presumably drawing for a straight or a flush. The lieutenant was probably holding a pair, but not a pair that could beat his aces. "I'll see your five and I'll raise you five."

"See me five and raise me five with what?" asked the lieutenant. Fitzgerald felt the blood rise in his face, felt the familiar pounding at his temple. He was down one hundred dollars — every penny from the pelts he had sold that afternoon to the sutler. He turned to the sutler. "Okay, old man — I'll sell you the second half of that pack of beaver. Same price — five bucks a plew."

A poor cards player, the sutler was a cagey trader. "Price has gone down since this afternoon. I'll give you three dollars a plew."

"You son of a bitch!" hissed Fitzgerald.

"Call me whatever you like," replied the sutler. "But that's my price."

Fitzgerald took another look at the pompous lieutenant, then nodded to the sutler. The sutler counted sixty dollars from a leather purse, stacking the coins in front of Fitzgerald. Fitzgerald pushed ten dollars to the center of the table.

The dealer threw a card to the boatman and three each to Fitzgerald and the lieutenant. Fitzgerald picked them up. *Seven . . . Jack . . . Three . . . Goddamn it!* He struggled to keep his face impassive. He looked up to see the lieutenant staring at him, the slightest hint of a smile at the corner of his mouth.

*You bastard.* Fitzgerald pushed the rest of his money to the center of the table. "Raise you fifty dollars."

The boatman whistled and threw his cards on the table.

The lieutenant's eyes traveled across the mound of money in the center of the table and came to rest on Fitzgerald. "That's a lot of money Mr . . . what was it — Fitzpatrick?"

Fitzgerald fought to control himself "Fit*zgerald.*"

"Fit*zgerald* — yes, sorry."

Fitzgerald gauged the lieutenant. *He'll fold. He hasn't got the nerve.* The lieutenant held his cards in one hand and drummed his fingers with the others. He pursed his lips, making his long mustache droop even further. It irritated Fitzgerald, especially the way that he stared.

"I'll see your fifty and call," said the lieutenant.

Fitzgerald felt his stomach sink. His jaw tensed as he turned over the pair of aces.

"Pair of aces," said the lieutenant. "Well, that would have beat my pair."

He threw down a pair of threes. "Except I got another one." He tossed another three on the table. "I

274

believe you're done for the evening, Mr. Fitz-whatever — unless the good sutler will buy your little canoe." The lieutenant reached for the mound of money in the center of the table.

Fitzgerald pulled the skinning knife from his belt and slammed it into the back of the lieutenant's hand. The lieutenant screamed as the knife pinned his hand to the table. Fitzgerald grabbed a whiskey bottle and shattered it on the pitiful lieutenant's head. He was poised to ram the jagged neck of the bottle into the lieutenant's throat when two soldiers grabbed him from behind, wrestling him to the ground.

Fitzgerald spent the night in the guardhouse. In the morning he found himself in shackles, standing before a major in a mess hall dressed up to look like a court of law.

The major talked for a long time in a stilted verse and cadence that made little sense to Fitzgerald. The lieutenant was there, his hand in a bloody bandage. The major interrogated the lieutenant for half an hour, then did the same thing with the sutler, the boatman, and three other witnesses from the bar. Fitzgerald found the whole proceeding curious, since he had no intention of denying that he'd stabbed the lieutenant.

After an hour the major told Fitzgerald to approach "the bench," which Fitzgerald assumed was the rather ordinary desk behind which the major had ensconced himself.

The major said, "This martial court finds you guilty of assault. You may choose between two sentences — five years imprisonment or three years enlistment in the

United States Army." One quarter of Fort Atkinson's men had deserted that year. The major took full advantage of opportunities to replenish his troops.

For Fitzgerald, the decision was simple. He'd seen the guardhouse. No doubt he could break out eventually, but enlistment presented a far easier path.

Later that day John Fitzgerald raised his right hand and swore an oath of allegiance to the Constitution of the United States of America as a new private in the Sixth Regiment of the U.S. Army. Until such time as he could desert, Fort Atkinson would be his home.

Hugh Glass was tying a pack on a horse when he saw Jim Bridger walking toward him across the yard. Before now, the boy had avoided him scrupulously. This time both his walk and his gaze were unwavering. Glass stopped his work and watched the boy approach.

When Bridger reached Glass he stopped. "I want you to know that I'm sorry for what I did." He paused for a moment before adding, "I wanted you to know that before you left."

Glass started to respond, then stopped. He had wondered if the boy would approach him. He had even thought about what he would say, rehearsed in his mind a lengthy lecture. Yet as he looked now at the boy, the particulars of his prepared speech eluded him. He felt something unexpected, a strange mixture of pity and respect.

Finally Glass said simply, "Follow your own lead, Bridger." Then he turned back to the horse.

An hour later, Hugh Glass and his three companions rode out of the fort on the Big Horn, bound for the Powder and the Platte.

# CHAPTER
# TWENTY-THREE

## *March 6, 1824*

Only the tops of the highest buttes held a grip on the few rays of sunlight. As Glass watched, even those were extinguished. It was an interlude that he held as sacred as Sabbath, the brief segue between the light of day and the dark of night. The retreating sun drew with it the harshness of the plain. Howling winds ebbed, replaced by an utter stillness that seemed impossible for a vista so grand. The colors too were transformed. Stark daytime hues blended and blurred, softened by a gentle wash of ever darkening purples and blues.

It was a moment for reflection in a space so vast it could only be divine.

And if Glass believed in a god, surely it resided in this great western expanse. Not a physical presence, but an idea, something beyond man's ability to comprehend, something larger.

The darkness deepened and Glass watched as the stars emerged, dim at first, later bright as lighthouse beacons. It had been a long time since he studied the stars, though the lessons of the old Dutch sea captain remained fixed in his mind: "Know the stars and you'll always have a compass." Glass picked out Ursa Major, followed its guide to the North Star. He searched for Orion, dominant on the eastern horizon. Orion, the hunter, his vengeful sword poised to strike.

Red interrupted the silence. "You get the late watch, Pig." Red kept a careful tally of the distribution of chores.

Pig needed no reminder. He pulled his blanket tightly over his head and closed his eyes.

They camped in a dry ravine that night, a ravine that cut the plain like a giant wound. Water had formed it, but not the gentle, nourishing rains of other places. Water came to the high plain in the torrential flood of spring runoff or as the violent spawn of a summer storm. Unaccustomed to moisture, the ground could not absorb it. The water's effect was not to nourish, but to destroy.

Pig was certain that he had just fallen asleep when he felt the persistent prodding of Red's foot. "You're up," said Red. Pig grunted, hoisting his body to a sitting position before working his way to his feet. The splash of the Milky Way was like a white river across the midnight sky. Pig looked up briefly, his only thought that the clear sky made it colder. He wrapped his blanket around his shoulders, picked up his rifle, and walked down the ravine.

Two Shoshone watched the changing of the guard from behind a clump of sagebrush. They were boys, Little Bear and Rabbit, twelve-year-olds on a quest not for glory but for meat. But it was glory that now stood before them in the form of five horses. The boys imagined themselves galloping into their village. They imagined the bonfires and feast that would celebrate them. They imagined the stories they would tell of their cunning and bravery. They could scarcely believe their good fortune as they stared into the ravine, though the nearness of the opportunity filled them with fear as much as excitement.

They waited until the last hour before dawn, hoping the guard's attentiveness would fade as the night wore on. It did. They could hear the man snoring as they crept from the sage. They let the horses see them and smell them as they crept up the ravine. The animals stood tense but quiet, ears perked as they watched the deliberate approach.

When the boys finally reached the horses, Little Bear slowly extended his arms, stroking the long neck of the nearest animal and whispering soothingly. Rabbit followed Little Bear's lead. They patted the horses for several minutes, gaining the animals' confidence before Little Bear pulled his knife and went to work on the hobbles that bound each animal's front legs together.

The boys had cut the hobbles from four of the five horses when they heard the sentry stir. They froze, each prepared to jump on a horse and gallop off. They stared at the dark hulk of the guard and he seemed to settle again. Rabbit motioned urgently to Little Bear — *Let's go!* Little Bear shook his head resolutely, pointing to the fifth horse. He walked to the animal and stooped to cut the hobble. His knife had grown dull, and it took an agonizing length of time to saw slowly through the twisted rawhide. In growing frustration and nervousness, Little Bear gave a hard tug at the knife. The rawhide snapped and his arm jerked backward. His elbow bashed into the horse's shin, eliciting a loud whinny from the animal in protest.

The sound jolted Pig from his sleep. He struggled to his feet, eyes wide and rifle cocked as he rushed toward the horses. Pig pulled up suddenly as a dark form appeared directly in front of him. He skidded to a halt, surprised to be confronted by a boy. The boy, Rabbit, looked about as menacing as his namesake, all wide eyes and spindly limbs. One of those limbs held a knife, though; another a length of rope. Pig struggled to know what to do. His job was to defend the horses, but even with the knife, the mere boy before him seemed a good measure short of threatening. Finally, Pig simply pointed his rifle and yelled, "Stop!"

Little Bear stared in horror at the scene before him. He had never seen a white man before that evening, and this one did not even appear to be human. He was enormous, with a chest like a bear and a face covered in fiery hair. The giant approached Rabbit, yelling wildly and pointing his gun. Without thinking, Little Bear rushed at the monster, burying his knife in its chest.

Pig saw a blur from his side before he felt the knife. He stood there, stunned. Little Bear and Rabbit stood there too, still terrified at the creature before them. Pig's legs felt suddenly weak and he dropped to his knees. Instinct told him to squeeze the trigger of his gun. It exploded, the bullet launching harmlessly toward the stars.

Rabbit managed to grab a horse by the mane, pulling himself to the animal's back. He yelled at Little Bear, who took one last look at the dying monster before leaping behind his friend. They had no control of the horse, which almost bucked them before all five animals galloped down the ravine.

Glass and the others arrived just in time to watch their horses disappear into the night. Pig still stood on his knees, his hands clutched to his chest. He fell to his side.

Glass bent over Pig, prying his hands away from the wound. He pulled back Pig's shirt. The three men stared grimly at the dark slit directly over his heart.

Pig looked up at Glass, his eyes a terrible mixture of pleading and fear.

"Fix me up, Glass."

Glass picked up Pig's massive hand and held it tightly. "I don't think I can, Pig."

Pig coughed. His big body gave a mighty shudder, like the ponderous moment before a great tree falls. Glass felt the hand go limp.

The giant man gave one final sigh and died there beneath the bright stars of the plain.

# CHAPTER
# TWENTY-FOUR

## *March 7, 1824*

Hugh Glass stabbed at the ground with his knife. It penetrated an inch at most; below that the frozen earth remained unpersuaded by the blade. Glass chipped away for almost an hour before Red observed, "You can't dig a grave in ground like that."

Glass sat back, his legs folded beneath him, panting from the exertion of the dig. "I'd make more progress if you pitched in."

"I'll pitch in — but I don't see much use in chipping away at ice." Chapman looked up from an antelope rib long enough to add, "Pig's gonna take a big hole."

"We could build him one of those scaffolds like they bury the Indians on," offered Red.

Chapman snorted. "What are you gonna build it with, sagebrush?"

Red looked around him, as if newly aware of the treeless plain. "Besides," continued Chapman, "Pig's too big for us to lift up on a scaffold."

"What if we just covered him with a big mound of rocks?" This idea had merit, and they spent half an hour scouring the area for stones. In the end, though, they managed to locate only a dozen or so. Most of those had to be extricated from the same frozen soil that prevented the digging of the grave.

"These are hardly enough to cover his head," said Chapman.

"Well," said Red. "If we covered up his head at least the magpies won't pick at his face."

Red and Chapman were surprised when Glass turned suddenly and walked away from the camp.

"Now where's he going?" asked Red. "Hey!" he shouted at Glass's back. "Where you going?"

Glass ignored them as he walked toward a small mesa, a quarter mile away.

"Hope those Shoshone don't come back while he's gone."

Chapman nodded his head in agreement. "Let's get a fire going and cook some more of the antelope."

Glass returned about an hour later. "There's an outcropping in the base of that mesa," he said. "It's big enough to hold Pig."

"In a cave?" said Red.

Chapman thought about it for a minute. "Well, I guess it's kinda like a crypt."

Glass looked at the two men and said, "It's the best we can do. Put out the fire and let's get on with it."

There was no dignified way to move Pig. There were no materials to build a litter and he was too heavy to carry. In the end, they put him facedown on a blanket and dragged him toward the mesa. Two men took turns with Pig while the third carried the four rifles. They did their best, with mixed results, to steer around the cactus and yucca that littered the ground. Twice Pig dropped to the ground, his rigid body landing in a plaintive, ungainly lump.

It took more than half an hour to reach the mesa. They rolled Pig on his back and covered him with the blanket while they gathered stones, now abundant, to seal the makeshift crypt. Sandstone formed the outcropping. It hung over a space about five feet in length and two feet in height. Glass used the butt of Pig's rifle to clear out the space inside. Some type of animal had nested in there, though there was no sign of recent occupation.

They piled up a great mound of loose sandstone, more than they needed, hesitant, it seemed, to move on to the final stage. Finally Glass threw a stone on the pile and said, "That's enough." He walked over to Pig's body and the other men helped him pull the dead man to the opening of the makeshift crypt. They lay him there, all of them staring.

The task of saying something fell to Glass. He removed his hat and the other men quickly followed suit, as if embarrassed at needing a prompt. Glass tried to clear his throat. He searched for the words to the verse about the "valley of death," but he couldn't remember enough to make it appropriate. In the end, the best he could come up with was the Lord's Prayer. He recited it in the strongest voice he could muster. It had been a long time since either Red or Chapman had said a prayer, but they mumbled along whenever a phrase evoked some distant memory.

When they were done, Glass said, "We'll take turns carrying his rifle."

Next he reached down and took the knife from Pig's belt. "Red, you look like you could use his knife. Chapman, you can have his powder horn."

Chapman accepted the horn solemnly. Red turned the knife in his hand. With a short smile and a brief flash of eagerness he said, "It's a pretty good blade."

Glass reached down and removed the small pouch that Pig wore around his throat. He dumped the contents onto the ground. A flint and steel tumbled out, along with several musket balls, patches — and a delicate pewter bracelet. It struck Glass as an odd possession for the giant man. *What story connected the dainty trinket to Pig? A dead mother? A sweetheart left behind?* They would never know, and the finality of the mystery filled Glass with melancholy thoughts of his own souvenirs.

Glass picked out the flint and steel, the balls and patches, transferring the items to his own possibles bag.

Sunlight gleamed off the bracelet. Red reached for it, but Glass caught his wrist.

Red's eyes flashed defensively. "He don't need that."

"You don't need it, either." Glass returned the bracelet to Pig's pouch, then lifted Pig's massive head to replace the pouch round his neck.

It took another hour to finish their work. They had to bend Pig's legs to make him fit. There was barely enough space between Pig and the walls of the outcropping to pull the blanket over his body. Glass did his best to tuck the fabric tightly over the dead man's face. They piled the rocks to seal the crypt as best they could. Glass placed the last stone, gathered his rifle, and walked away. Red and Chapman stared for a

286

moment at the stone wall they had built, then scampered after Glass.

They walked down the Powder River along the face of the mountains for two more days, until the river took a sharp turn west. They found a creek heading south and followed that until it petered out, swallowed in the alkali flats of the most wretched land they had crossed. They kept heading south toward a low mountain shaped flat on top like a table. In front of the mountain ran the wide, shallow water of the North Platte River.

The day after they reached the Platte a big wind picked up and the temperature began a rapid plunge. By late morning close clouds filled the air with big, puffy flakes. Glass's memory of the blizzard on the Yellowstone remained vivid, and this time he vowed to take no chances. They stopped at the next stand of cottonwoods. Red and Chapman built a crude but solid lean-to while Glass shot and dressed a deer.

By late afternoon a full-fledged blizzard raged down the North Platte valley. The great cottonwoods creaked at the strain of the howling wind and wet snow piled up rapidly all around them, but their shelter held firm. They wrapped themselves in blankets and kept an enormous fire burning in front of the lean-to. Heat seeped from the great mound of crimson embers that accumulated as the night wore on. They roasted venison on the fire and the hot food warmed them from within. The wind began to subside about an hour before dawn, and by sunrise the storm had blown past.

The sun rose on a world so uniformly white that it forced them to squint against its brilliant reflection.

Glass scouted downstream while Red and Chapman broke camp. Glass struggled to walk through the snow. A thin crust on the surface supported each step for an instant, but then his foot would break through and sink to the ground below. Some of the drifts measured more than three feet high. He guessed that the March sun would melt it all within a day or two, but in the meantime the snow would cripple their progress on foot. Glass cursed again the loss of their horses. He wondered whether they should wait, use the time to lay in a supply of jerky. A good supply of meat would relieve the need for daily foraging. And, of course, the faster they moved the better. A number of tribes considered the Platte their hunting ground — the Shoshone, the Cheyenne, the Pawnee, the Arapaho, the Sioux. Some of these Indians might be friendly, though Pig's death certainly underscored the hazards.

Glass crested a butte and stopped dead in his tracks. A hundred yards in front of him, a small herd of fifty or so buffalo huddled together, holding a protective, circular formation from their own recent battle with the storm. The lead bull spotted him immediately. The animal pivoted into the herd and the great mass of animals began to move. *They're going to stampede.*

Glass dropped to his knee and brought his rifle to his shoulder. He aimed at a fat cow and fired. He saw the cow stagger at the shot, but she held her feet. *Not enough powder at this range.* He doubled the charge, reloading in ten seconds. He sighted again on the

288

cow and pulled the trigger. The cow pitched into the snow.

He scanned the horizon as he jammed the ramrod down the barrel.

When he looked back at the herd, Glass was surprised that they hadn't stampeded out of range — and yet every animal seemed in flailing motion. He watched a bull struggling at the front of the herd. The bull lunged forward, sinking to his chest in the deep, wet snow. *They can barely move.*

Glass wondered if he should shoot another cow or calf, but quickly decided that they had more than enough meat. *Too bad*, he thought. *I could shoot a dozen if I wanted.*

Then an idea struck him, and he wondered why he hadn't thought of it before. He moved to within forty yards of the herd, aimed at the biggest bull he could find and fired. He reloaded and quickly shot another bull. Suddenly two shots rang out behind him. A calf fell into the snow and he turned to see Chapman and Red. "Yee-haw!" yelled Red.

"Just the bulls!" yelled Glass.

Red and Chapman moved up beside him, eagerly reloading. "Why?" asked Chapman. "The calves is better eating."

"It's the hides I'm after," said Glass. "We're making a bull-boat."

Five minutes later eleven bulls lay dead in the little vale. It was more than they needed, but Red and Chapman were caught in a frenzy once the shooting started. Glass pushed his ramrod hard to reload. The flurry of shooting had fouled his barrel. Only when the charge was seated and the pan primed did he approach the closest bull. "Chapman, get up on that ridgeline and take a look around. That's a lot of noise we just made. Red, start putting that new knife to use."

Glass approached the closest bull. In his glazed eye shone the last dim spark of vitality as its lifeblood pooled around him on the snow. Glass walked from the bull to the cow. He pulled out his knife and cut her throat. This is the one they would eat and he wanted to be sure she was properly bled. "Come over here, Red. It's easier if we skin them together." They rolled the cow on her side and Glass made a deep cut the length of the belly. Red used his hands to pull the hide back while Glass cut it away from the carcass. They laid the hide fur-side down while they carved out the best cuts: the tongue, the liver, the hump, and the loins. They threw the meat on the hide and then went to work on the bulls.

Chapman returned and Glass set him to work, too. "We need to cut as big a square as we can out of each hide, so don't be hacking away."

His arms already red to the shoulder, Red looked up from the great carcass beneath him. Shooting the buffalo had been exhilarating; skinning them was just a big damn mess. "Why don't we just make a raft?" he complained. "There's plenty of timber along the river."

"Platte's too shallow — especially this time of year." Aside from the abundance of building materials, the great benefit of the bullboat was its draft — barely nine inches. The mountain runoff that would flood the banks was still months away. In early spring the Platte hardly trickled.

Around noon Glass sent Red back to camp to set fires for jerking meat.

Behind him Red dragged the cow's hide across the snow, piled high with choice cuts. They took the tongues from the bulls, but otherwise worried only about the hides. "Roast up that liver and a couple of those tongues for tonight," yelled Chapman.

Skinning the bulls was the first of many steps. With each hide, Glass and Chapman worked to cut the largest square possible — they needed uniform edges. Their knives dulled quickly against the thick winter fur, forcing them to stop frequently and sharpen their blades. When they finished it took three trips to drag the hides back to camp. A new moon danced merrily on the North Platte by the time they laid out the last skin in a clearing near the camp.

To his credit, Red had worked diligently. Three low fires burned in rectangular pits. All the meat had been cut into thin slices and hung over willow racks. Red had been gorging himself all afternoon, and the smell of the roasting meat was overwhelming. Glass and Chapman stuffed mouthful after mouthful of the succulent meat. They ate for hours, contented not only by the abundant food, but also by the absence of wind and cold. It seemed incredible that they had huddled in a blizzard the night before.

"You ever make a bullboat?" asked Red at one point.

Glass nodded. "Pawnee use them on the Arkansas. Takes a while, but there's not much to it — frame of branches wrapped in skin — like a big bowl."

"I don't see how they float."

"The hides stretch tight as drums when they dry. You just caulk up the seams every morning."

It took a week to build the bullboats. Glass opted for two smaller boats rather than one large one. All of them could fit into one in a pinch. The smaller craft were also lighter and could float easily in any water deeper than a foot.

They spent the first day cutting sinews from the buffalo carcasses and building the frames. They used large cotton-wood branches for the gunwales, bent in the shape of a ring. From the gunwales they worked their way down with progressively narrower rings. Between the rings they braided vertical supports with stout willow branches, tying the joints with sinew.

Working the hides took the longest. They used six per boat. Stitching the skins together was tedious work. They used their knife tips to auger holes, then sewed the skins tightly together with the sinew. When they finished, they had two giant squares, each consisting of four hides laid out two-by-two.

In the center of each rectangle they placed their wooden frames. They pulled the hides over the gunwale with the fur toward the inside of the boat. They trimmed the excess, then used sinew to stitch around the top. When they were finished, they set the boats upside down to dry.

Caulk required another trip to the dead buffalo in the vale. "Jesus it stinks," said Red. Sunny weather since the blizzard had melted the snow and set the carcasses to rot. Magpies and crows swarmed over the plentiful meat, and Glass worried that the circling carrion eaters would signal their presence. Not much they could do about it, except finish the boats and leave.

They cut tallow from the buffalo and used their hatchets to hack off slices from the hooves. Back at the camp they combined the reeking mixture with water and ash, melting it together slowly over coals into a sticky, liquid mass. Their cooking pot was small, so it took two days to prepare the dozen batches necessary to render the quantity they required.

They applied the caulk mixture to the seams, liberally smearing the mixture. Glass checked the boats as they dried in the March sun. A stiff, dry wind helped the process along. He was pleased with the work.

They left the next morning, Glass in one boat with their supplies, Red and Chapman in the other. It took a few miles to get the feel for their clumsy craft, pushing with cottonwood poles along the banks of the Platte, but the boats were sturdy.

A week had passed since the blizzard, a long time to sit in one place. But Fort Atkinson was a straight shot now, five hundred miles down the Platte. They would more than make up the time on the boats, floating all the way. *Twenty-five miles a day?* They could be there in three weeks if the weather held.

Fitzgerald must have passed through Fort Atkinson, thought Glass.

Glass pictured him, sauntering into the fort with the Anstadt. What lies had he invented to explain his presence? One thing was certain: Fitzgerald would not go unnoticed. Not many white men coming down the Missouri in winter. Glass pictured Fitzgerald's fishhook scar. Man like that makes an impression. With the confidence of a relentless predator, Glass knew that his quarry lay somewhere before him, nearer and nearer with each passing hour. Glass would find Fitzgerald, because he would never rest until he did.

Glass planted his long pole against the bottom of the Platte and pushed.

# CHAPTER
# TWENTY-FIVE

## *March 28, 1824*

The Platte carried Glass and his companions steadily downstream. For two days the river flowed due east along the buckskin foothills of low mountains. On the third day the river took a sharp turn south. A snowcapped peak rose above the others like a head on broad shoulders. For a while it seemed they were headed straight toward the peak, until the Platte veered again, settling finally on a southeastern course.

They made good time. Occasional headwinds slowed their progress, but more common was a stiff western breeze at their tail. Their supply of buffalo jerky eliminated the need to hunt. When they camped, the upside-down bullboats made good shelter. It took an hour every morning to recaulk the bullboats' seams with the supply they'd carried with them, but otherwise they could spend almost every daylight hour on the water, drifting toward Fort Atkinson with minimal exertion. Glass was grateful to let the river do their work.

It was the morning of the fifth day on the boats. Glass was spreading caulk when Red came tumbling back into camp. "There's an Indian over the rise! A brave on a horse!"

"Did he see you?"

Red shook his head vigorously. "Don't think so. There's a creek — looked like he was checking a trap line."

"You make out the tribe?" asked Glass.

"Looked like a Ree."

"Shit!" said Chapman. "What're Rees doing on the Platte?"

Glass questioned the reliability of Red's report. He doubted Arikara would wander this far from the Missouri. More likely Red had seen a Cheyenne or a Pawnee. "Let's go take a look." For Red's benefit he added, "Nobody shoots unless I do."

They moved forward on hands and knees as they approached the crest of the butte, their rifles in the crooks of their arms. The snow had long since melted, so they picked their way through clumps of sage and dry stalks of buffalo grass.

From the top of the hill they saw the rider, or rather his back, as he rode down the Platte at a distance of a half mile. They could barely make out the horse, a piebald. There was no way to know his tribe, only that Indians were close.

"Now what do we do?" asked Red. "He ain't alone. And you know they must be camped on the river."

Glass shot an irritated glance at Red, who had an uncanny knack for spotting problems and an utter inability for crafting solutions. That said, he was probably right. The few creeks they'd passed had been small. Any Indians in the area would hug tight to the

296

Platte, directly in their path. *But what choice do we have?*

"Not much we can do," said Glass. "We'll put someone up on the bank to scout when we hit an open stretch."

Red started to mutter something and Glass cut him off. "I can pole my own boat. You men are free to go where you want — but I intend to float down this river." He turned and walked back toward the bullboats. Chapman and Red took a long look at the fading rider, then turned to follow Glass.

After two more good days in the boats, Glass guessed they had covered a hundred and fifty miles. It was nearly dusk when they approached a tricky bend in the Platte. Glass thought about stopping for the night, waiting to navigate the stretch in better light, but there was no good spot to put ashore.

Bookend hills forced the river to narrow, which deepened the water and sped the current. On the north bank, a cottonwood had fallen partway across the river, trapping a wild tangle of debris behind it. Glass's boat led the other by ten yards. The current carried him straight toward the downed tree. He sunk his pole to steer around. *No bottom.*

The current accelerated, and the protruding branches of the cottonwood appeared suddenly like spears. One good poke and the bullboat would sink. Glass raised himself on one knee and braced the other foot against the boat's ribbing. He lifted his pole and searched for a place to plant it. He saw a flat surface on the trunk and thrust his pole forward. The pole caught.

Glass used all his strength to heave the clumsy craft against the current. He heard the rush of water against the boat as the current lifted its backside, pivoting the craft around the tree.

Glass faced backward now, giving him a direct view of Red and Chapman. Both braced for impact, rocking the boat precariously. When Red raised his pole he nearly bashed Chapman in the face. "Watch out, you idiot!" Chapman pushed his pole against the cottonwood as the current pressed hard from behind. Red finally extricated his pole and planted it loosely on the debris.

Both men heaved against the river, then ducked low as the current pushed them through the top of the half-submerged tree. Red's shirt caught a branch, bending it sharply back. The shirt ripped and the branch whipped backward, catching Chapman squarely in the eye. He cried out at the stinging pain, dropping his pole as he pressed his hands to his face.

Glass continued to stare backward as the current pushed both boats around the hill and toward the southern bank. Chapman stood on his knees in the bottom of their bullboat, facedown with his palm still pressed to his eye. Red looked downstream, past Glass and his boat. Glass watched as a terrified look captured Red's face. Red dropped his pole, desperately reaching for his rifle. Glass spun around.

Two dozen teepees stood on the south bank of the Platte, less than fifty yards in front of them. A handful of children played near the water. They spotted the bullboats and erupted in screams. Glass watched as two braves by a campfire jumped to their feet. Red had been right, he realized too late. *Arikara!* The current drove both boats directly toward the camp. Glass heard a shot as he watched the men in the camp grab weapons and rush toward the high bank along the river. Glass gave a final push with his pole and grabbed his gun.

Red fired a shot and an Indian tumbled down the bank. "What's happening?" yelled Chapman, struggling to see through his one clear eye.

Red started to say something when he felt a burning sensation in his belly. He looked down and saw blood oozing from a hole in his shirt. "Oh shit, Chapman, I'm shot!" He rose up in panic, ripping at his shirt to inspect the wound. Two more shots hit simultaneously, pitching him backward. His legs hooked the gunwale as he fell, tipping the rim of the bullboat into the rushing flow of the river. Water spilled across the gunwale and the boat flipped.

Half blind, Chapman found himself suddenly underwater. He felt the jarring chill of the river. For an instant, the wild rush seemed to slow, and Chapman struggled to process the lethal events surrounding him. Through his good eye he saw Red's body floating downstream, his blood leaching into the river like black ink. He heard the watery echo of legs crashing toward him from the river's edge. *They're coming for me!* He desperately needed to breathe, yet he knew with terrible certainty what waited on the surface.

Finally he could stand it no more. His head broke the surface and he gasped to fill his lungs. He would never draw another breath. His eyes had not yet cleared, so Chapman never saw the swinging ax.

Glass leveled his rifle on the nearest Arikara and fired. He watched in horror as several Arikara waded into the river, hacking at Chapman when his head broke the surface. Red's body floated forlornly downstream. Glass reached for Pig's rifle as he heard a wild cry. An enormous Indian hurled a spear from the shoreline. Glass ducked instinctively. The spear cleanly penetrated the side of the boat, burying its tip in the ribbing on the opposite side. Glass raised above the gunwale and fired, killing the big Indian on the shore.

He saw a flash of motion and looked up on the bank. Three Arikara stood in a deadly gauntlet, barely twenty yards away. *They can't miss.* He threw himself backward into the Platte as their trio of shots exploded.

For an instant he tried to hold on to the rifle. Just as quickly he let go.

He dismissed the idea of trying to make his escape by swimming downstream. He was already numb from the icy water. Besides, the Arikara would find their mounts in a few minutes — maybe they already had. A racing horse would easily outpace the meandering Platte. His only chance was to stay submerged as long as possible and get to the opposite bank. Put the river between him and them — then hope to find cover. He kicked furiously and used both arms to propel himself.

The channel ran deep in the middle of the river, deeper than a man's head. A sudden streak cut the water in front of him and Glass realized it was an arrow. Bullets pierced the water too, like mini torpedoes, searching for him. *They can see me!* Glass struggled to go deeper below the surface, but already his chest constricted for lack of breath. *What's on the opposite bank?* He hadn't even managed to look before chaos erupted. *Must breathe!* He pushed himself toward the surface.

His head cleared the water and he heard the quick staccato of shots.

He grimaced as he drew a deep breath, expecting the crash of a ball against his skull. Musket balls and arrows splashed around him — but none hit. He scanned the north bank before diving back below the surface. What he saw gave him hope. The river ran for forty yards or so along a sandbar. No cover there; if he climbed out they would shoot him down. At the end of the sandbar, though, the water joined with a low, grassy bank. It was his only chance.

Glass dug deep and pulled hard against the water, the current aiding his stroke. He thought he could just make out the end of the sandbar through the murky water. *Thirty yards.* The musket balls and arrows stabbed at the water. *Twenty yards.* He veered toward the bank as his lungs screamed for air. *Ten yards.* His feet hit the rocks of the bottom but he stayed submerged, his desperation to breathe still less than his fear of the Arikara guns. When the water became too shallow to remain submerged, he stood up, sucking for air as he dove for the tall grass on the bank. He felt a sharp sting in the back of his leg and ignored it, scrambling into a thick stand of willows.

From the temporary cover of the willows he looked back. Four riders coaxed their horses down the steep bank across the river. A half dozen Indians stood at the water's edge, pointing toward the willows. Something caught his eye farther upstream. Two Arikara were dragging Chapman's body up the bank. Glass turned to flee, sharp pain shooting up his leg. He looked down to find an arrow protruding from his calf. It had not hit a bone. He reached down, wincing as he ripped the arrow backward in a single, swift motion. He threw it aside and crawled deeper into the willows.

Glass's first lucky turn came in the form of an independent-minded filly, the first of the four horses to hit the water of the Platte. Aggressive quirting goaded her into the shallows, but the animal balked when the bottom disappeared and she was forced to swim. She whinnied and thrashed her head, ignoring the hard rein as she turned stubbornly back to shore. The other three horses had their own reservations about cold water and were happy to follow the filly's lead. The balking animals bumped into each other, churning the Platte and dumping two of their riders into the river.

By the time the riders regained control and whipped their mounts back into the river, precious seconds had passed.

Glass crashed through the willows, emerging suddenly at a sandy embankment. He scrambled to the top and looked down at a narrow back channel. Shaded from the sun during most of the day, the still water of the channel lay frozen, a thin dusting of snow on its icy surface. Across the channel, another steep embankment led to a thick mass of willows and trees. *There*.

Glass slid down the slope and leapt onto the frozen surface of the channel. The thin layer of snow gave way to the ice beneath. His moccasins gained no traction and he flipped backward, landing flat on his back. For an instant he lay stunned, staring up at the fading light of the evening sky. He rolled to his side, shaking his head to clear it. He heard the whinny of a horse and pushed himself to his feet. Gingerly this time, he picked his way across the narrow channel and clambered up the opposite bank. He heard the crash of horses behind him as he scrambled into the brush.

The four Arikara riders crested the embankment, peering down. Even in the dim light, the tracks on the surface of the channel were clear. The lead rider kicked his pony. The pony hit the ice and fared no better than Glass. Worse, in fact, as the animal's flat hooves found nothing to grip. Its four legs flailed spastically as it crashed to its side, crushing its rider's leg in the process. The rider cried out in pain. Heeding the clear lesson, the three other horsemen quickly dismounted, continuing their pursuit on foot.

Glass's trail faded quickly in the thick brush across the back channel.

It would have been obvious in daylight. In his desperate flight, Glass paid no heed to the branches he broke or even the footprints trailing behind him. But now there remained no more than a faint glow of the day. The shadows themselves had disappeared, dissolving into uniform darkness.

Glass heard the scream of the downed rider behind him and stopped.

*They're on the ice.* He guessed there were fifty yards of brush between them. In the growing darkness, he realized, the peril was not being seen, but being heard. A large cottonwood loomed beside him. He reached for a low branch and pulled himself up.

The tree's main branches formed a broad crotch at a height of about eight feet. Glass hunkered low, struggling to quiet his heaving chest. He reached down to his belt, relieved to touch the pommel of his knife, still secure in its scabbard. There, too, was the *sac au feu*. Inside were his flint and steel. Though his rifle lay on the bottom of the Platte, his powder horn still hung round his neck. At least starting fires would pose no problems. The thought of fire made him suddenly aware of his sopping clothing and the bone-deep chill from the river. His body began to shiver uncontrollably and he fought to keep still.

A twig snapped. Glass peered into the clearing beneath him. A lanky warrior stood in the brush. His eyes scanned the clearing, searching the ground for sign of his quarry. He gripped a long trading musket and wore a hatchet on his belt. Glass held his breath as the Arikara stepped into the clearing. The warrior held his gun ready as he walked slowly toward the cottonwood. Even in the darkness, Glass could see clearly the white gleam of an elk-tooth necklace around his neck, the shiny brass of twin bracelets on his wrist. *God, don't let him look up.* His heart hammered with such force that it seemed his chest could not contain its beating.

The Indian reached the base of the cottonwood and stopped. His head was no more than ten feet below Glass. The brave studied the ground again, then the surrounding brush. Glass's first instinct was to hold perfectly still, hope that the warrior would pass. But as he stared down he began to calculate the odds of another course — killing the Indian and taking his gun. Glass reached slowly for his knife. He felt its reassuring grip and began to slide it slowly from its sheath.

Glass focused on the Indian's throat. A swift cut across the jugular would not only kill him, but also prevent him from crying out. With excruciating slowness he raised his body, tensing for the pounce.

Glass heard an urgent whisper from the edge of the clearing. He looked up to see a second warrior step out of the brush, a stout lance in his hand. Glass froze. He had moved from the relative concealment of the tree's crotch, poising himself to leap. From where he was now perched, only darkness concealed him from the two warriors hunting him.

The Indian below him turned, shaking his head and pointing to the ground, then motioning toward the thick brush. He whispered something in response. The Indian with the lance walked up to the cottonwood. Time seemed suspended as Glass struggled to maintain his composure. *Hold tight*. Finally the Indians settled on a course, and each disappeared into a separate gap in the brush.

Glass didn't move from the cottonwood for more than two hours. He listened to the off-and-on sounds of his searchers as he plotted his next move. After an hour one of the Arikara cut back through the clearing, apparently on his way toward the river.

When Glass finally climbed down his joints felt like they had frozen in place. His foot had fallen asleep, and it took several minutes before he could walk normally.

He would survive the night, though Glass knew that the Arikara would return at dawn. He also knew that the brush would not conceal him or his tracks in the glaring light of day. He picked his way through the dark tangle, careful to stay parallel with the Platte. Clouds blocked the light of the moon, though they also kept the temperature above freezing. He could not shake the chill of his wet clothing, but at least the constant motion kept his blood pumping hard.

After three hours he reached a small spring creek. It was perfect. He waded into the water, careful to leave a few telltale tracks pointing up the stream — away from the Platte. He waded more than a hundred yards up the creek until he found the right terrain, a rocky shoreline that would conceal his tracks. He picked a path out of the water and across the rocks, working his way toward a grove of stumpy trees.

They were hawthorns, whose thorny branches made them favorites of nesting birds. Glass stopped, reaching for his knife. He cut a small, ragged patch from his red cotton shirt and stuck the cloth on one of the thorns. *They won't miss that.* He turned then, picking his way back across the rocks to the creek, careful not to leave a trace. He waded to the middle of the creek and began to work his way back down.

The little creek meandered lazily across the plain before joining with the Platte. Glass tripped repeatedly on the slippery rocks of the dark creek bed. The dousings kept him wet and he tried not to think about the cold. He had no sensation in his feet by the time he reached the Platte. He stood shivering in the knee-deep water, dreading what he had to do next.

He peered across the river, trying to make out the contour of the opposite bank. There were willows and a few cotton-woods. *Don't make any tracks crawling out.* He waded into the water, his breaths coming shorter and shorter as the water rose up to his waist. Darkness concealed a shelf beneath the water. Glass stepped off and found himself suddenly submerged to his neck. Gasping at the shock of the icy water on his chest, he swam hard for the opposite bank. When he could stand again he still stayed in the river, walking along the shoreline until he found a good spot to get out — a rocky jetty leading into willows.

Glass worked his way carefully through the willows and the cottonwoods behind them, mindful of every step. He hoped that the Arikara would fall for his ruse up the spring creek — they certainly wouldn't expect him to come back across the Platte. Still, he left nothing to chance. Glass was defenseless if they picked up his trail, so he did everything in his power not to leave one.

A faint glow lit the eastern sky when he emerged from the cottonwoods. In the predawn light he saw the dark profile of a large plateau, a mile or two away. The plateau ran parallel to the river as far as he could see.

He could lose himself there, find a sheltered draw or cave to hide, build a fire — dry out and get warm. When things settled down he could return to the Platte, continue his trek toward Fort Atkinson.

Glass walked toward the looming plateau in the growing glow of the coming day. He thought about Chapman and Red and felt a sudden stab of guilt. He pushed it from his mind. *No time for that now.*

# CHAPTER
# TWENTY-SIX

## *April 14, 1824*

Lieutenant Jonathon Jacobs raised his arm and barked out an order. Behind him a column of twenty men and their mounts reined to a dusty halt. The lieutenant patted his horse's sweaty flank and reached for his canteen. He tried to affect nonchalance as he drew a long swig from the canteen. In truth, he hated any moment away from the relative safety of Fort Atkinson.

He particularly hated this moment, when the galloping return of his scout could herald a wide variety of misfortunes. The Pawnee and a renegade band of Arikara had been raiding up and down the Platte since the snow began melting. The lieutenant tried to check his imagination as he awaited the scout's report.

The scout, a grizzled plainsman named Higgins, waited until he was practically on top of the column before he reined his own mount. The fringe on his leather jacket bounced as the big buckskin slid to a sideways halt.

"There's a man walking this way — up over the ridgeline."

"You mean an Indian?"

"'Sume so, Lieutenant. Didn't get close enough to find out." Lieutenant Jacobs's first instinct was to send Higgins back out with the sergeant and two men. Reluctantly, he came to the conclusion that he should go himself.

As they neared the ridgeline they left one man to hold the horses while the rest of them crawled forward on their bellies. The wide valley of the Platte spread before them for a hundred miles. Half a mile away, a solitary figure picked his way down the near bank of the river. Lieutenant Jacobs pulled a small looking glass from the breast pocket of his tunic. He extended the brass instrument to its full length and peered through.

The magnified view bobbed up and down the riverbank as Jacobs steadied the scope. He found his target, holding on the buckskin-clad man. He couldn't make out the face — but he could see the bushy smudge of a beard.

"I'll be damned," said Lieutenant Jacobs with surprise. "It's a white man. What the hell is he doing out here?"

"He ain't one of ours," said Higgins. "All the deserters head straight for St. Louis."

Perhaps because the man appeared to be in no immediate danger, the lieutenant felt suddenly gripped by chivalry. "Let's go get him."

Major Robert Constable represented, albeit not by choice, the fourth generation of Constable men to pursue a career in the military. His great-grandfather fought the French and Indians as an officer of His

**310**

Majesty's Twelfth Regiment of Foot. His grandfather stayed true to his family's vocation, if not to its king, fighting against the British as an officer of Washington's Continental Army.

Constable's father had poor luck when it came to military glory — too young for the Revolution and too old for the War of 1812. Given no opportunity to win distinction of his own, he felt the least he could do was to offer up his only son. Young Robert had yearned to pursue a career in the law and dreamed of wearing the robes of a judge. Robert's father refused to stain the family lineage with a pettifogger, and used a friendship with a senator to secure a spot for his son at West Point. So for twenty unremarkable years, Major Robert Constable inched his way up the military ladder. His wife had stopped trailing after him a decade earlier, and now resided in Boston (in close proximity to her lover, a well-known judge). When General Atkinson and Colonel Leavenworth returned east for the winter, Major Constable inherited temporary command of the fort.

Over what did he reign supreme? Three hundred infantrymen (equally divided between recent immigrants and recent convicts), a hundred cavalrymen (with, in an unfortunate bit of asymmetry, only fifty horses), and a dozen rusty cannons. Still, reign supreme he would, passing on the bitter brine of his career to the subjects of his tiny kingdom.

Major Constable was sitting behind a large desk flanked by an aide, when Lieutenant Jacobs presented the weather-beaten plainsman he had rescued. "We found him on the Platte, sir," reported Jacobs, breathlessly. "He survived an Arikara attack on the north fork."

Lieutenant Jacobs stood beaming in the bright light of his heroism, awaiting the certain accolades for his brave act. Major Constable barely looked at him before he said, "Dismissed."

"Dismissed, sir?"

"Dismissed."

Lieutenant Jacobs continued to stand there, somewhat dumbfounded at this brusque reception. Constable put his command more bluntly: "Go away." He held his hand in the air and whisked it, as if shooing a gnat. Turning to Glass, he asked, "Who are you?"

"Hugh Glass." His voice was as scarred as his face.

"And how is it that you find yourself wandering down the Platte River?"

"I'm a messenger for the Rocky Mountain Fur Company."

If the arrival of a badly scarred white man had not piqued the major's jaded interest, mention of the Rocky Mountain Fur Company did. Fort Atkinson's future, not to mention the major's ability to salvage his own career, depended on the commercial viability of the fur trade. What other significance could be found in a wasteland of uninhabitable deserts and impassable peaks?

"From Fort Union?"

"Fort Union's abandoned. Captain Henry moved to Lisa's old post on the Big Horn."

The major leaned forward in his chair. All winter he had dutifully filed dispatches to St. Louis. None contained anything more compelling than bleak reports about dysentery among his men, or the dwindling number of cavalrymen in possession of a horse. Now he had something! Rescue of a Rocky Mountain man! The abandonment of Fort Union! A new fort on the Big Horn!

"Tell the mess to send hot food for Mr. Glass."

For an hour, the major peppered Glass with questions about Fort Union, the new fort on the Big Horn, the commercial viability of their venture.

Glass carefully avoided a discussion of his own motivation for returning from the frontier. Finally, though, Glass asked a question of his own. "Did a man with a fishhook scar pass through here — coming down the Missouri?" Glass used his finger to trace a fishhook beginning at the corner of his mouth.

Major Constable searched Glass's face. Finally he said, "Pass through, no . . ."

Glass felt the sharp pang of disappointment.

"He stayed on," said Constable. "Chose enlistment over incarceration after a brawl in our local saloon."

*He's here!* Glass fought to steady himself, to erase any emotion from his face.

"I gather you know this man?"

"I know him."

"Is he a deserter from the Rocky Mountain Fur Company?"

"He's a deserter from many things. He's also a thief."

"Now, that's a very serious allegation." Constable felt the latent stirring of his judicial ambitions.

"Allegation? I'm not here to register a complaint, Major. I'm here to settle my account with the man who robbed me."

Constable inhaled deeply, his chin rising slowly with the breath. He exhaled loudly, then spoke as if patiently lecturing a child. "This is not the *wilderness*, Mr. Glass, and I would advise you to keep your tone respectful. I am a major in the United States Army and the commanding officer of this fort. I take your charges seriously. I will ensure that they are properly investigated. And, of course, you'll have an opportunity to present your evidence . . ."

"My evidence! He's got my rifle!"

"Mr. Glass!" Constable's irritation was growing. "If Private Fitzgerald has stolen your property, I will punish him in accordance with military law."

"This isn't very complicated, Major." Glass could not keep the derision from his tone.

"Mr. Glass!" Constable spit out the words. His pointless career on a godforsaken outpost provided daily tests of his ability to rationalize. He would not tolerate disrespect for his authority. "This is the last time I'll warn you. It's *my* job to administer justice on this post!"

Major Constable turned to an aide. "Do you know the whereabouts of Private Fitzgerald?"

"He's with Company E, sir. They're out on wood detail, coming back tonight."

"Arrest him when he arrives at the fort. Search his quarters for the rifle. If he has it, seize it. Bring the private to the courtroom tomorrow morning at eight. Mr. Glass, I expect you to be present — and clean yourself up before you do so."

A jury-rigged mess hall served as Major Constable's courtroom. Several soldiers carried Constable's desk from his office, then set it up on a makeshift riser. The elevated seat allowed Constable to survey the proceedings from an appropriately judicious altitude. Lest there be any question about the official sanction of his courtroom, Constable flew two flags behind the desk.

If it lacked the splendor of a true courtroom, at least it was big. A hundred spectators could pack the room when the tables were removed. To ensure an appropriate audience, Major Constable usually canceled other duties for all but a few of the fort's inhabitants. With little competition in the way of entertainment, the major's official performances always played to a packed house. Interest in the current proceeding ran particularly high. Word of the scarred frontiersman and his wild accusations had spread quickly through the fort.

From a bench near the major's desk, Hugh Glass watched as the door of the mess hall burst open. "A-ten-SHUN!" The spectators rose to attention as Major Constable strode into the room. Constable was attended by a lieutenant named Neville K. Askitzen, dubbed "Lieutenant Ass-Kisser" by the enlisted men.

Constable paused to survey his audience before strolling regally to the front, Askitzen skittering behind him. Once seated, the major nodded to Askitzen, who gave an order permitting the spectators to sit.

"Bring forth the accused," ordered Major Constable. The doors opened again and Fitzgerald appeared in the doorway, his hands in shackles and a guard at either arm. The audience squirmed for a glimpse as the guards led Fitzgerald to the front, where a sort of holding pen had been constructed perpendicular and to the right of the major's desk. The pen placed him directly across from Glass, who sat to the major's left.

Glass's eyes bored into Fitzgerald like an auger in soft wood. Fitzgerald had cut his hair and shaved his beard. Navy blue wool replaced his buckskins. Glass felt revulsion at the sight of Fitzgerald, shrouded in the respectability that a uniform implied.

It seemed unreal, suddenly to be in his presence. He fought against the desire to rush at Fitzgerald, wrap his hands around the man's throat, choke the life from him. *I can't do that. Not here.* Their eyes met for a brief instant. Fitzgerald nodded — as if to politely acknowledge him!

Major Constable cleared his throat and said, "This martial court is hereby convened. Private Fitzgerald, it is your right to be confronted by your accuser, and to hear formally the charges brought against you. Lieutenant, read the charges."

Lieutenant Askitzen unfolded a piece of paper and read to the chamber in a stately voice: "We hear today the complaint of Mr. Hugh Glass, of the Rocky

Mountain Fur Company, against Private John Fitzgerald, United States Army, Sixth Regiment, Company E. Mr. Glass alleges that Private Fitzgerald, while himself in the employ of the Rocky Mountain Fur Company, did steal from Mr. Glass a rifle, a knife, and other personal effects. If found guilty, Mr. Fitzgerald faces court-martial and imprisonment of ten years."

A murmur rippled through the crowd. Major Constable banged a gavel against the desk and the room fell silent. "Will the complainant approach the bench." Confused, Glass looked up at the major, who gave an exasperated look before motioning him toward the desk.

Lieutenant Askitzen stood there with a Bible. "Raise your right hand," he said to Glass. "Do you swear to tell the truth, so help you God?" Glass nodded and said yes in the weak timbre that he hated but could not change.

"Mr. Glass — you heard the reading of the charges?" asked Constable.

"Yes."

"And they are accurate?"

"Yes."

"Do you wish to make a statement?"

Glass hesitated. The formality of the proceeding had taken him completely by surprise. Certainly he had not expected a hundred spectators. He understood that Constable commanded the fort. But this was a matter between him and Fitzgerald — not a spectacle for the amusement of an arrogant officer and a hundred bored enlisted men.

"Mr. Glass — do you wish to address the court?"

"I told you yesterday what happened. Fitzgerald and a boy named Bridger were left to tend me after a grizzly attacked me on the Grand River. They abandoned me instead. I don't fault them for that. But they robbed me before they ran off. Took my rifle, my knife, even my flint and steel. They took from me the things I needed to have a chance on my own."

"Is this the rifle you claim is yours?" The major produced the Anstadt from behind his desk.

"That's my rifle."

"Can you identify it by any distinguishing marks?"

Glass felt his face grow flush at the challenge. *Why am I the one being questioned?* He took a deep breath. "The barrel is engraved with the name of the maker — J. Anstadt, Kutztown, Penn."

The major pulled a pair of spectacles from his pocket and examined the barrel. He read aloud, "J. Anstadt, Kutztown, Penn." Another murmur filled the room.

"Do you have anything further to say, Mr. Glass?" Glass shook his head no.

"You are dismissed."

Glass returned to his place across from Fitzgerald as the major continued. "Lieutenant Askitzen, swear in the defendant." Askitzen walked to Fitzgerald's pen. The shackles on Fitzgerald's hands clanked as he placed his hand on the Bible. His strong voice filled the mess hall as he solemnly stated the oath.

Major Constable rocked back in his chair. "Private Fitzgerald — you've heard the charges of Mr. Glass. How do you account for yourself?"

**318**

"Thank you for the opportunity to defend myself, Your Hon — I mean Major Constable." The major beamed at the slip as Fitzgerald continued. "You probably expect me to tell you that Hugh Glass is a liar — but I'm not going to do that, sir." Constable leaned forward, curious. Glass's eyes narrowed as he too wondered what Fitzgerald was up to.

"In fact, I know Hugh Glass to be a good man, respected by his peers in the Rocky Mountain Fur Company.

"I believe that Hugh Glass believes every word he said to be the God's honest truth. The problem, sir, is that he believes a whole bunch of things that never happened.

"Truth is, he'd been delirious for two days before we left him. Fever spiked up that last day, especially — death sweats, we thought. He moaned and cried out — we could tell he was hurting. I felt bad there wasn't more we could do."

"What *did* you do for him?"

"Well, I'm no doctor, sir, but I did my best. I made up a poultice for his throat and for his back. I made a broth to try and feed him. Course his throat was so bad he couldn't swallow or talk."

This was too much for Glass. In the firmest voice he could muster, he said, "Lying comes easy to you, Fitzgerald."

"Mr. Glass!" roared Constable, his face twisted suddenly into a stiff knot of indignation. "This is *my* proceeding. I will cross-examine the witnesses. And *you* will keep your mouth shut or I'll hold you in contempt!"

Constable let the weight of his pronouncement sink in before turning back to Fitzgerald. "Go on, Private."

"I don't blame him for not knowing, sir." Fitzgerald tossed Glass a pitiful glance. "He was out — or feverish — most of the time we tended him."

"Well, that's all well and good, but do you deny that you abandoned him? Robbed him?"

"Let me tell you what happened that morning, sir. We'd been camped for four days by a spring creek off the Grand. I left Bridger with Hugh and went down on the main river to hunt — been gone most of the morning. About a mile from camp I all but stepped on an Arikara war party." Another ripple of excitement passed through the spectators, most of them veterans of the dubious fight at the Arikara village.

"The Rees didn't see me at first, so I made my way back toward camp as quick as I could. They spotted me just about when I got to the creek. They came charging, while I went running up to our camp.

"When I got there, I told Bridger that the Rees were right behind me — told him to help me get the camp ready to make a stand. That's when Bridger told me that Glass was dead."

"You bastard!" Glass spat the words as he stood and moved toward Fitzgerald. Two soldiers with rifles and bayonets blocked his path.

"Mr. Glass!" yelled Constable, beating a gavel on the table. "You will hold your seat and hold your tongue or I will have you jailed!"

It took the major a moment to regain his composure. He paused to adjust the collar of his brass-buttoned jacket before returning to the interrogation of Fitzgerald. "Obviously Mr. Glass was not dead. Did you examine him?"

"I understand why Hugh's angry, sir. I shouldn't have taken Bridger's word. But when I looked at Glass that day he was pale as a ghost — not moving a twitch. We could hear the Rees coming up the creek. Bridger started yelling that we had to get out of there. I was sure Glass was dead — so we ran for cover."

"But not before taking his rifle."

"Bridger did that. He said it was stupid to leave a rifle and knife behind for the Rees. There wasn't time to argue about it."

"But you're the one with the rifle now."

"Yes, sir, I am. When we got back to Fort Union, Captain Henry didn't have the cash to pay us for staying back with Glass. Henry asked me to take the rifle as payment. Of course, Major, I'm glad for the chance to give it back to Hugh."

"What about his flint and steel?"

"We didn't take them, sir. I expect the Rees got that."

"Why wouldn't they have killed Mr. Glass — lifted his scalp in the usual manner?"

"I imagine they thought he was dead, same as we did. No offense to Hugh, but there wasn't much scalp left to lift. The bear carved him up so bad the Rees probably figured there wasn't no mutilating left to be done."

"You've been on this post for six weeks, Private. Why haven't you unburdened yourself of this story before today?"

Fitzgerald allowed a carefully calibrated pause, bit at his lip, and hung his head. Finally he raised his eyes and then his head. In a quiet voice he said, "Well, sir — I guess I was ashamed."

Glass stared in utter disbelief. Not so much at Fitzgerald, from whom no treachery arrived completely unexpected. But more so at the major, who had begun to nod along with Fitzgerald's story like a rat to the piper's tune. *He believes him!*

Fitzgerald continued. "I didn't know before yesterday that Hugh Glass was alive — but I did think that I'd abandoned a man without so much as a decent burial. Man deserves that, even on the front —"

Glass could bear it no longer. He reached beneath his capote for the pistol concealed at his belt. He pulled out the gun and fired. The ball strayed just wide of its mark, burying itself in Fitzgerald's shoulder. Glass heard Fitzgerald cry out and at the same time felt strong arms grabbing him from both sides. He struggled to break their grip. Pandemonium erupted in the courtroom. He heard Askitzen yell something, caught a flash of the major and his golden epaulettes. He felt a sharp pain at the back of his skull and all went black.

# CHAPTER
# TWENTY-SEVEN

## *April 28, 1824*

Glass awoke in musty darkness with a throbbing headache. He lay facedown on a rough-hewn floor. He rolled slowly to his side, bumping against a wall. Above his head he saw light, streaming through a narrow slot in a heavy door. Fort Atkinson's guardhouse consisted of a large holding pen, for drunks and other common truants, and two wooden cells. From what Glass could hear, three or four men occupied the pen outside his cell.

The space seemed to shrink as he lay there, closing in like the sides of a casket. It reminded him suddenly of the dank hold of a ship, of the stifling life at sea that he had come to hate. Beads of sweat formed on his brow, and his breath came in short, sporadic spurts. He struggled to control himself, to replace the image of imprisonment with that of the open plain, a waving sea of grass, unbroken but for a mountain on a horizon far away.

He measured the passage of days by the daily routine of the guardhouse: change of guard at dawn; delivery of bread and water around noon; change of guard at dusk; then night. Two weeks had passed when he heard the creak of the outside door opening and felt the suction of fresh air. "Stay back you stinking idiots or I'll smash your skulls," said a smoky voice that walked deliberately toward his cell. Glass heard the jangling of keys, then the play of a key in the lock. A bolt turned and his door swung open.

He squinted at the light. A sergeant with yellow chevrons and gray muttonchops stood in the doorway. "Major Constable issued an order. You can go. Actually, you have to go. Off the post by noon tomorrow or you'll be tried for stealing a pistol and for using it to poke a hole in Private Fitzgerald."

The light outside was blinding after two weeks in the dark cell. When someone said, "Bonjour, Monsieur Glass," it took Glass a minute to focus on the fat, bespeckled face of Kiowa Brazeau.

"What are you doing here, Kiowa?"

"On my way back from St. Louis with a keelboat of supplies."

"You spring me loose?"

"Yes. I'm on good terms with Major Constable. You, on the other hand, seem to have gotten yourself into a bit of trouble."

"Only trouble is that my pistol didn't shoot straight."

"As I understand it, it wasn't your pistol. This, though, I think belongs to you." Kiowa handed Glass a rifle as Glass finally focused enough to see.

The Anstadt. He gripped the gun at the wrist and the barrel, remembering the sturdy weight. He examined the trigger works, which were in need of fresh grease.

Several new abrasions marred the dark stock, and Glass noticed a small bit of carving near the buttplate — "JF."

Anger flooded over him. "What happened to Fitzgerald?"

"Major Constable is returning him to his duties."

"No punishment?"

"He has to forfeit two months' pay."

"Two months' pay!"

"Well, he's also got a hole in his shoulder where there didn't used to be one — and you get your rifle back."

Kiowa stared at Glass, easily reading his face. "In case you're getting any ideas — I'd avoid using the Anstadt on the premises of this fort. Major Constable fancies his judicial responsibilities and he's eager to try you for attempted murder. He only relented because I convinced him you're a protégé of Monsieur Ashley."

They walked together across the parade ground. A flagpole stood there, its support ropes straining to hold firm against a stiff spring breeze. The flag itself snapped in the wind, its edges frayed by the constant beating.

Kiowa turned to Glass: "You're thinking stupid thoughts, my friend."

Glass stopped and looked directly at the Frenchman.

Kiowa said, "I'm sorry that you never had a proper rendezvous with Fitzgerald. But you should have figured out by now that things aren't always so tidy."

They stood there for a while, with no sound but the flapping of the flag.

"It's not that simple, Kiowa."

"Of course it's not simple. Who said it was simple? But you know what? Lots of loose ends don't ever get tied up. Play the hand you're dealt. Move on."

Kiowa pressed on. "Come with me to Fort Brazeau. If it works out, I'll bring you in as a partner."

Glass slowly shook his head. "That's a generous offer, Kiowa, but I don't think I could stay planted in one spot."

"So what then? What's your plan?"

"I have a message to deliver to Ashley in St. Louis. From there, I don't know yet." Glass paused a minute before adding, "And I still have business here."

Glass said nothing more. Kiowa too was silent for a long time. Finally he said quietly, "*Il n'est pire sourd que celui qui ne veut pas entendre.* Do you know what that means?"

Glass shook his head.

"It means *there are none so deaf as those that will not hear.* Why did you come to the frontier?" demanded Kiowa. "To track down a common thief? To revel in a moment's revenge? I thought there was more to you than that."

Still Glass said nothing. Finally Kiowa said, "If you want to die in the guardhouse, that's for you to decide." The Frenchman turned and walked across the parade ground. Glass hesitated a moment, then followed behind.

"Let's go drink whiskey," yelled Kiowa over his shoulder. "I want to hear about the Powder and the Platte."

326

Kiowa loaned Glass the money for a few supplies and a night's lodging at Fort Atkinson's equivalent of an inn — a row of pallets in the sutler's attic. Whiskey usually made Glass drowsy, but that night it did not. Nor did it clarify the jumble of thoughts in his head. He struggled to think clearly. What was the answer to Kiowa's question?

Glass took the Anstadt and walked outside into the crisp air of the parade ground. The night was perfectly clear with no moon, reserving the sky for a billion stars, piercing pinpricks of light. He climbed crude steps to the narrow palisade that circled the wall of the fort. The view from the top was commanding.

Glass looked behind him into the confines of the fort. Across the parade ground lay the barracks. *He's there.* How many hundreds of miles had he traversed to find Fitzgerald? And now his quarry lay sleeping, a handful of steps away. He felt the cold metal of the Anstadt in his hand. *How can I walk away now?*

He turned his back, looking across the ramparts of the fort toward the Missouri River.

Stars danced on the dark water, their reflection like a marker of the heavens against the earth. Glass searched the sky for his beacons. He found the sloping tails of Ursa Major and Ursa Minor, the steady comfort of the North Star. *Where's Orion? Where's the hunter with his vengeful sword?*

The brilliant sparkle of the great star Vega seemed suddenly to fight for Glass's attention. Next to Vega he picked out the Cygnus, the Swan.

Glass stared at Cygnus, and the more he stared, the more its perpendicular lines seemed clearly to form a cross. *The Northern Cross.* That was the common name for Cygnus, he remembered. It seemed more fitting.

He stood there on the high rampart for a long time that night, listening to the Missouri and staring at the stars. He wondered at the source of the waters, of the mighty Big Horns whose tops he had seen but never touched. He wondered at the stars and the heavens, comforted by their vastness against his own small place in the world. Finally he climbed down from the ramparts and went inside, quickly finding the sleep that had eluded him before.

# CHAPTER
# TWENTY-EIGHT

## *May 7, 1824*

Jim Bridger started to knock on Captain Henry's door, then stopped. It had been seven days since anyone had seen the captain outside of his quarters. Seven days ago was when the Crow stole back the horses. Not even Murphy's successful return from a hunt could entice Henry from his seclusion.

Bridger took a deep breath and knocked. He heard a rustling sound from inside, then silence. "Captain?" More silence. Bridger paused again, then pushed open the door.

Henry sat hunched behind a desk made from two barrels and a plank.

A wool blanket draped his shoulders in a fashion that reminded Bridger of an old man huddled over the stove at a general store. The captain held a quill in one hand and a piece of paper in the other. Bridger glanced at the paper. Long columns of numbers crowded the page from left to right, top to bottom. Blotches of ink spotted the text, as if his quill had encountered frequent obstacles and stopped, spilling itself like blood onto the page. Wadded paper lay strewn across the desk and the floor.

Bridger waited for the captain to say something, or at least to look up.

For a long time, he didn't do either. Finally the captain raised his head. He looked like he hadn't slept for days, his bloodshot eyes peering out above sagging gray bags. Bridger wondered if it was true what some of the men were saying, that Captain Henry had gone over the edge.

"You know anything about numbers, Bridger?"

"No sir."

"Me neither. Not much, anyway. In fact, I keep hoping that I've just been too stupid to make all this add up." The captain stared back down at the paper. "Trouble is, I keep doing it over and over and it keeps coming out the same way. I think the problem's not my math — it's just that it doesn't come out the way I want."

"I don't know what you mean, Captain."

"What I mean is that we're belly-up. We're thirty thousand dollars in the hole. Without horses, we can't keep enough men in the field to get it back. And we got nothing left to trade for horses."

"Murphy just came in with two packs from the Big Horns."

The captain absorbed the news through the thick filter of his own past.

"That's nothing, Jim. Two packs of fur won't put us back on our feet. Twenty packs won't put us back on our feet."

The conversation was not moving in the direction Jim had hoped. It had taken two weeks for him to raise

**330**

the gumption to come see the captain. Now the whole thing was off track. He fought the instinct to retreat. *No. Not this time.* "Murphy says you're sending some men over the mountains to look for Jed Smith."

The captain offered no confirmation, but Bridger plowed forward anyway. "I want you to send me with them."

Henry looked at the boy. The eyes staring back at him gleamed as hopeful as the dawn of a spring day. How long had it been since he felt even an ounce of that youthful optimism? *A long time — and good riddance.*

"I can save you some trouble, Jim. I've been over those mountains. They're like the false front on a whorehouse. I know what you're looking for — and it's just not there."

Jim had no idea how to respond. He could not imagine why the captain was acting so strangely. Maybe he really had gone mad. Bridger didn't know about that, but what he did know, what he believed with unshakeable faith — was that Captain Henry was wrong.

They fell into another long period of silence. The feeling of discomfort grew, but Jim would not leave. Finally the captain looked at him and said, "It's your choice, Jim. I'll send you if you want to go."

Bridger walked out into the yard, squinting at the bright morning sunlight. He barely noticed the crisp air that nipped at his face, the vestige of a season about to pass. More snow would fall before winter at last gave way, but spring had fixed its grip on the plains.

Jim climbed a short ladder to the palisade. He perched his elbows on the top of the wall, gazing toward the Big Horn Mountains. With his eyes he traced again a deep canyon that seemed to penetrate the mountain's very core. *Did it?* He smiled at the infinite prospect of what might lay up the canyon, of what might lay on the mountaintops, of what might lay beyond.

He raised his eyes to a horizon carved from snowy mountain peaks, virgin white against the frigid blue sky. He could climb up there if he wanted. Climb up there and touch the horizon, jump across and find the next.

# Historical Note

Readers may wonder about the historical accuracy of the events in this novel. The fur trade era contains a murky mixture of history and legend, and some legend no doubt has invaded the history of Hugh Glass. *The Revenant* is a work of fiction. That said, I endeavored to stay true to history in the main events of the story.

What is certainly true is that Hugh Glass was attacked by a grizzly bear while scouting for the Rocky Mountain Fur Company in the fall of 1823; that he was horribly mauled; that he was abandoned by his compatriots, including two men left to tend for him; and that he survived to launch an epic quest for revenge. The most comprehensive historical work on Glass was done by John Myers Myers in his entertaining biography *The Saga of Hugh Glass*. Myers makes a strong case for even some of the most remarkable aspects of Glass's life, including his imprisonment by the pirate Jean Lafitte and, later, by the Pawnee Indians.

There is some division among historians as to whether Jim Bridger was one of the two men left to care for Glass, though most historians believe that he was. (The historian Cecil Alter, in a 1925 biography of

Bridger, makes a passionate contrary case.) There is considerable evidence that Glass confronted and then forgave Bridger at the fort on the Big Horn.

I took literary and historical liberties in a couple of places that I wish to note. There is persuasive evidence that Glass did finally catch up with Fitzgerald at Fort Atkinson, finding his betrayer in the uniform of the U.S. Army. However, accounts of the encounter are cursory. There is no evidence of a formal proceeding such as I portrayed. The character of Major Constable is wholly fictional, as is the incident in which Glass shoots Fitzgerald in the shoulder. There is also evidence that Hugh Glass had separated from the party of Antoine Langevin prior to the Arikara attack on the voyageurs. (Toussaint Charbonneau does appear to have been with Langevin, and to have survived the attack, although the circumstances are not clear.) The characters of Professeur, Dominique Cattoire, and La Vierge Cattoire are wholly fictional.

Fort Talbot and its inhabitants are invented. Otherwise, the geographic reference points are as accurate as I could make them. A spring 1824 attack against Glass and his companions by the Arikara Indians did take place, reportedly at the confluence of the North Platte River and the (later named) Laramie River. Eleven years later, Fort William — the predecessor of Fort Laramie — would be established at that site.

Readers interested in the fur trade era would enjoy historical treatments including Hiram Chittenden's classic *The American Fur Trade of the Far West* and

Robert M. Utley's more recent work *A Life Wild and Perilous*.

In the years following the events portrayed in this novel, many of the central characters went on to continued adventure, tragedy, and glory. The following are notable:

Captain Andrew Henry: In the summer of 1824, Henry and a group of his men rendezvoused with Jed Smith's troop in what is now Wyoming. Though not enough to cover the company's debts, Henry had collected a significant number of furs. Smith stayed in the field, with Henry responsible for returning to St. Louis with their harvest. Though modest at best, Ashley believed the quantity of furs justified an immediate return to the field. He secured funding for another expedition, which left St. Louis under Henry's command on October 21, 1824. For reasons not recorded by history, Henry appears to have retreated from the frontier not long after.

Had Henry held his stake in the Rocky Mountain Fur Company for another year, he — like the other principals in the syndicate — might have retired a wealthy man. But once again, Henry demonstrated his peculiar propensity for bad luck. He sold his share in the company for a modest sum. Even this could have provided a comfortable life, but Henry took up the surety business. When several of his debtors defaulted, he lost everything. Andrew Henry died penniless in 1832.

William H. Ashley: It is remarkable that two partners in the same enterprise could ride it to such different conclusions. Though faced with mounting debts, Ashley remained steadfast in the belief that a fortune could be made in furs. After losing a bid for the governorship of Missouri in 1824, Ashley led a party of trappers down the south fork of the Platte. He became the first white man to attempt a navigation of the Green River, an effort that nearly ended in disaster near the mouth of what is today called the Ashley River.

With few furs to show for his adventure, Ashley and his men met up with a dispirited group of trappers from the Hudson Bay Company. Through a mysterious transaction, Ashley came into possession of a hundred packs of beaver. Some allege the Americans plundered the HBC's cache. More credible reports say Ashley did nothing more spurious than strike a hard bargain. In any event, Ashley sold the furs in St. Louis in the fall of 1825 for more than $200,000 — securing a fortune for life.

At the rendezvous of 1826, Ashley sold his share of the Rocky Mountain Fur Company to Jedediah Smith, David Jackson, and William Sublette. Having created the rendezvous system, launched the careers of several legends of the fur trade era, and secured his own place in history as a successful fur baron, Ashley retired from the trade.

In 1831, the people of Missouri elected Ashley to replace Congressman Spencer Pottis (Pottis had died in a duel). Ashley twice won reelection, retiring from politics in 1837. William H. Ashley died in 1838.

Jim Bridger: In the fall of 1824, Jim Bridger crossed the Rockies and became the first white man to touch the waters of the Great Salt Lake. By 1830, Bridger had become a partner in the Rocky Mountain Fur Company, then rode the fur trade era to its crash in the 1840s. As the fur trade ebbed, Bridger caught the next wave of westward expansion. In 1838, he built a fort in what is now Wyoming. "Fort Bridger" became an important trading post on the Oregon Trail, later serving as a military post and Pony Express station. In the 1850s and 1860s, Bridger served often as a guide for settlers, exploration parties, and the U.S. Army.

Jim Bridger died on July 17, 1878, near Westport, Missouri. For his lifetime of accomplishment as a trapper, explorer, and guide, Bridger is often referred to as the "King of the Mountain Men." Today mountains, streams, and towns throughout the West bear his name.

John Fitzgerald: Little is known about John Fitzgerald. He did exist, and is generally regarded as one of the two men who abandoned Hugh Glass. He is also believed to have deserted the Rocky Mountain Fur Company, and then to have enlisted in the U.S. Army at Fort Atkinson. I have fictionalized other parts of his life.

Hugh Glass: From Fort Atkinson, Glass appears to have traveled downriver to St. Louis, delivering Henry's message to Ashley. In St. Louis, Glass met a party of traders bound for Santa Fe. He joined them, and spent a year trapping on the Helo River. By around 1825, Glass was in Taos, a center of the southwestern fur trade.

The arid streams of the Southwest played out quickly, and Glass again turned north. He trapped his way up the Colorado, the Green, and the Snake, eventually finding himself on the headwaters of the Missouri River. In 1828, the so-called free trappers elected Glass to represent their interests in negotiations to break the monopoly of the Rocky Mountain Fur Company. After trapping as far west as the Columbia River, Glass turned most of his attention to the eastern face of the Rockies.

Glass spent the winter of 1833 at an outpost called "Fort Cass," near Henry's old fort at the confluence of the Yellowstone and Big Horn rivers. On a February morning, Glass and two companions were crossing the frozen Yellowstone at the outset of a trapping foray. They were ambushed by thirty Arikara warriors and killed.

# Acknowledgments

Many of my friends and family (and a couple of kind strangers) made the generous gift of their time, reading early drafts of this book and improving it through their critique and encouragement. Thanks to Sean Darragh, Liz and John Feldman, Timothy and Lori Otto Punke, Peter Scher, Kim Tilley, Brent and Cheryl Garrett, Marilyn and Butch Punke, Randy and Julie Miller, Kelly MacManus, Marc Glick, Bill and Mary Strong, Mickey Kantor, Andre Solomita, Ev Ehrlich, Jen Kaplan, Mildred Hoecker, Monte Silk, Carol and Ted Kinney, Ian Davis, David Kurapka, David Marchick, Jay Ziegler, Aubrey Moss, Mike Bridge, Nancy Goodman, Jennifer Egan, Amy and Mike McManamen, Linda Stillman, and Jacqueline Cundiff.

Thanks to a group of outstanding teachers from Torrington, Wyoming: Ethel James, Betty Sportsman, Edie Smith, Rodger Clark, Craig Sodaro, Randy Adams, and Bob Latta. If you ever wonder whether teachers make a difference, please know that you did for me.

Particular thanks to the fantastic Tina Bennett at William Morris Endeavor. While I take all responsibility for its short-comings, Tina helped make this book better and then worked to make it a film. Thanks to Tina's talented assistant, Svetlana Katz, who (among other things) gave this book a name. I am grateful for early editing advice from Philip Turner. Stephen Morrison at Picador, with assistance from P. J. Horoszko, helped *The Revenant* return to life.

In 2002, Keith Redmon saw film potential in *The Revenant* and has worked steadfastly ever since to make a movie happen, along with his Anonymous Content colleagues Steve Golin and David Kanter.

Most important, special thanks to my family. Thank you, Sophie, for helping me experiment with deadfall traps. Thank you, Bo, for your uncanny imitation of a grizzly. And thank you, Traci, for your steadfast support and patient attention through a hundred labored readings.

# Key Sources

Alter, Cecil J.: *Jim Bridger*, 1925.

Ambrose, Stephen E.: *Undaunted Courage*, 1996.

Brown, Tom: *Tom Brown's Field Guide to Wilderness Survival*, 1983.

Chittenden, Hiram Martin: *The American Fur Trade of the Far West*, Volumes I and II, 1902.

DeVoto, Bernard: *Across the Wide Missouri*, 1947.

Garcia, Andrew: *Montana 1878, Tough Trip through Paradise*, 1967.

Knight, Dennis H.: *Mountains and Plains: The Ecology of Wyoming Landscapes*, 1994.

Lavender, David: *The Great West*, 1965.

Library of Congress, *The North American Indian Portfolios*, 1993.

McMillion, Scott: *Mark of the Grizzly*, 1998.

Milner, Clyde A, et al.: *The Oxford History of the American West*, 1994.

Morgan, Ted: *A Shovel of Stars*, 1995.

——: *Wilderness at Dawn: The Settling of the North American Continent*, 1993.

Myers, John Myers: *The Saga of Hugh Glass: Pirate, Pawnee, and Mountain Man*, 1963.

Nute, Grace Lee: *The Voyageur*, 1931.

Russell, Carl P.: *Firearms, Traps, & Tools of the Mountain Men*, 1967.

Utley, Robert M.: *A Life Wild and Perilous: Mountain Men and the Paths to the Pacific*, 1997.

Vestal, Stanley: *Jim Bridger, Mountain Man*, 1946.

Willard, Terry: *Edible and Medicinal Plants of the Rocky Mountains and Neighbouring Territories*, 1992.

**Other titles published by Ulverscroft:**

# A PERFECT HOME

## Kate Glanville

Claire appears to have it all — the kind of life you read about in magazines: a beautiful cottage, three gorgeous children, a handsome husband in William, and her own flourishing vintage textile business. But when an interiors magazine sends a good-looking photographer to take pictures of Claire's perfect home, he makes her wonder if the house means more to William than she does, and question whether home really is where the heart is . . .

# YANTO'S SUMMER

## Ray Pickernell

Post-war Gloucestershire: Yanto Gates, invalided out of the Army towards the end of the war, enjoys civilian life in the small village of Purton East, but he misses the thrill and risk of combat. He's had to readjust to a sedate life of dock work, fishing, and 'going steady' — but things don't stay that way for long, especially not when an old flame of his returns to a nearby town. There are dark secrets and old feuds at play in this sleepiest of villages . . .